D1265091

FANTAGRAPHICS BOOKS, INC.
Seattle, Washington, USA

ISBN 978-1-60699-983-7

Third Printing: July 2018

Printed in Hong Kong

FOR MELISSA

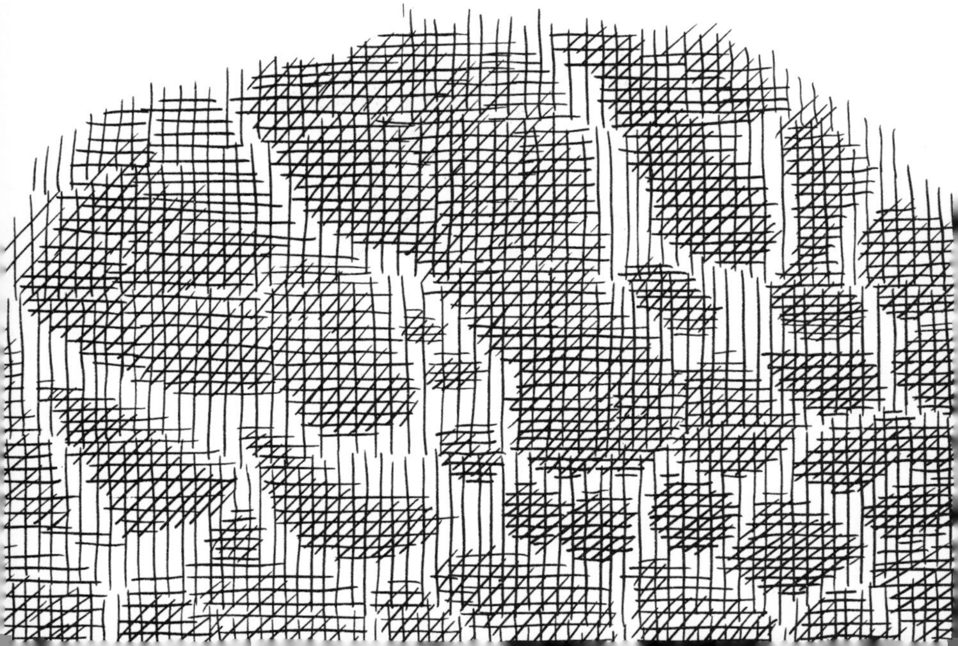

THE

END

OF

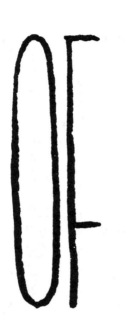

THE

FUCKING

WORLD

HARD TO BE AROUND

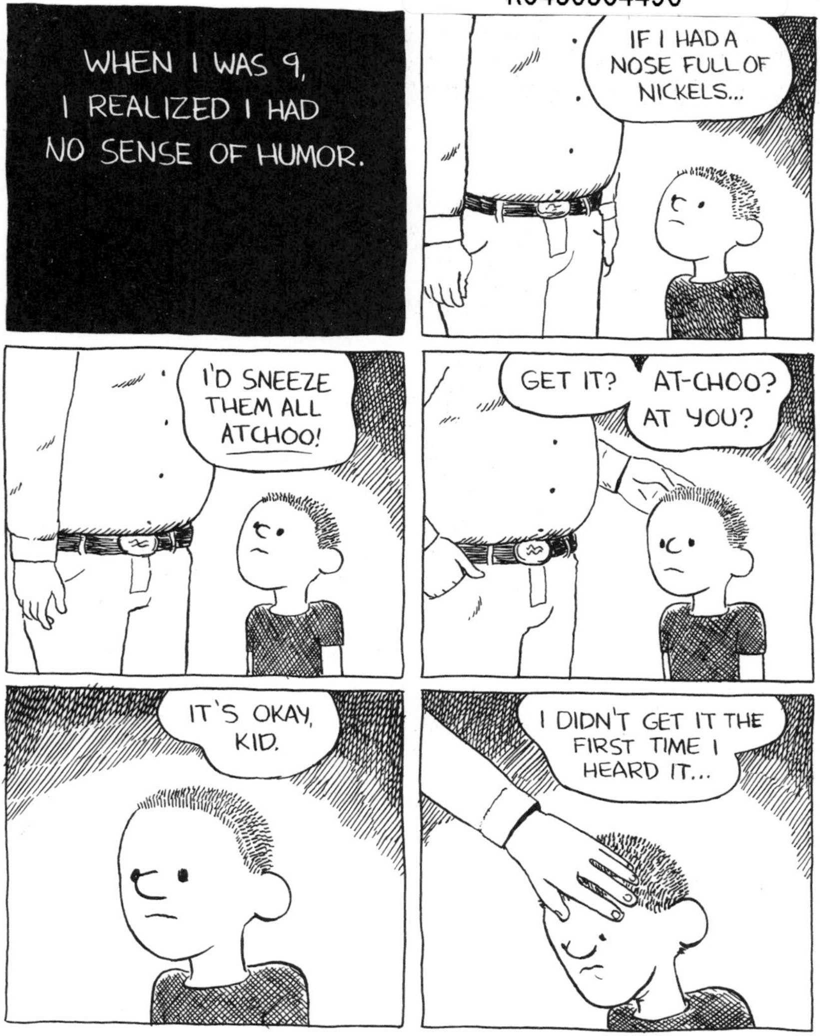
WHEN I WAS 9, I REALIZED I HAD NO SENSE OF HUMOR.
IF I HAD A NOSE FULL OF NICKELS...
I'D SNEEZE THEM ALL ATCHOO!
GET IT?
AT-CHOO? AT YOU?
IT'S OKAY, KID.
I DIDN'T GET IT THE FIRST TIME I HEARD IT...

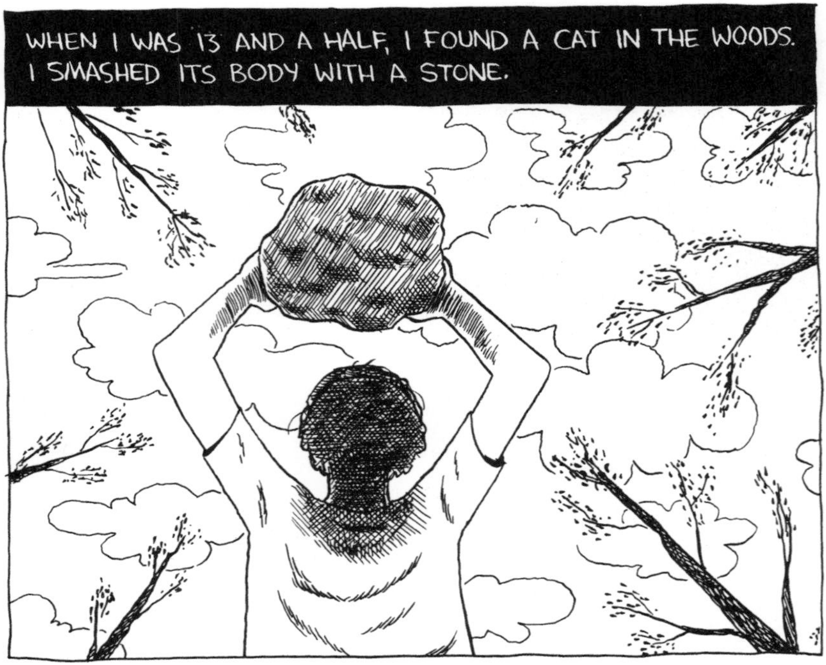
WHEN I WAS 13 AND A HALF, I FOUND A CAT IN THE WOODS.
I SMASHED ITS BODY WITH A STONE.

AFTER THAT, I KILLED MORE ANIMALS. I REMEMBER THEM ALL.

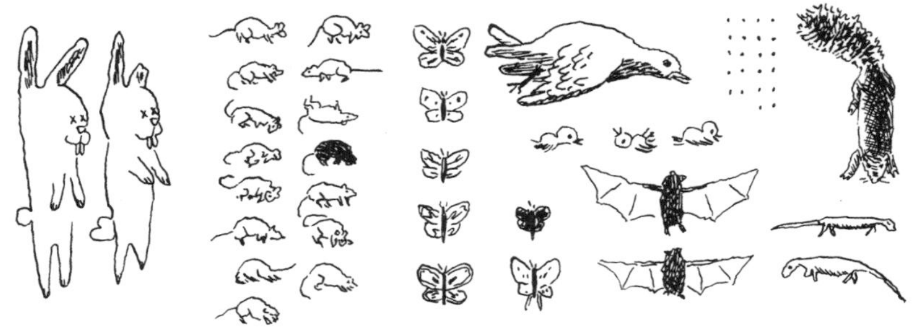

AT 15, I STUCK MY HAND INTO THE GARBAGE DISPOSAL.
WIRRRRRRRR
WIRRRRR
WIRRRRRRRR
GROA

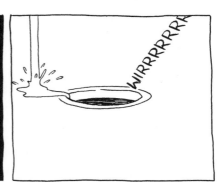

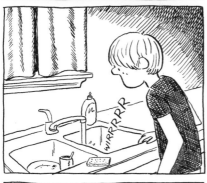

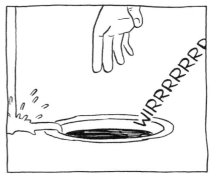

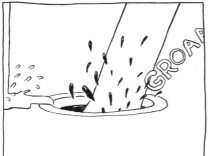

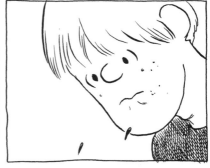

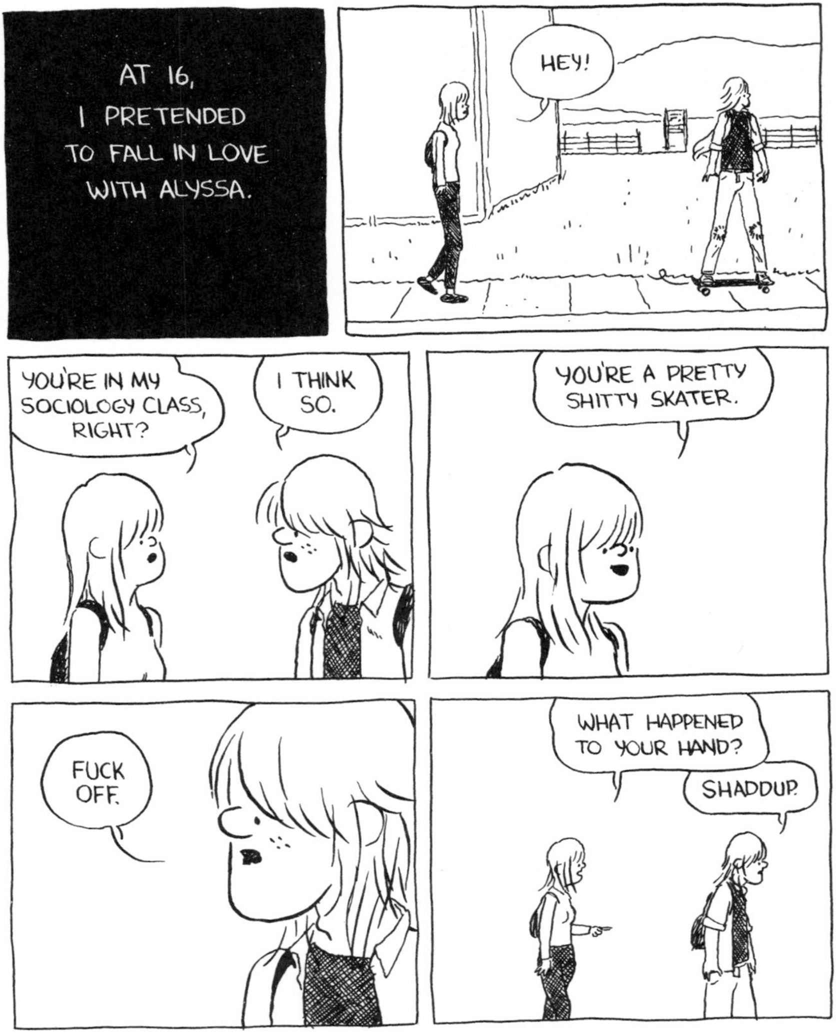
AT 16, I PRETENDED TO FALL IN LOVE WITH ALYSSA.
HEY!
YOU'RE IN MY SOCIOLOGY CLASS, RIGHT?
I THINK SO.
YOU'RE A PRETTY SHITTY SKATER.
FUCK OFF.
WHAT HAPPENED TO YOUR HAND?
SHADDUP.

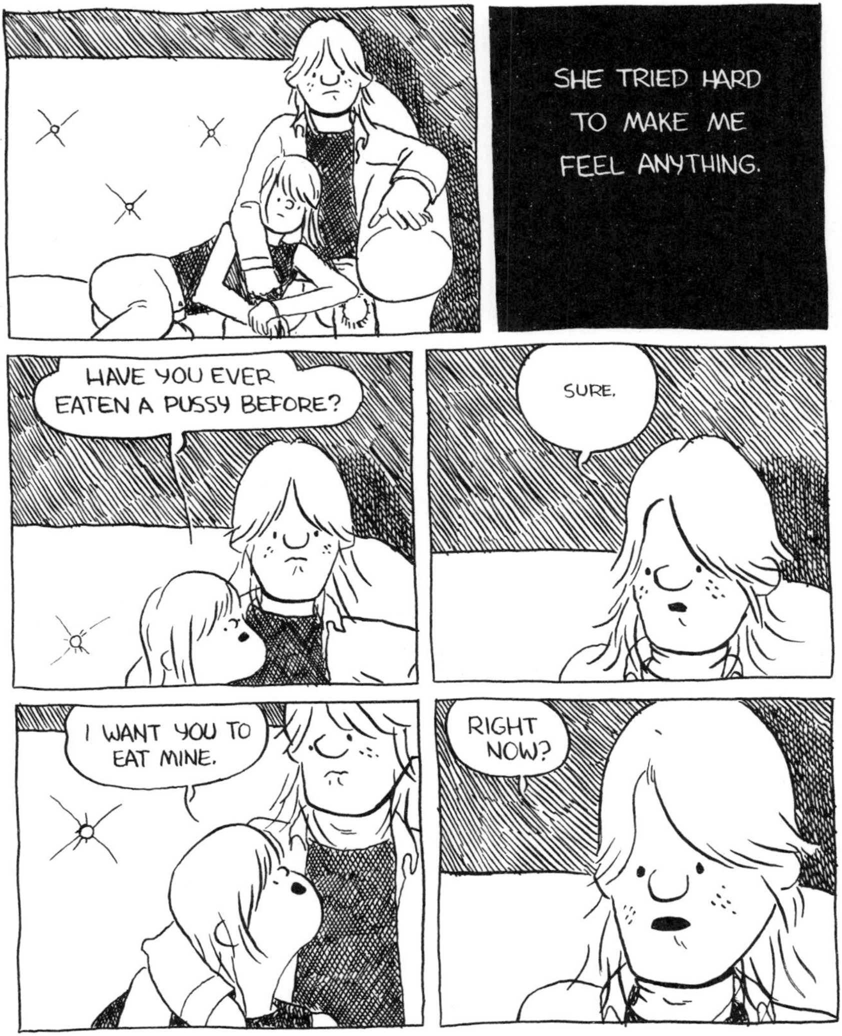
SHE TRIED HARD TO MAKE ME FEEL ANYTHING.
HAVE YOU EVER EATEN A PUSSY BEFORE?
SURE.
I WANT YOU TO EAT MINE.
RIGHT NOW?

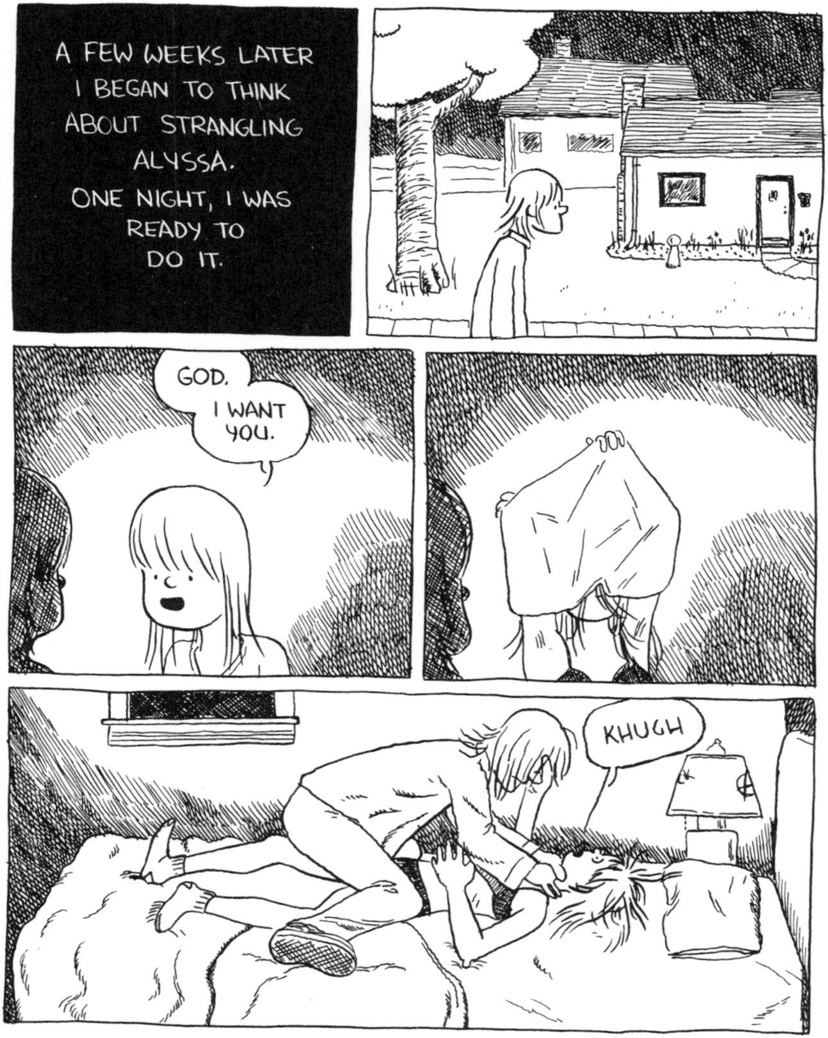
A FEW WEEKS LATER I BEGAN TO THINK ABOUT STRANGLING ALYSSA.
ONE NIGHT, I WAS READY TO DO IT.
GOD. I WANT YOU.
KHUGH

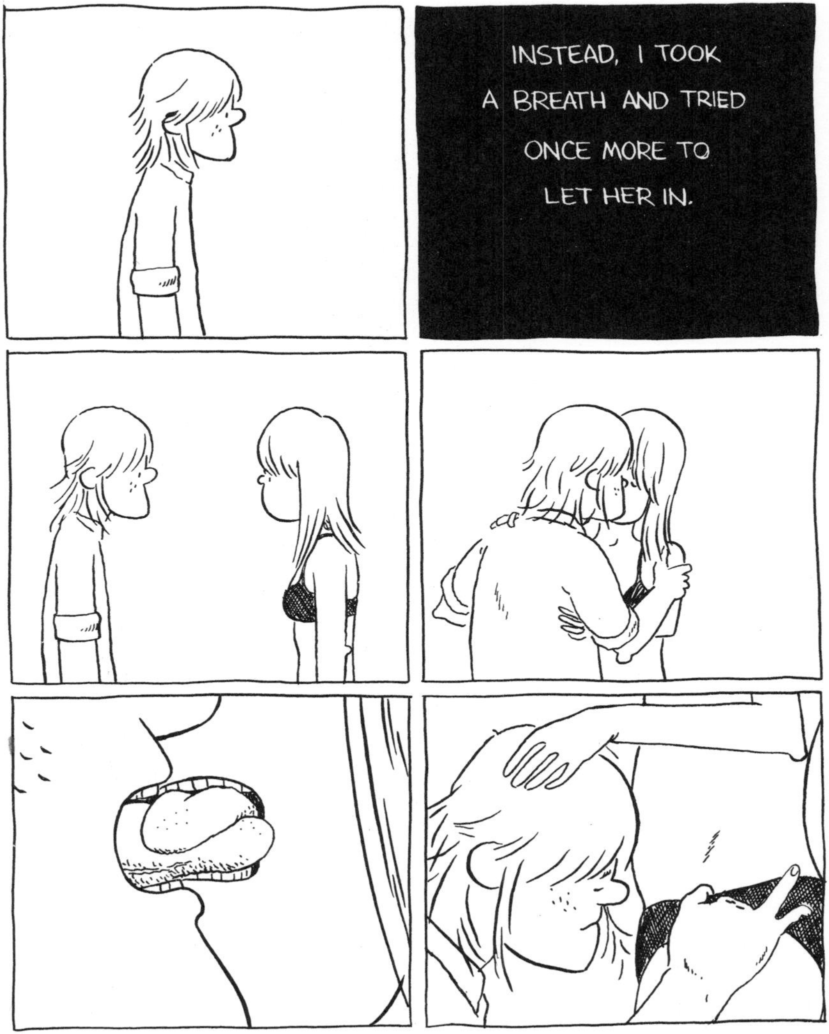
INSTEAD, I TOOK A BREATH AND TRIED ONCE MORE TO LET HER IN.

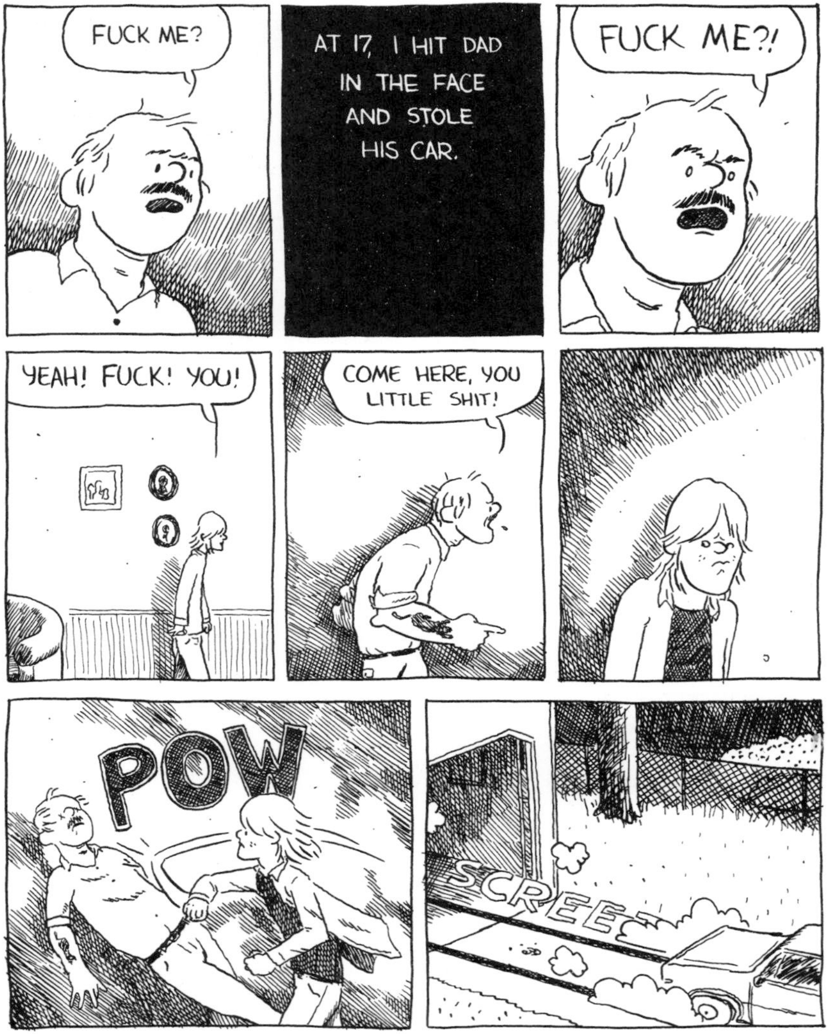
FUCK ME?
AT 17, I HIT DAD IN THE FACE AND STOLE HIS CAR.
FUCK ME?!
YEAH! FUCK! YOU!
COME HERE, YOU LITTLE SHIT!
POW
SCREEE

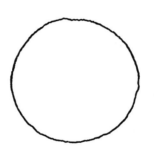

FIRE ON THE OUTSIDE

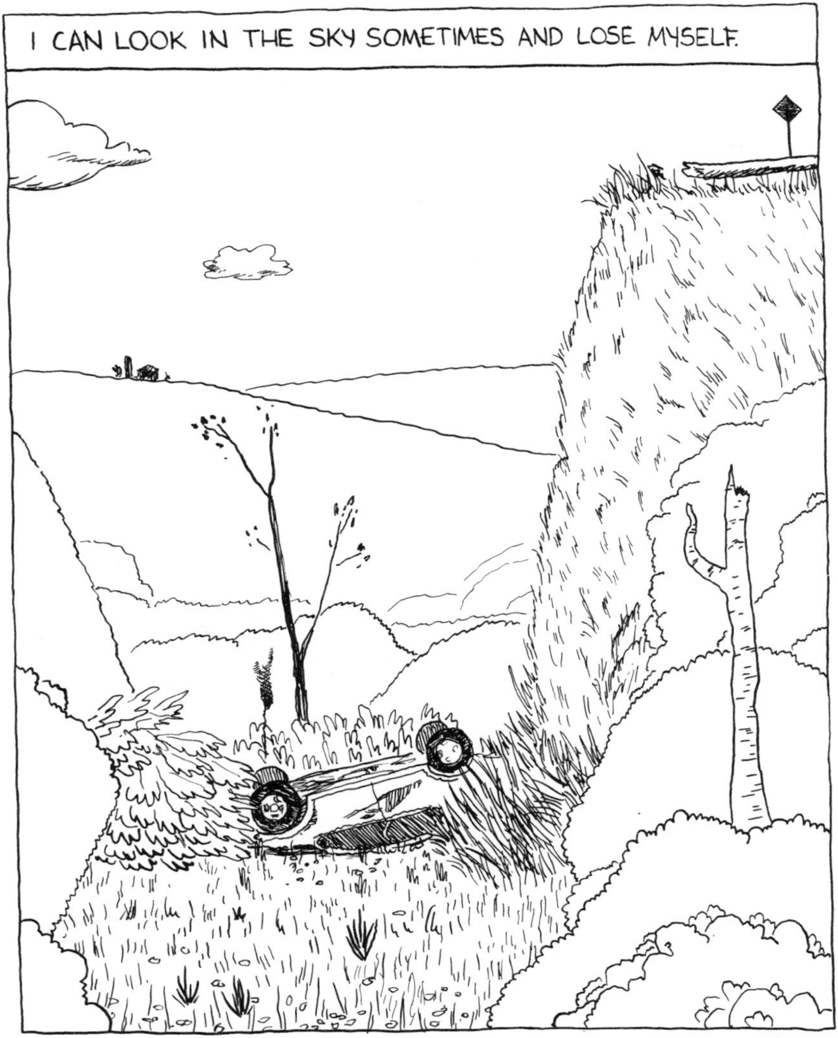
I CAN LOOK IN THE SKY SOMETIMES AND LOSE MYSELF.

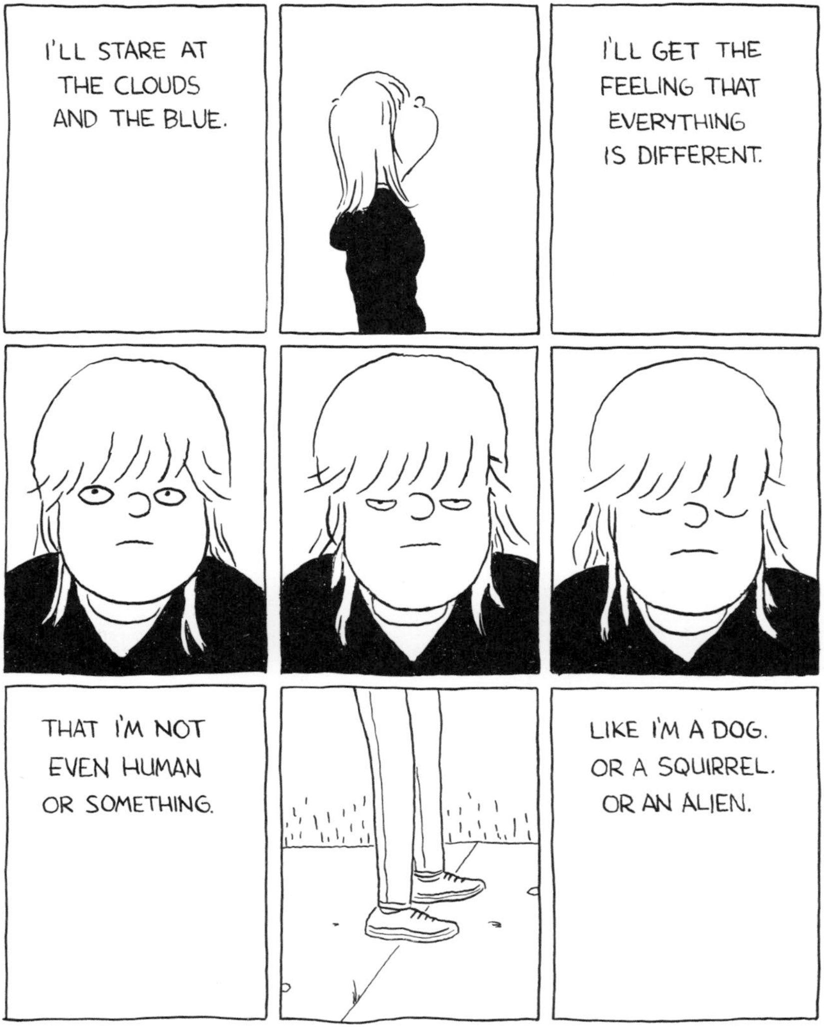
I'LL STARE AT THE CLOUDS AND THE BLUE.
I'LL GET THE FEELING THAT EVERYTHING IS DIFFERENT.
THAT I'M NOT EVEN HUMAN OR SOMETHING.
LIKE I'M A DOG. OR A SQUIRREL. OR AN ALIEN.

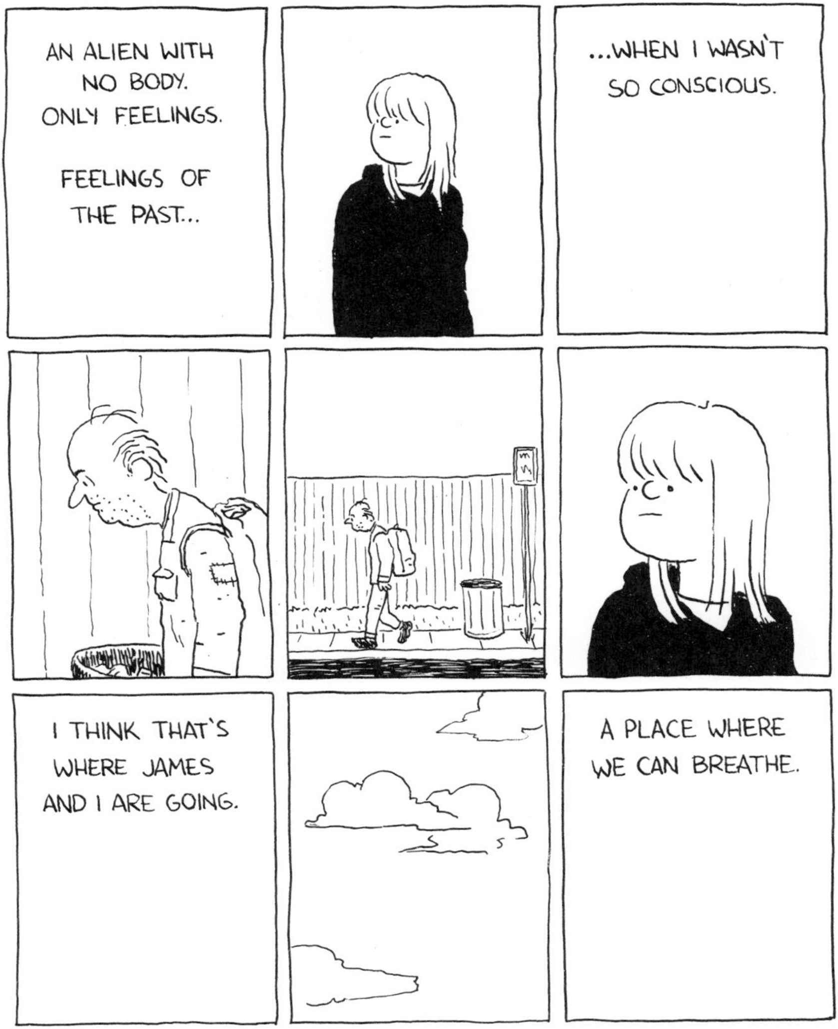
AN ALIEN WITH NO BODY. ONLY FEELINGS.
FEELINGS OF THE PAST...
...WHEN I WASN'T SO CONSCIOUS.
I THINK THAT'S WHERE JAMES AND I ARE GOING.
A PLACE WHERE WE CAN BREATHE.

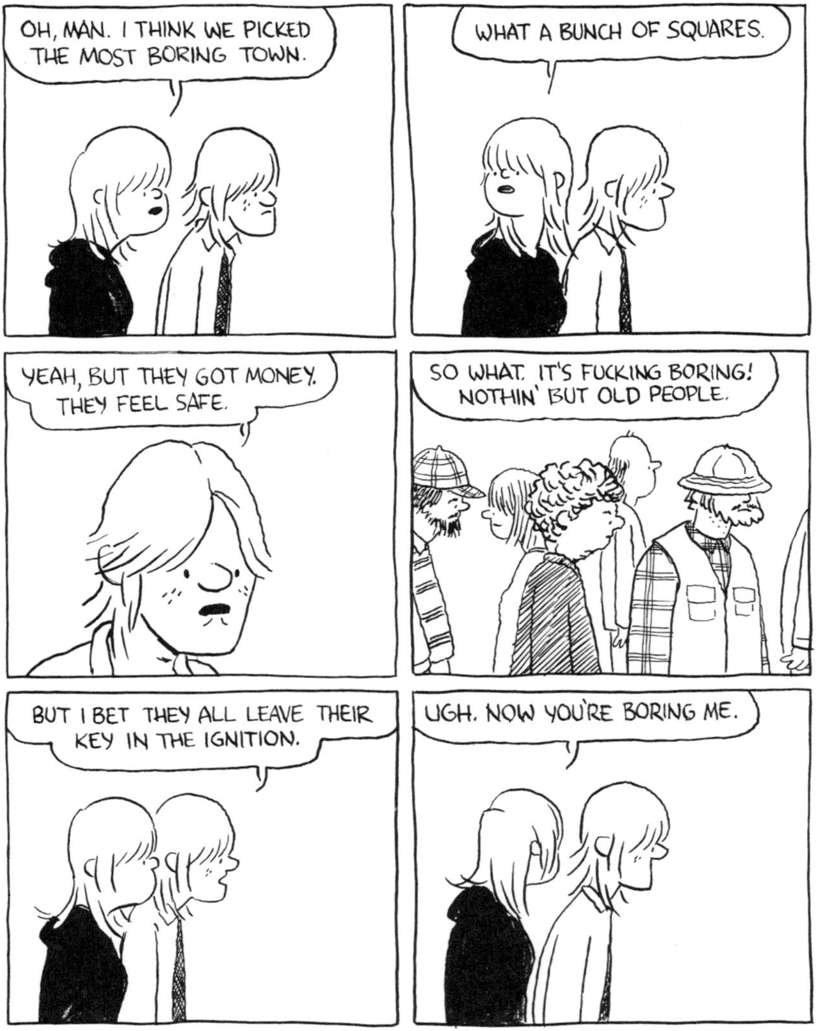
OH, MAN. I THINK WE PICKED THE MOST BORING TOWN.
WHAT A BUNCH OF SQUARES.
YEAH, BUT THEY GOT MONEY. THEY FEEL SAFE.
SO WHAT. IT'S FUCKING BORING! NOTHIN' BUT OLD PEOPLE.
BUT I BET THEY ALL LEAVE THEIR KEY IN THE IGNITION.
UGH. NOW YOU'RE BORING ME.

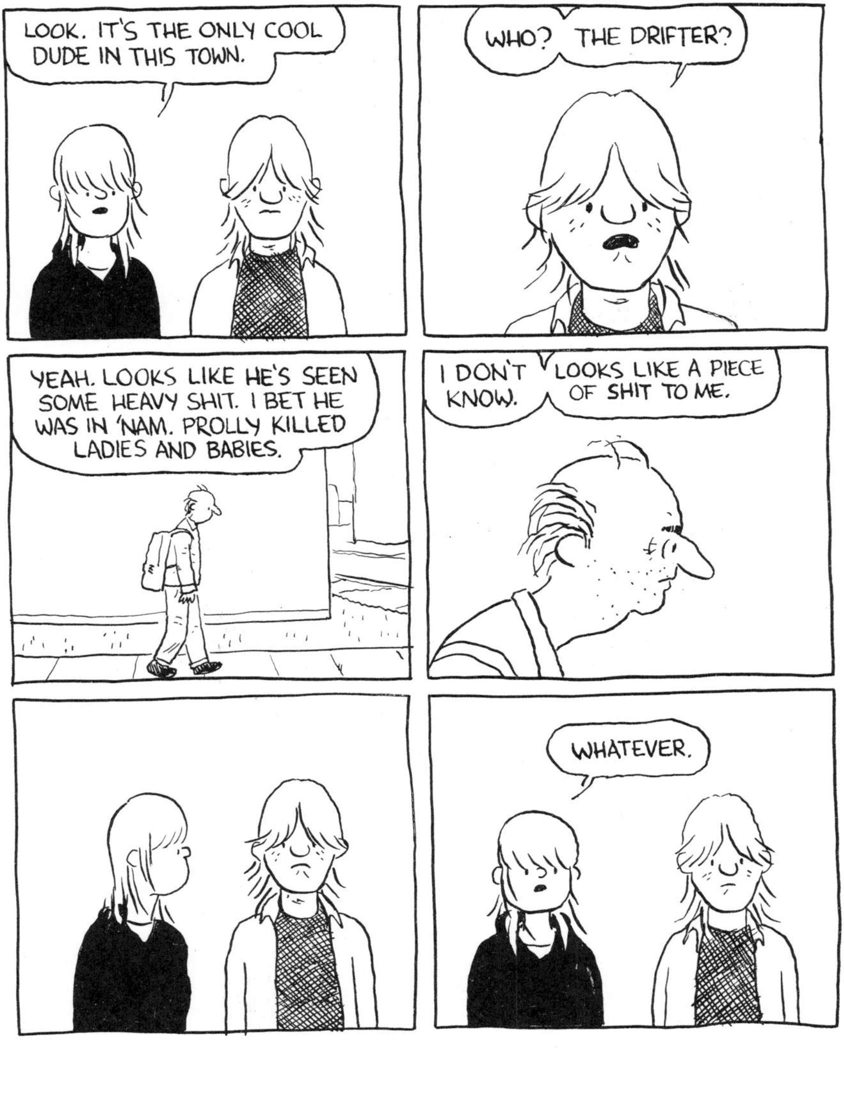
LOOK. IT'S THE ONLY COOL DUDE IN THIS TOWN.
WHO?
THE DRIFTER?
YEAH. LOOKS LIKE HE'S SEEN SOME HEAVY SHIT. I BET HE WAS IN 'NAM. PROLLY KILLED LADIES AND BABIES.
I DON'T KNOW.
LOOKS LIKE A PIECE OF SHIT TO ME.
WHATEVER.

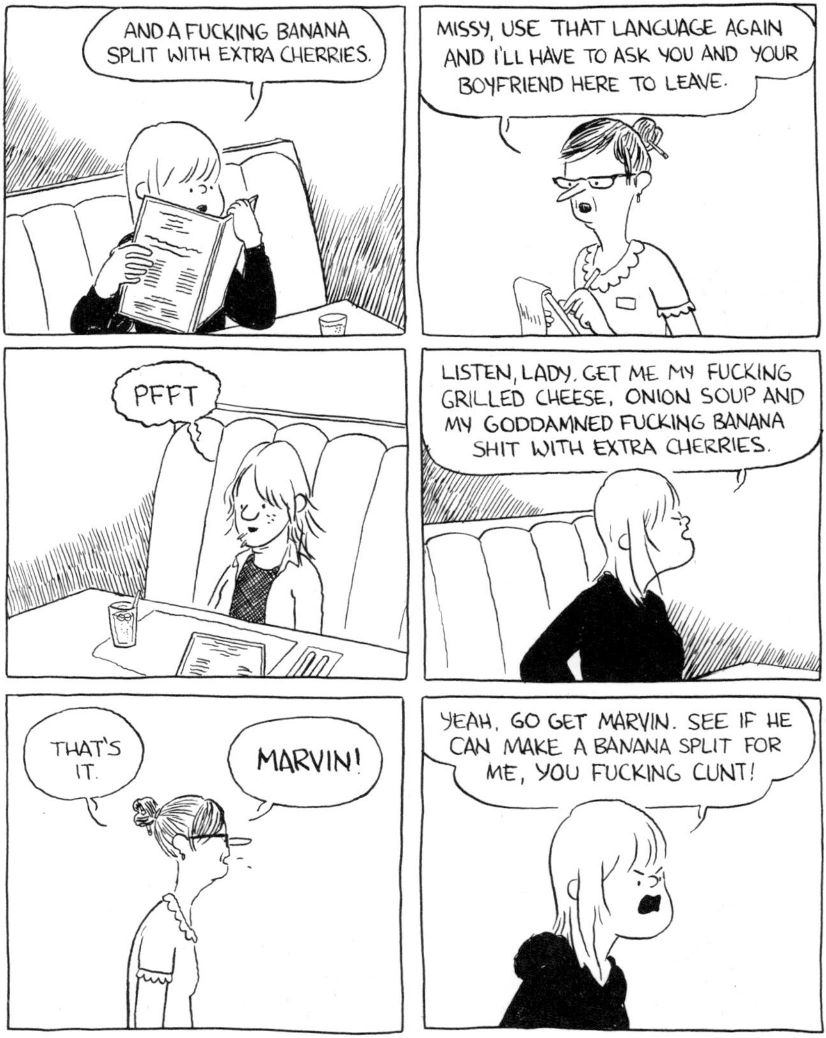
AND A FUCKING BANANA SPLIT WITH EXTRA CHERRIES.
MISSY, USE THAT LANGUAGE AGAIN AND I'LL HAVE TO ASK YOU AND YOUR BOYFRIEND HERE TO LEAVE.
PFFT
LISTEN, LADY. GET ME MY FUCKING GRILLED CHEESE, ONION SOUP AND MY GODDAMNED FUCKING BANANA SHIT WITH EXTRA CHERRIES.
THAT'S IT.
MARVIN!
YEAH, GO GET MARVIN. SEE IF HE CAN MAKE A BANANA SPLIT FOR ME, YOU FUCKING CUNT!

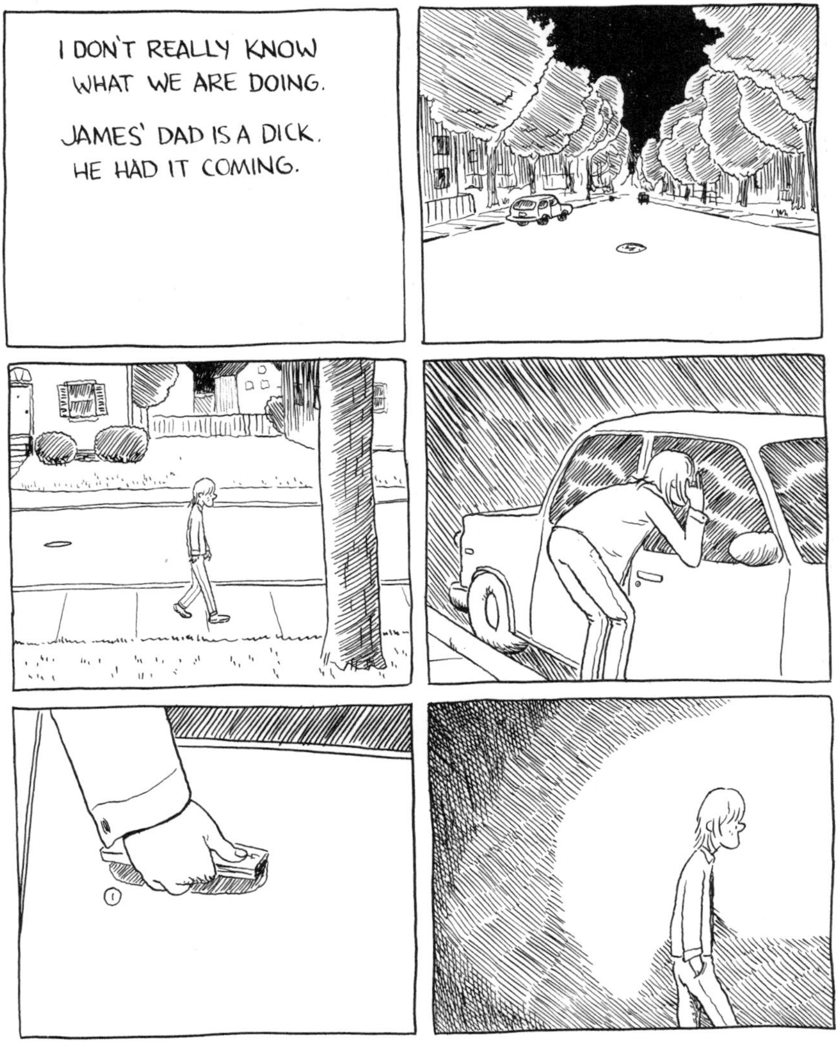
I DON'T REALLY KNOW WHAT WE ARE DOING.
JAMES' DAD IS A DICK. HE HAD IT COMING.

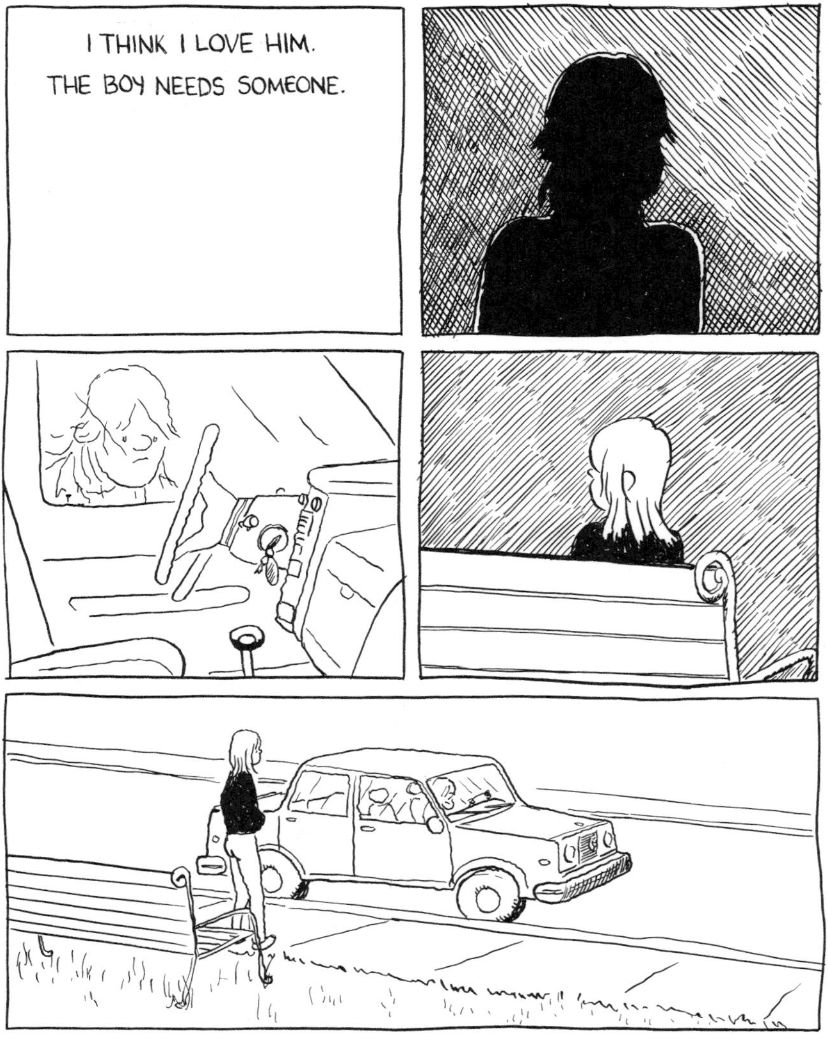
I THINK I LOVE HIM.
THE BOY NEEDS SOMEONE.

HOME

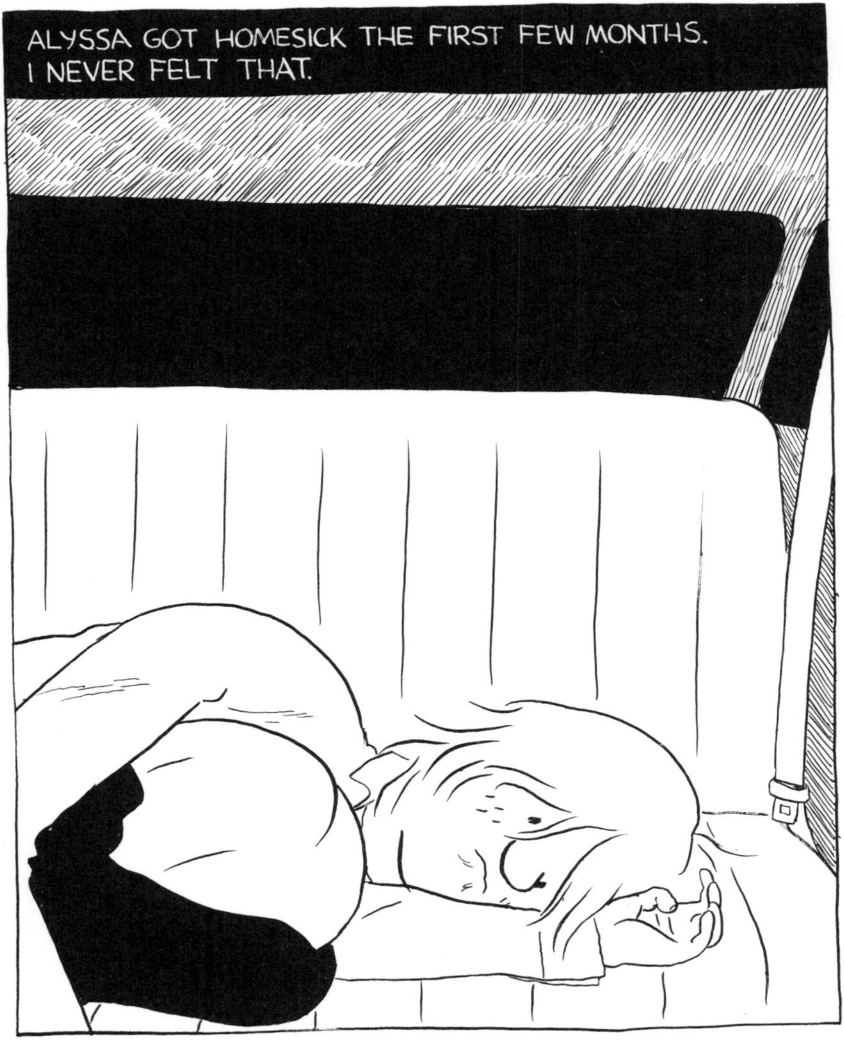
ALYSSA GOT HOMESICK THE FIRST FEW MONTHS.
I NEVER FELT THAT.

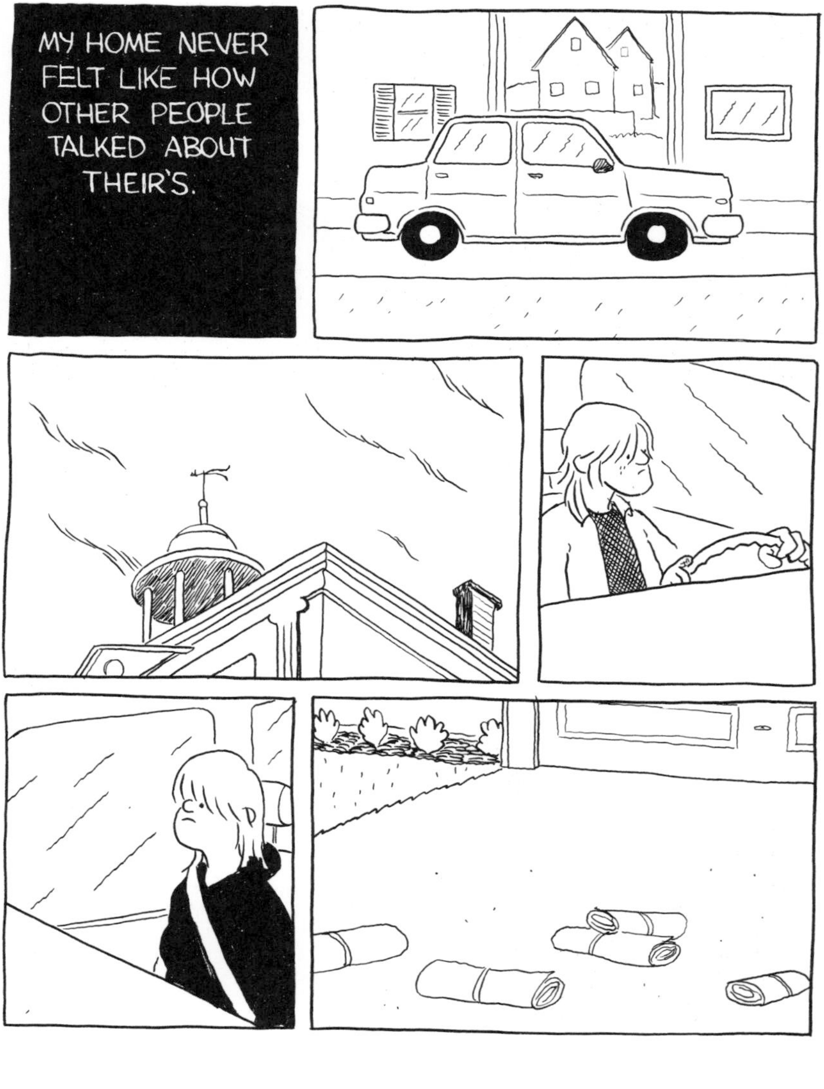
MY HOME NEVER FELT LIKE HOW OTHER PEOPLE TALKED ABOUT THEIR'S.

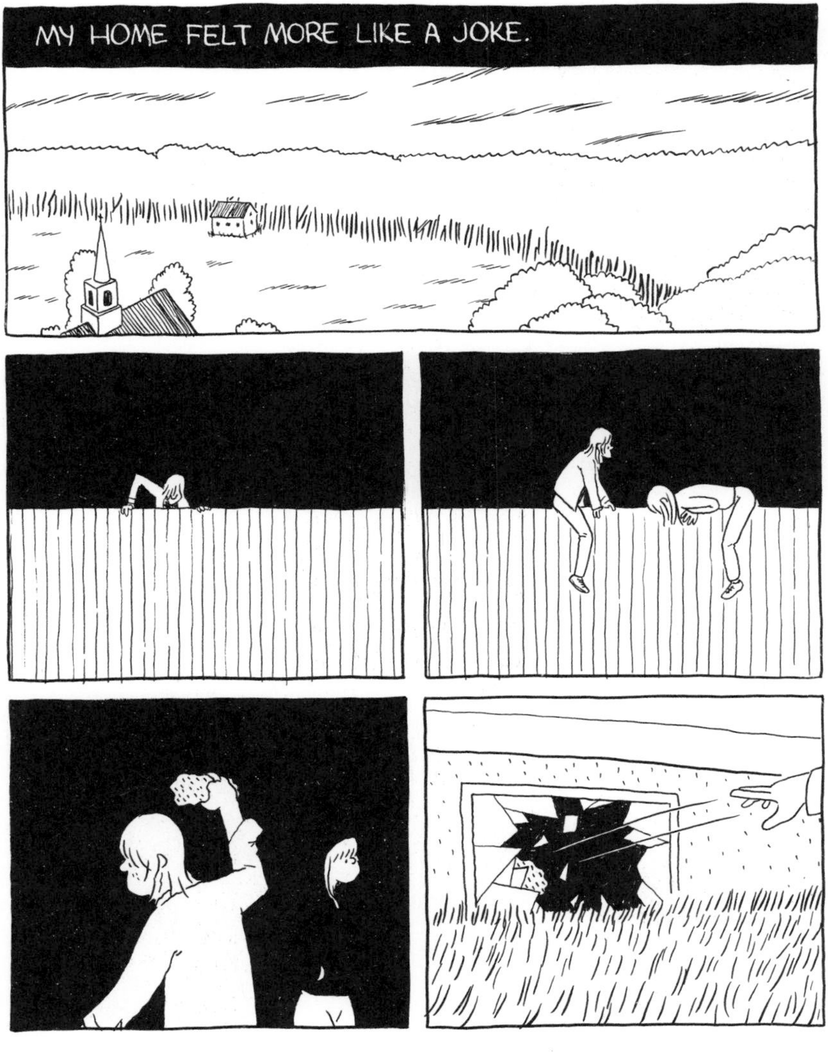
MY HOME FELT MORE LIKE A JOKE.

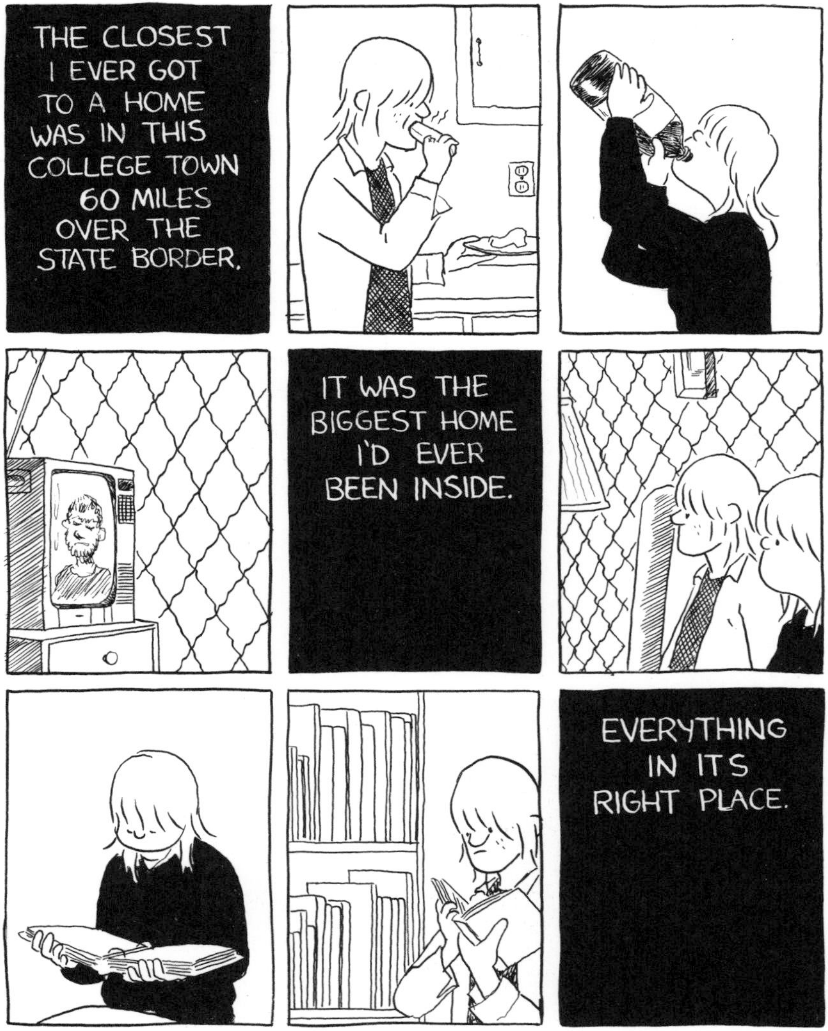
THE CLOSEST I EVER GOT TO A HOME WAS IN THIS COLLEGE TOWN 60 MILES OVER THE STATE BORDER.
IT WAS THE BIGGEST HOME I'D EVER BEEN INSIDE.
EVERYTHING IN ITS RIGHT PLACE.

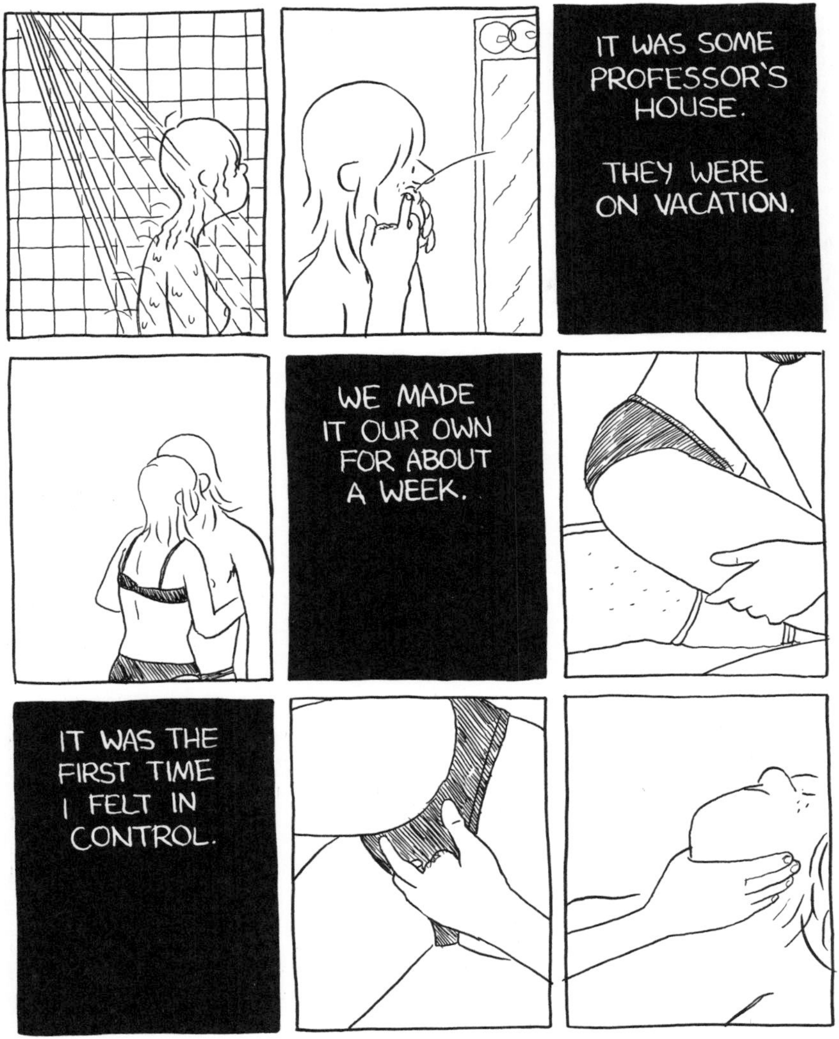
IT WAS SOME PROFESSOR'S HOUSE.
THEY WERE ON VACATION.
WE MADE IT OUR OWN FOR ABOUT A WEEK.
IT WAS THE FIRST TIME I FELT IN CONTROL.

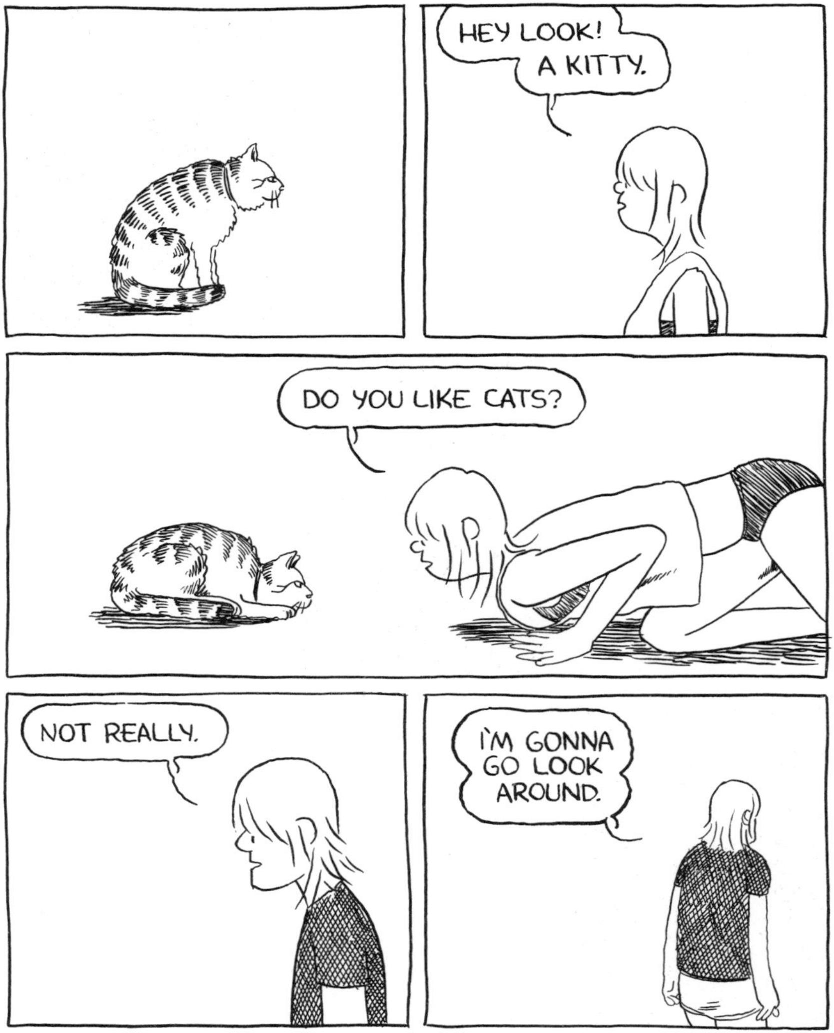
HEY LOOK! A KITTY.
DO YOU LIKE CATS?
NOT REALLY.
I'M GONNA GO LOOK AROUND.

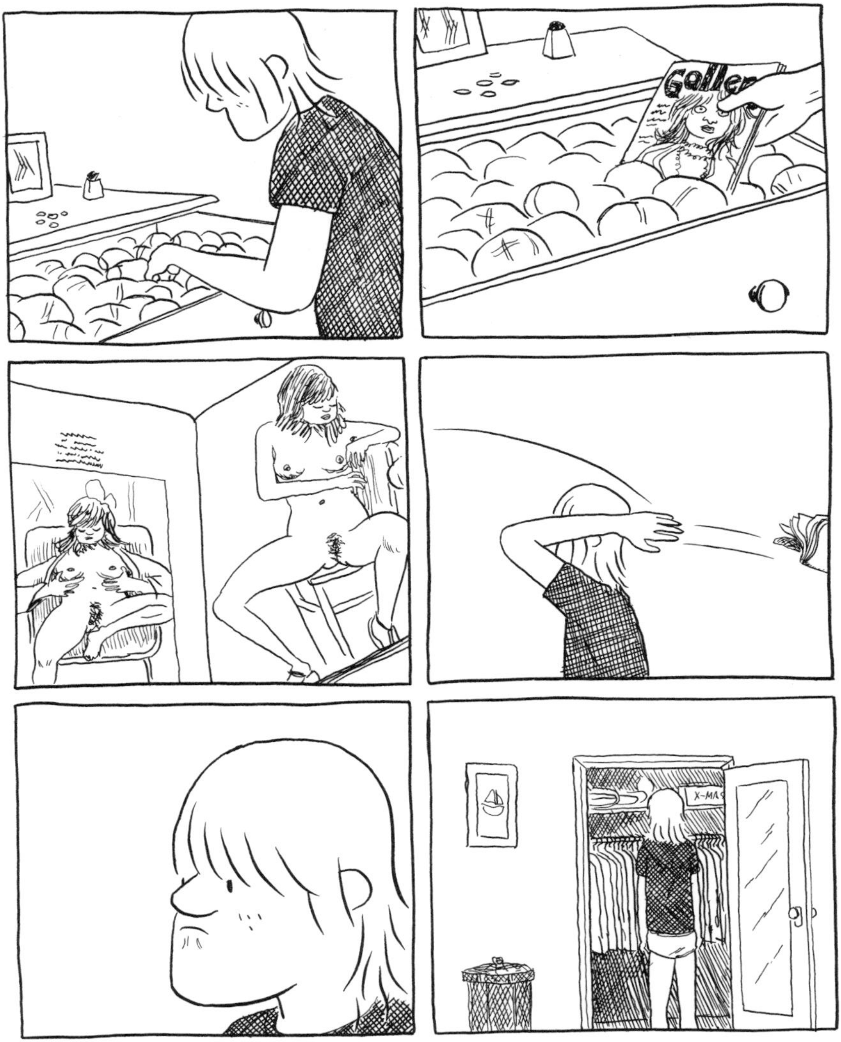
Galler
X-MA

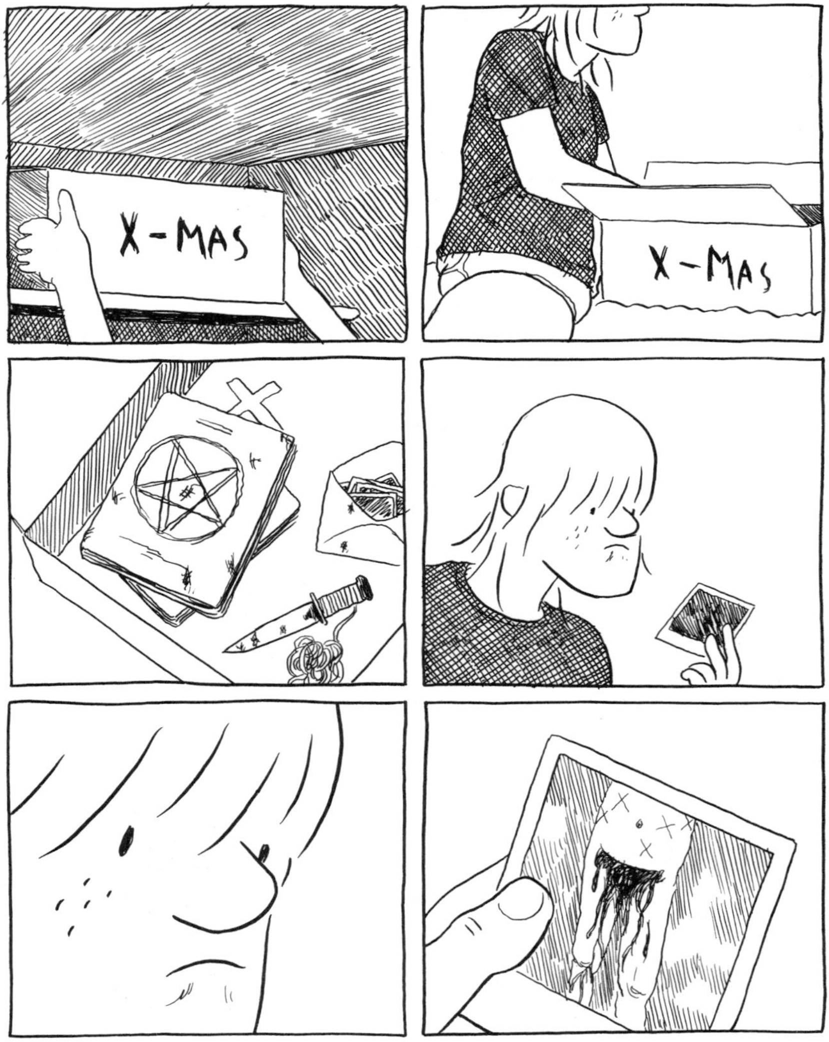
X-MAS
X-MAS

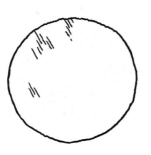

SAFE AND SOUND

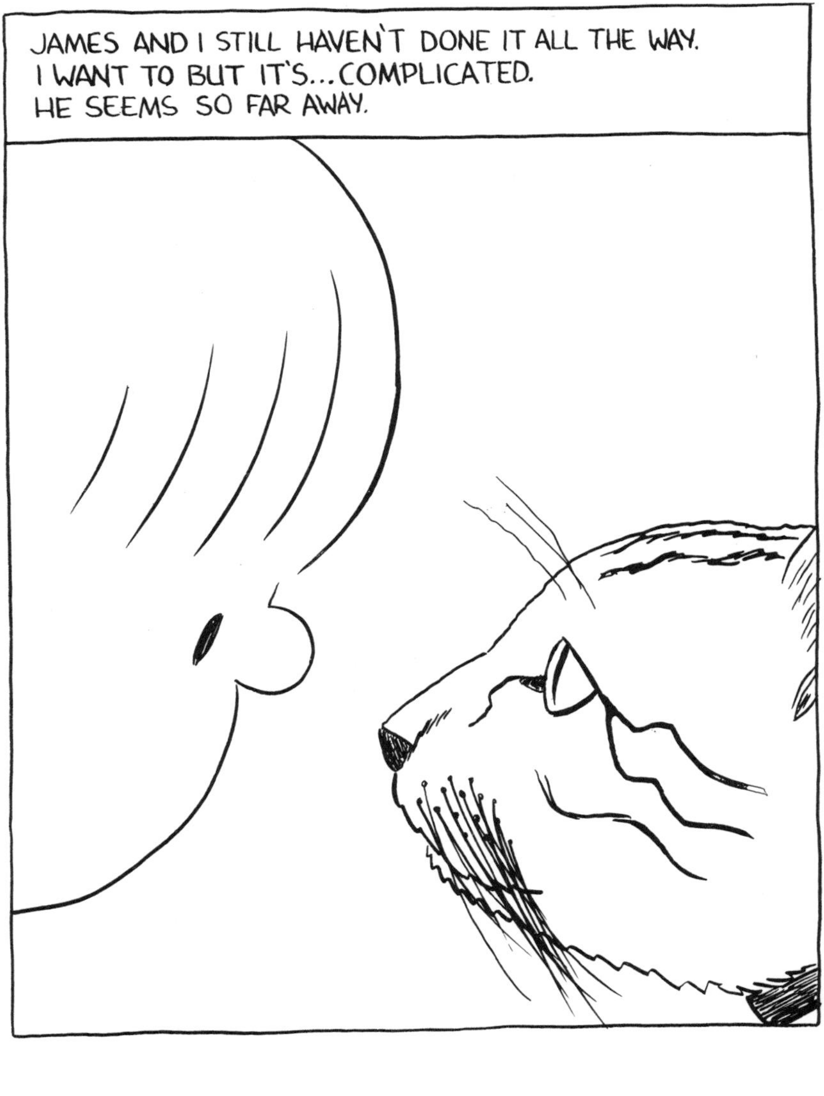
JAMES AND I STILL HAVEN'T DONE IT ALL THE WAY.
I WANT TO BUT IT'S...COMPLICATED.
HE SEEMS SO FAR AWAY.

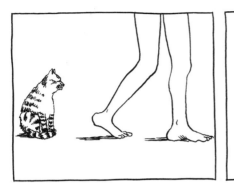

I'M HAVING FUN THOUGH.

I COULDN'T TAKE ANOTHER FUCKING MINUTE WITH MOM AND HER PERVERT BOYFRIEND.

I WISH MY DAD WAS THERE. I HAVEN'T SEEN HIM IN LIKE 10 YEARS SINCE MOM KICKED HIM OUT OF THE HOUSE.

JAMES SAID THAT WE SHOULD GO SEE HIM.

IF WE CAN FIND HIM.

I HOPE HE REMEMBERS ME.

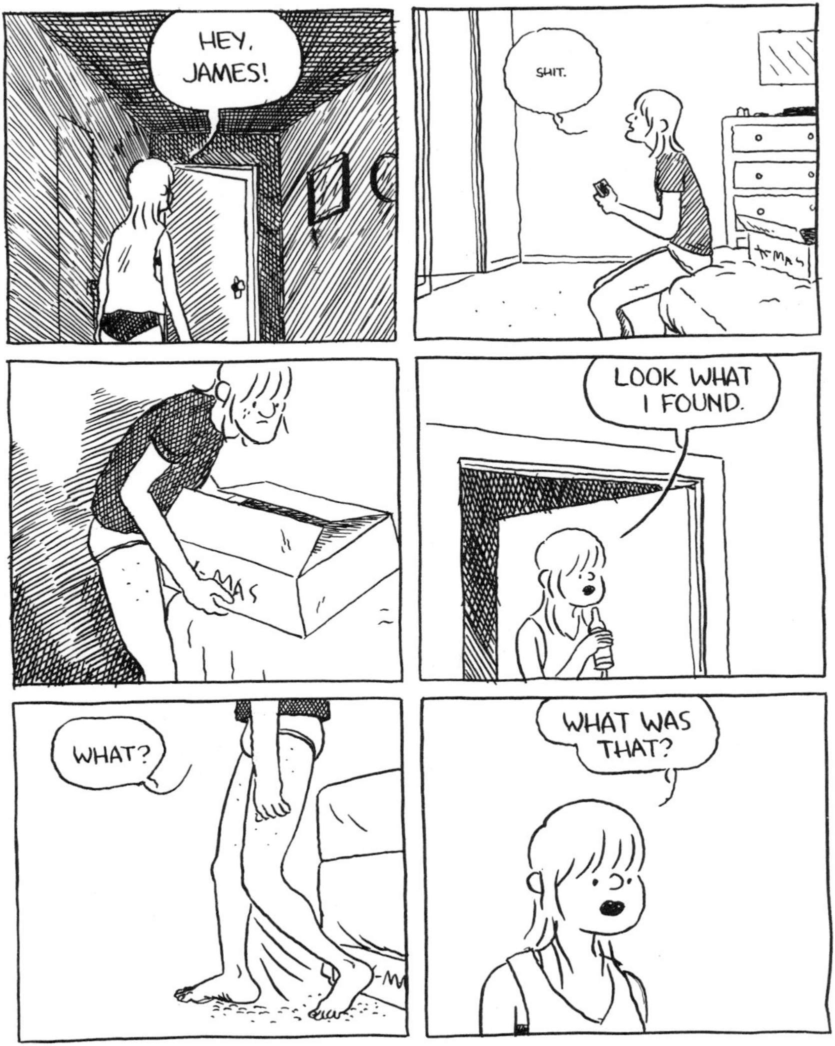
HEY, JAMES!
SHIT.
X-MAS
LOOK WHAT I FOUND.
WHAT?
WHAT WAS THAT?

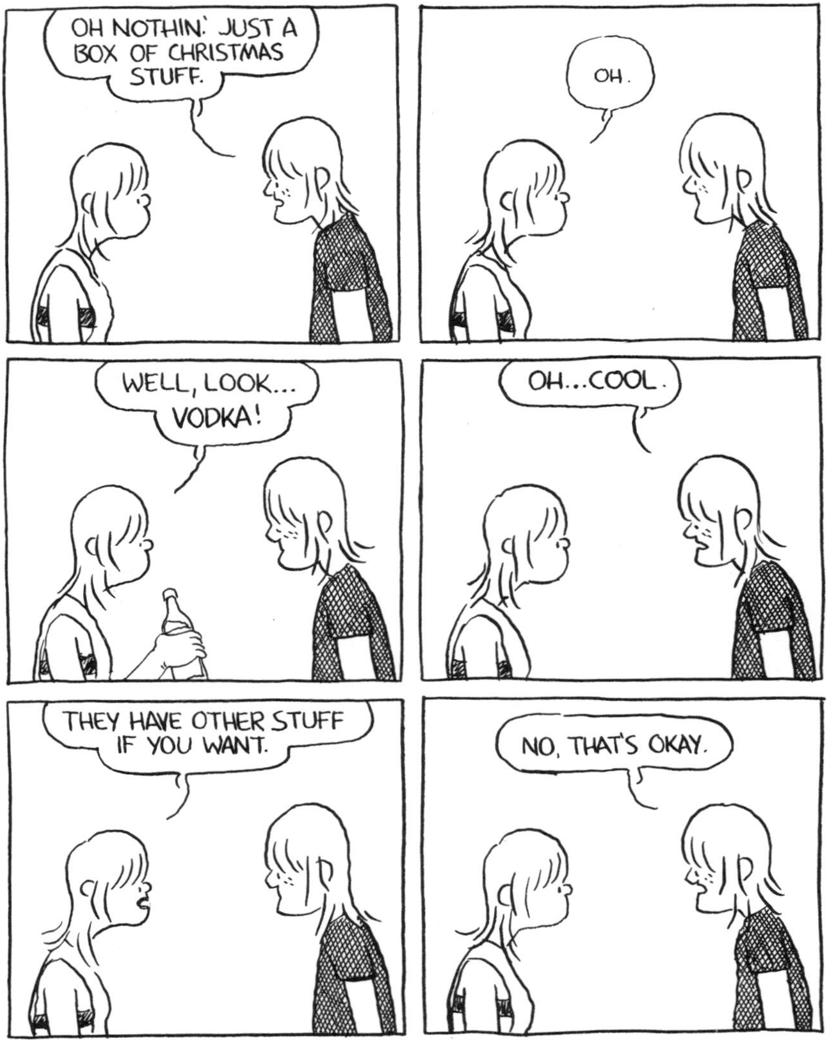
OH NOTHIN'. JUST A BOX OF CHRISTMAS STUFF.
OH.
WELL, LOOK... VODKA!
OH...COOL.
THEY HAVE OTHER STUFF IF YOU WANT.
NO, THAT'S OKAY.

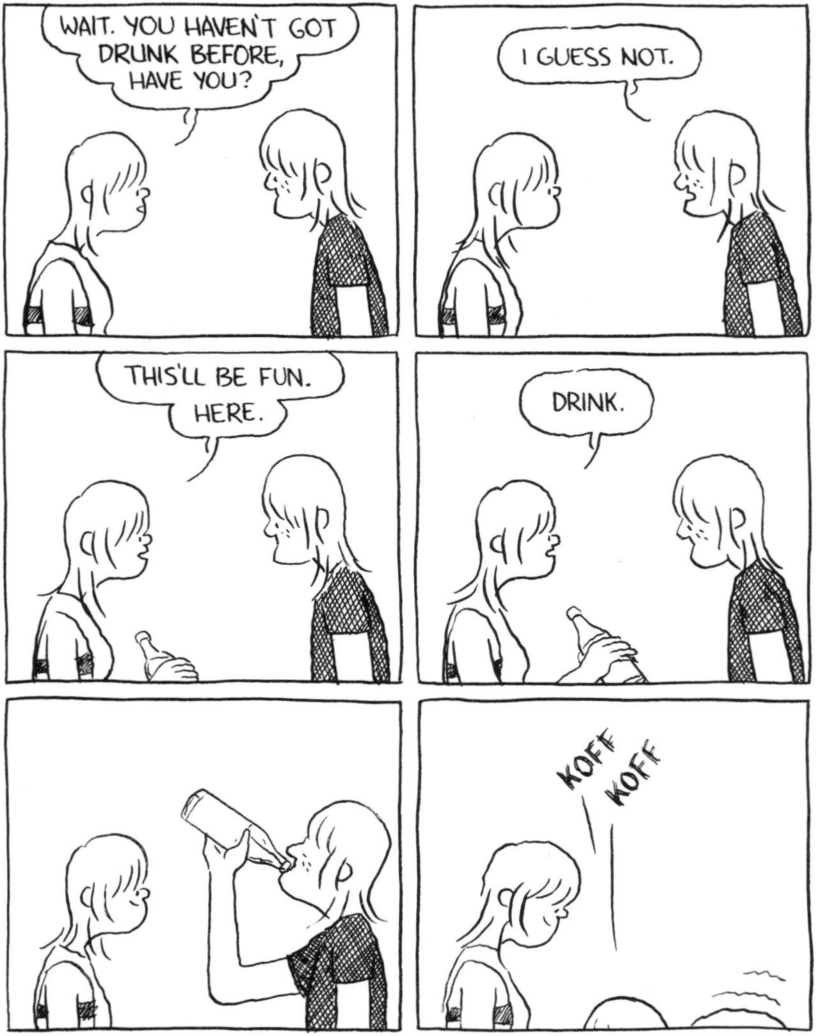

WAIT. YOU HAVEN'T GOT DRUNK BEFORE, HAVE YOU?
I GUESS NOT.
THIS'LL BE FUN. HERE.
DRINK.
KOFF KOFF

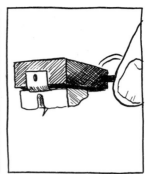

♪ FRANKIE AND JOHNNY ✓
WERE LOVERS

✓ O LORDY, HOW THEY ♪♪
COULD LOVE

♪ THEY SWORE TO BE TRUE
TO EACH OTHER ♪

♪ JUST AS TRUE AS ♪♪
THE STARS ABOVE

♪ HE WAS HER MAN ♪

✓ BUT HE DONE ♪♪
HER WRONG

O ROLL ME OVER SO EASY
ROLL ME OVER SO SLOW
ROLL ME OVER EASY BOYS
CAUSE MY WOUNDS THEY HURT ME SO
I WAS HER MAN
BUT I DONE HER WRONG
BRING OUT YOUR LONG BLACK COFFIN
BRING OUT YOUR FUNERAL CLOTHES
TO THE GRAVEYARD JOHNNY GOES

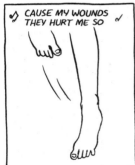

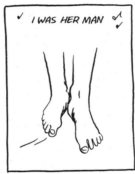

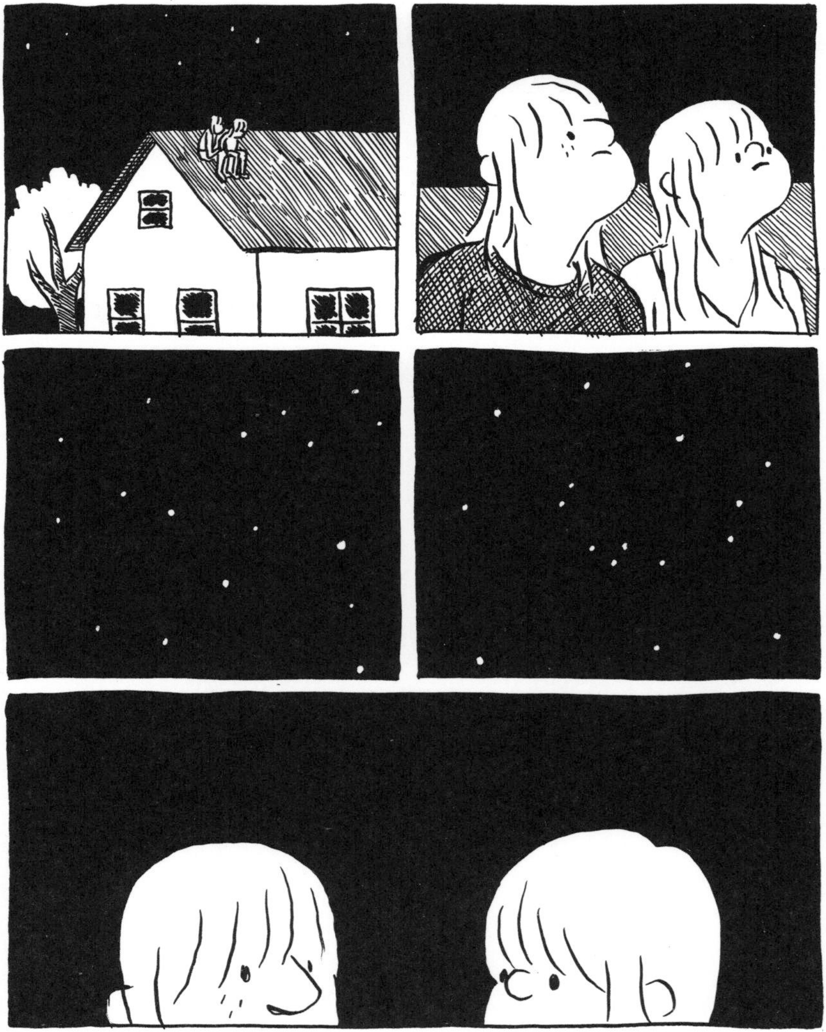

FAST FRIENDS

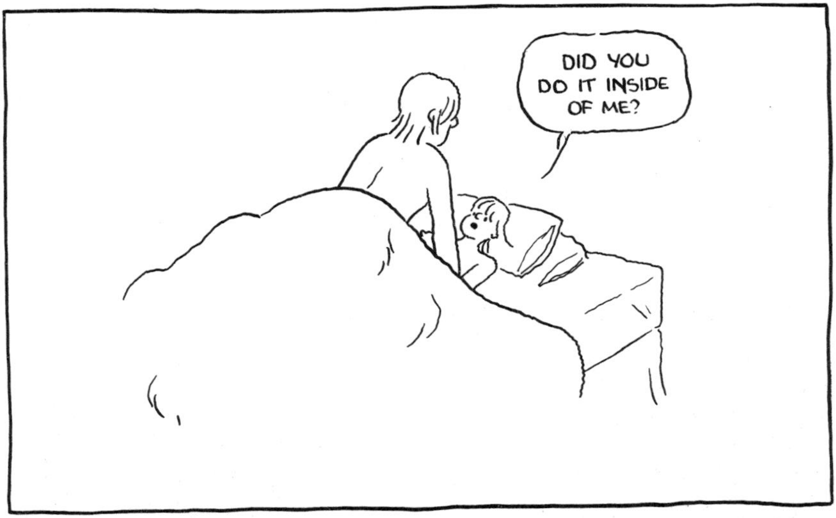
DID YOU
DO IT INSIDE
OF ME?

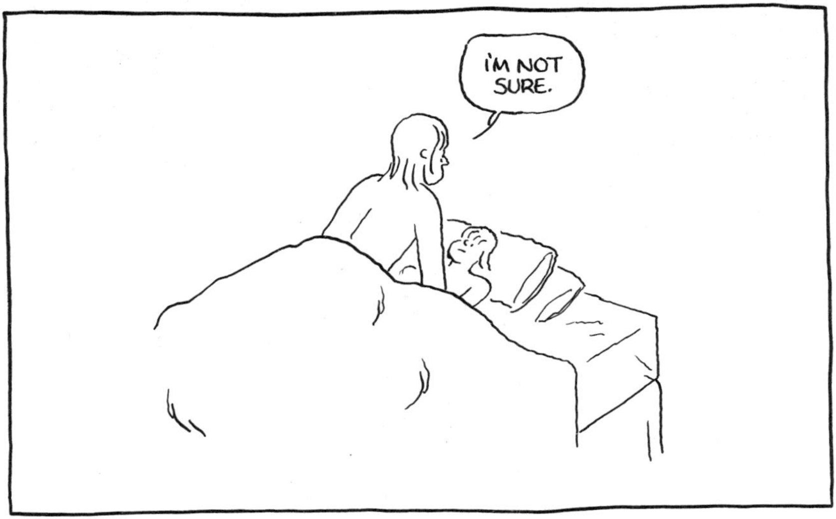
I'M NOT
SURE.

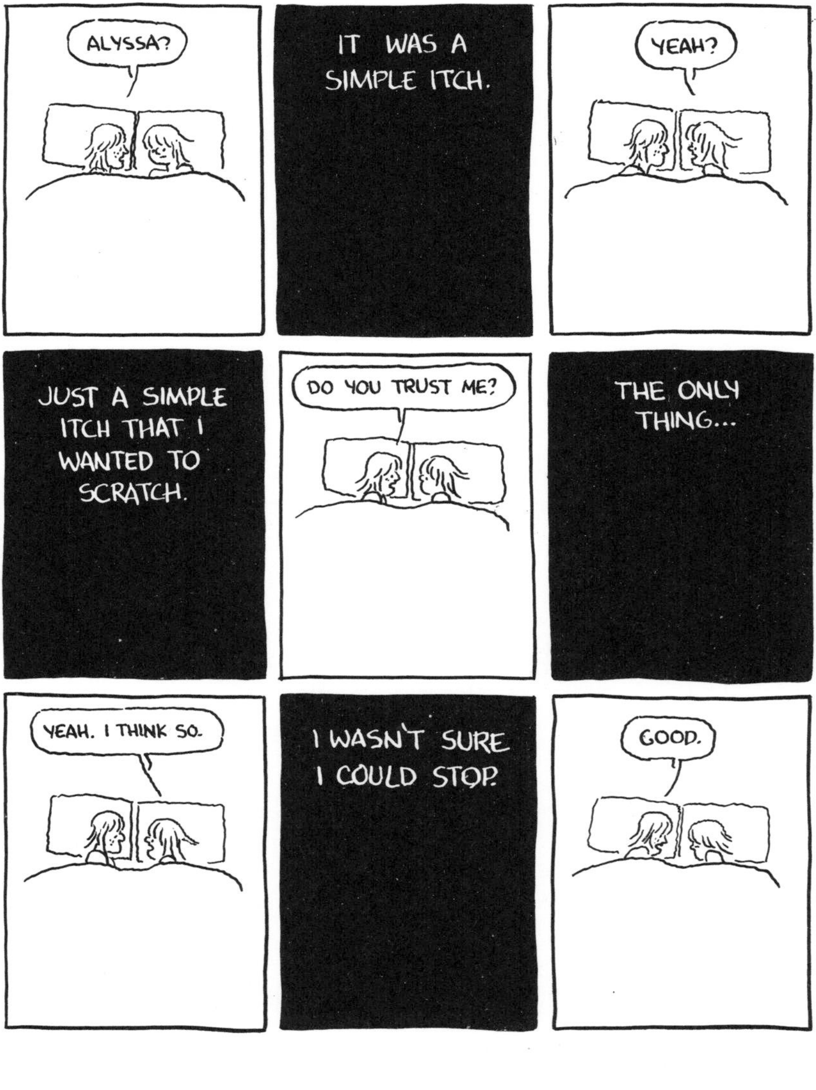
ALYSSA?
IT WAS A SIMPLE ITCH.
YEAH?
JUST A SIMPLE ITCH THAT I WANTED TO SCRATCH.
DO YOU TRUST ME?
THE ONLY THING...
YEAH. I THINK SO.
I WASN'T SURE I COULD STOP.
GOOD.

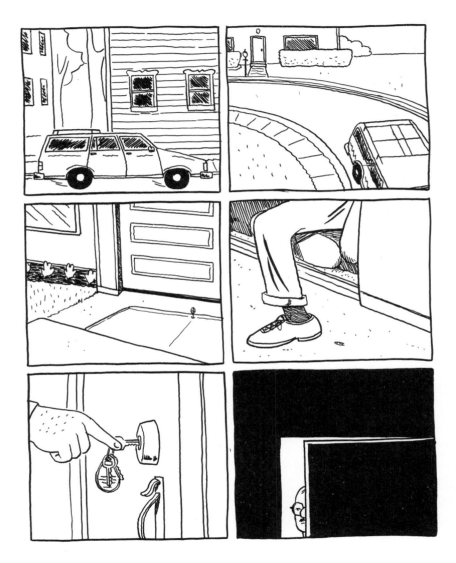

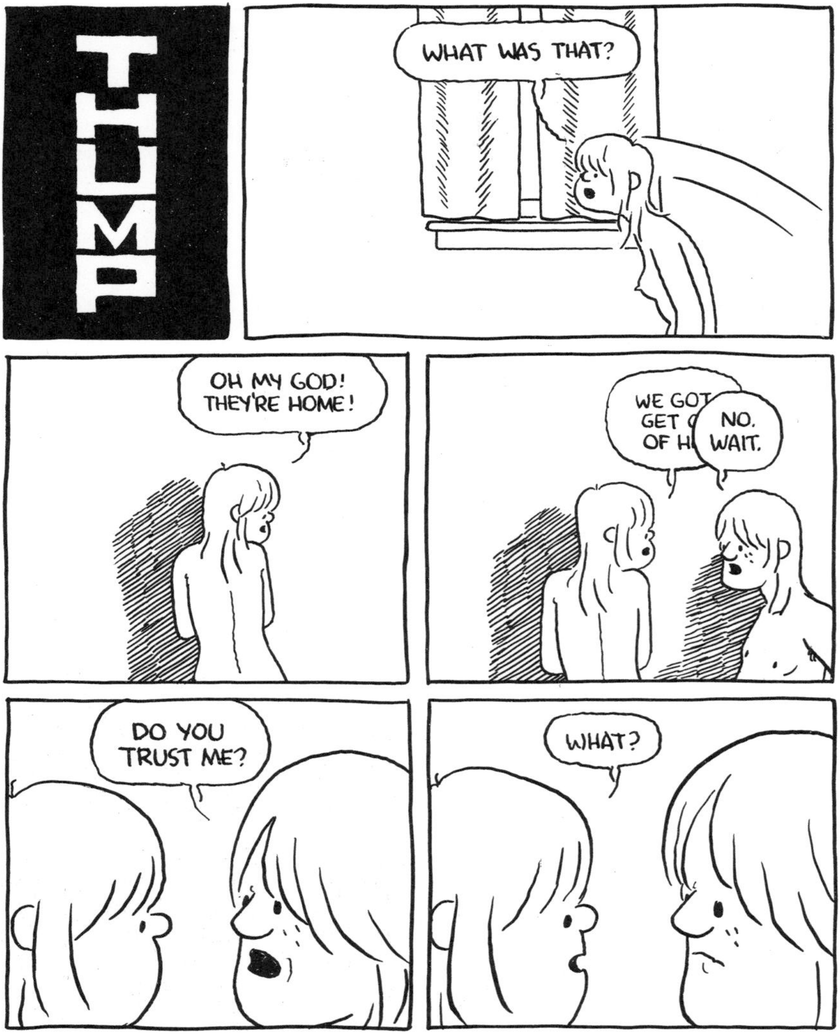
THUMP
WHAT WAS THAT?
OH MY GOD! THEY'RE HOME!
NO. WAIT.
DO YOU TRUST ME?
WHAT?

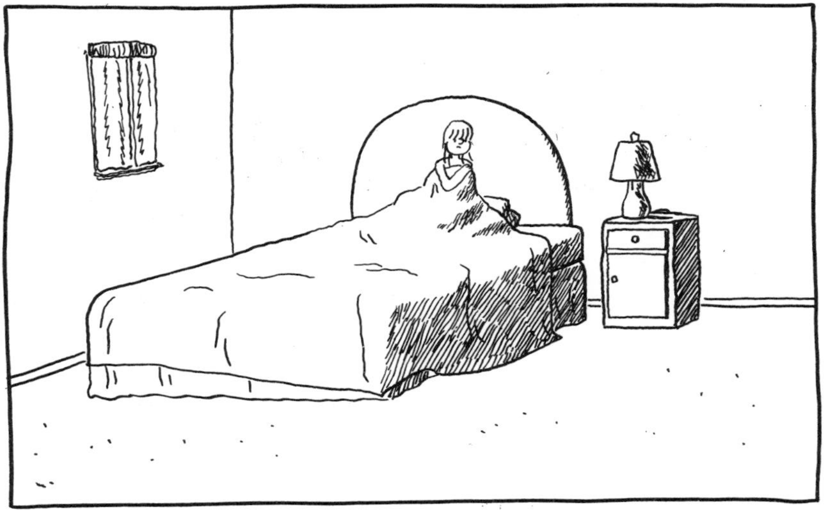

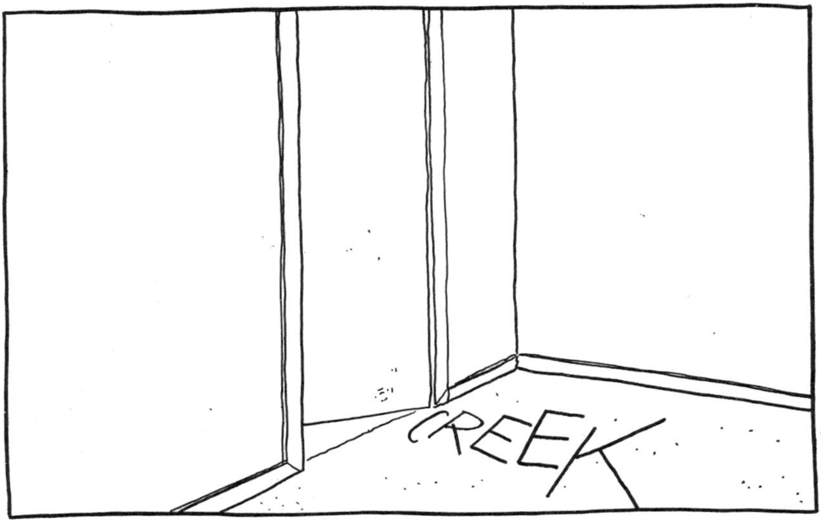
CREEK

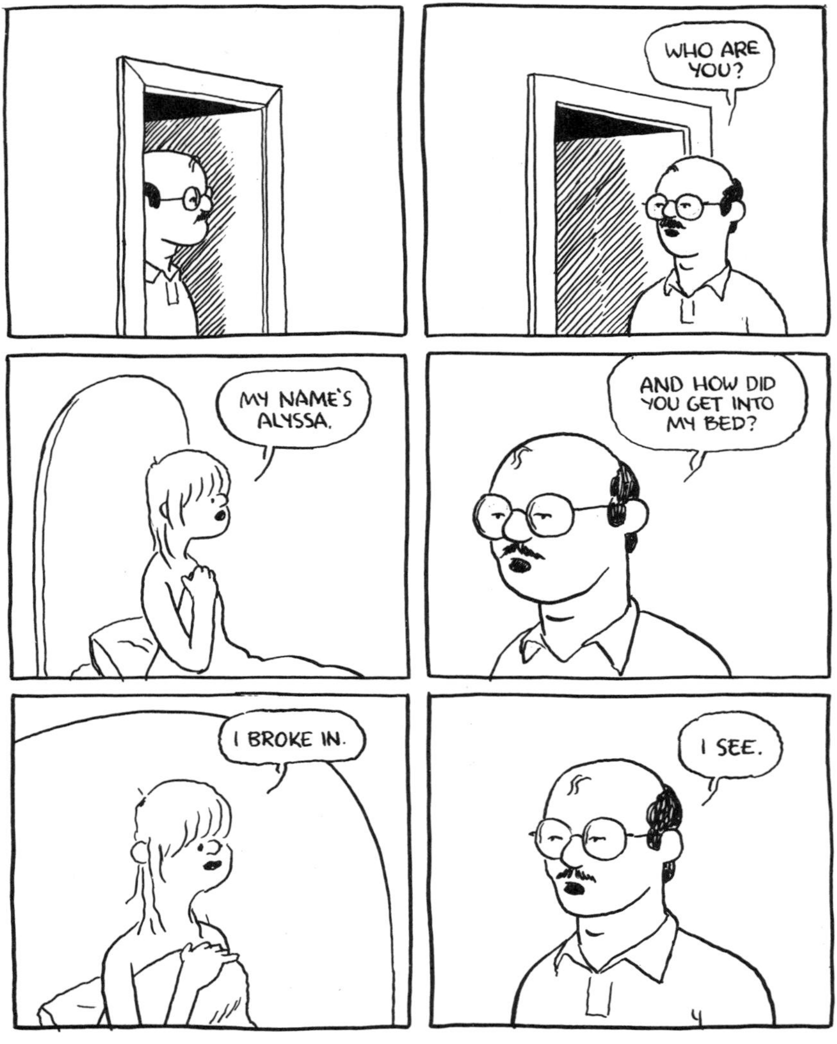
WHO ARE YOU?
MY NAME'S ALYSSA.
AND HOW DID YOU GET INTO MY BED?
I BROKE IN.
I SEE.

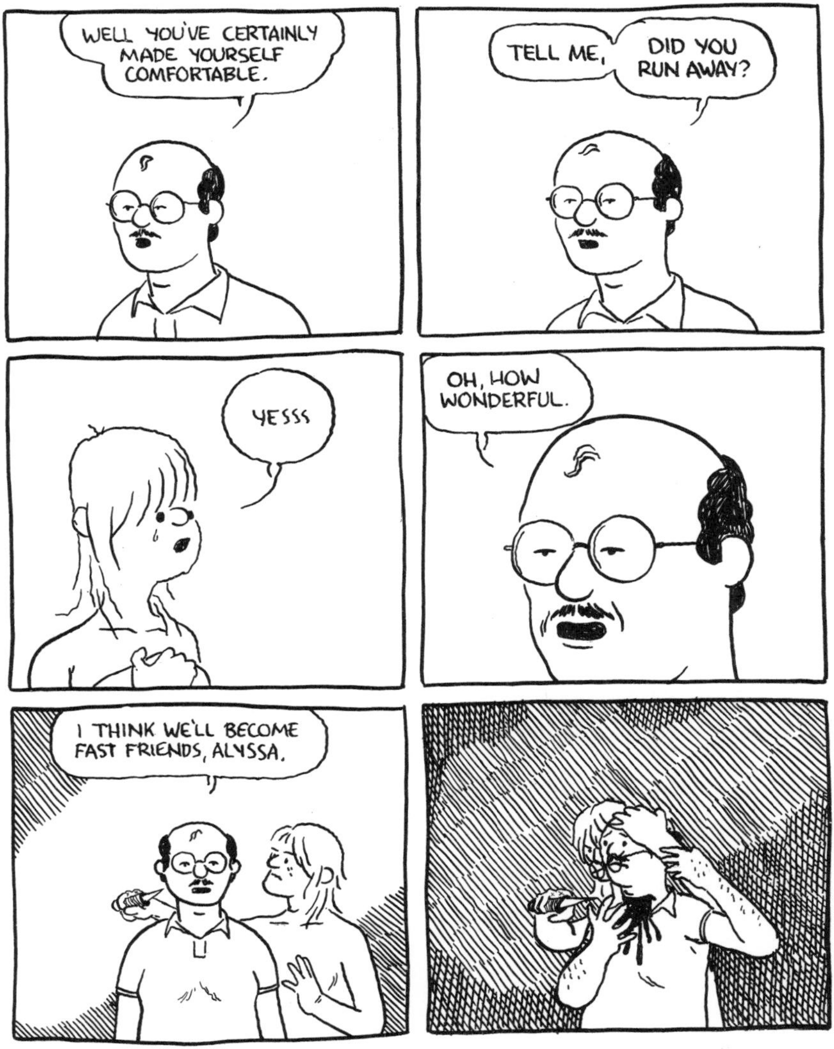
WELL YOU'VE CERTAINLY MADE YOURSELF COMFORTABLE.
TELL ME,
DID YOU RUN AWAY?
YESSS
OH, HOW WONDERFUL.
I THINK WE'LL BECOME FAST FRIENDS, ALYSSA.

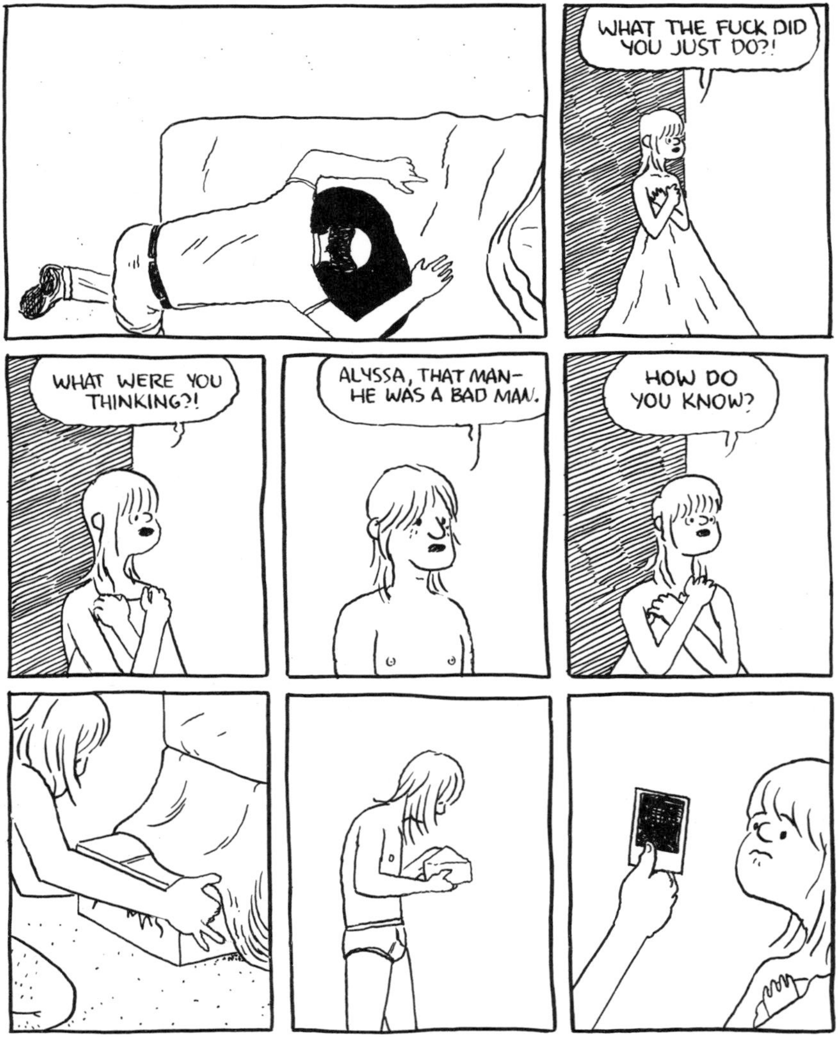
WHAT THE FUCK DID YOU JUST DO?!
WHAT WERE YOU THINKING?!
ALYSSA, THAT MAN- HE WAS A BAD MAN.
HOW DO YOU KNOW?

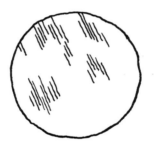

WORSE PROBABLY

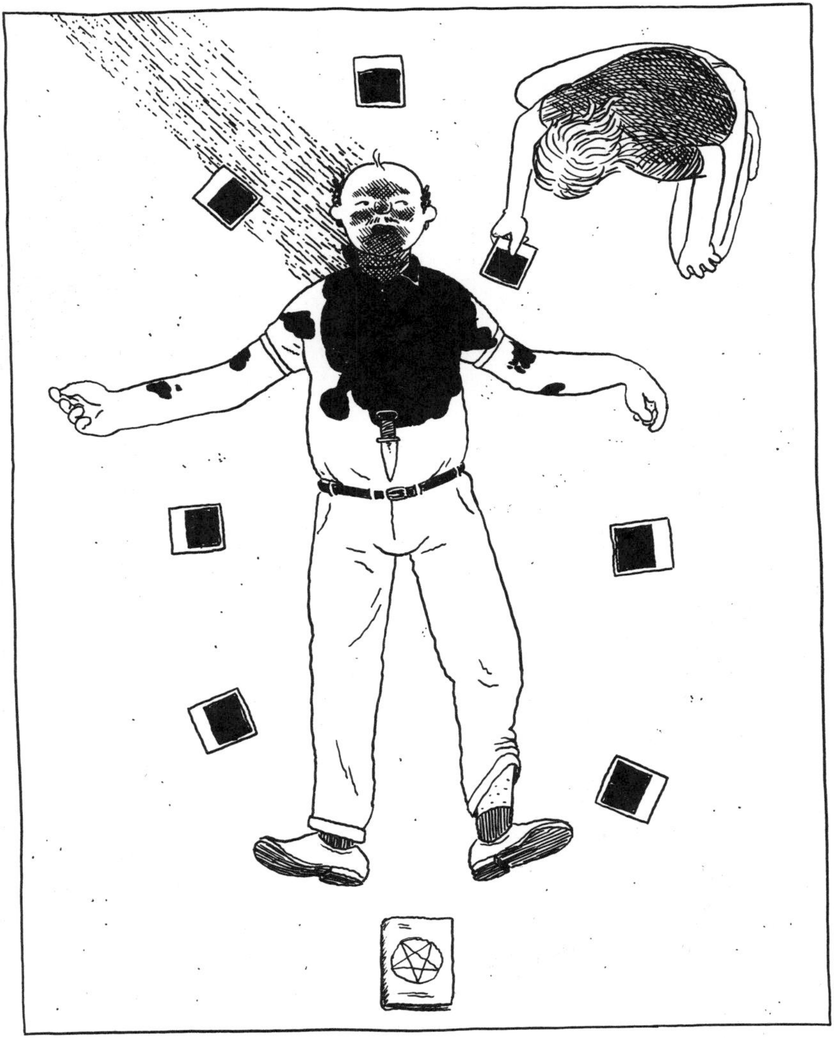

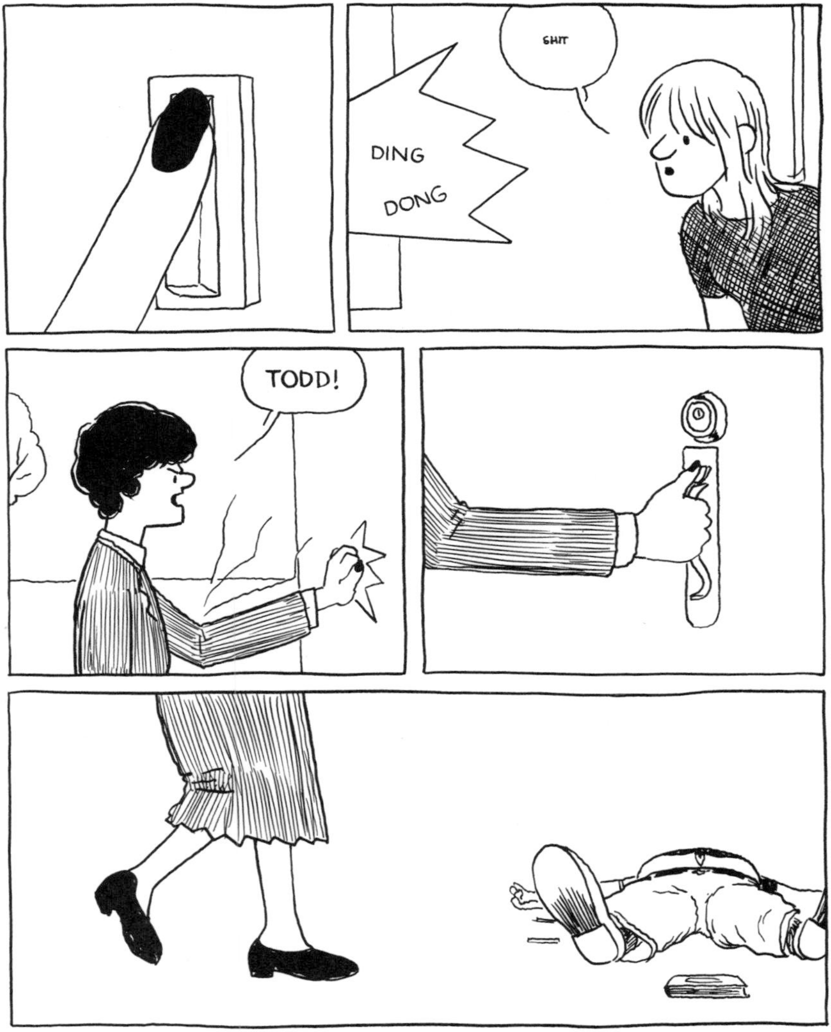
DING
DONG
SHIT
TODD!

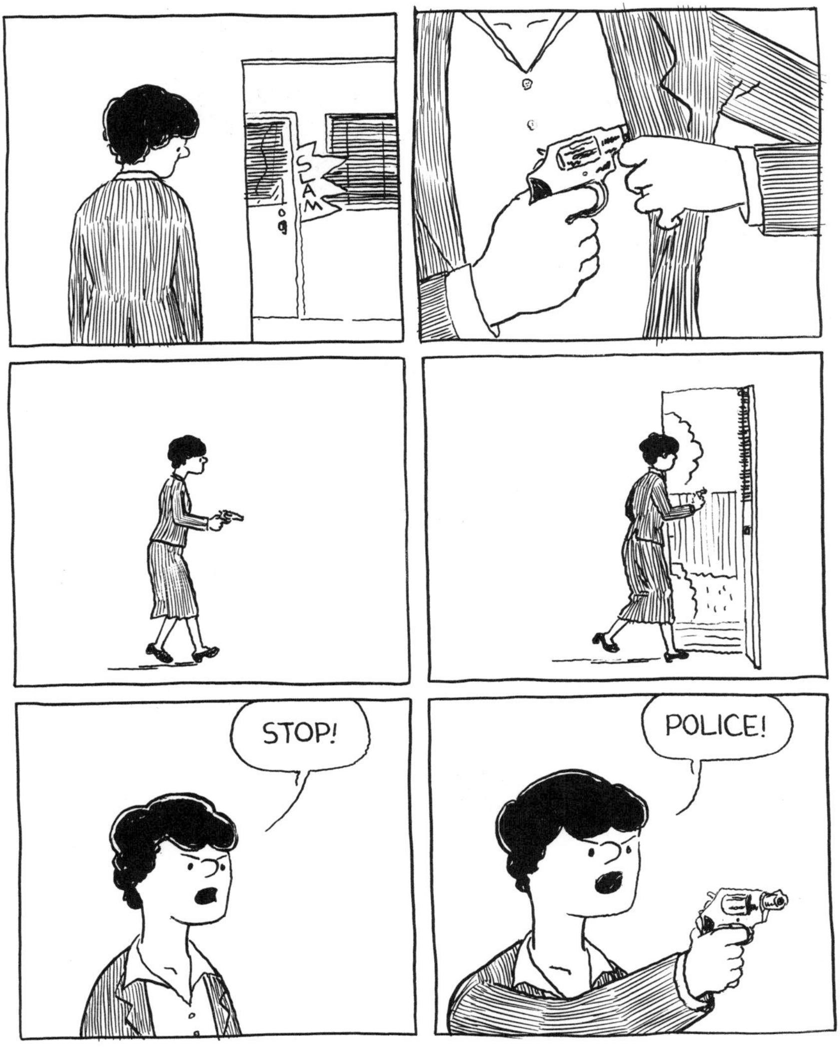
SLAM
STOP!
POLICE!

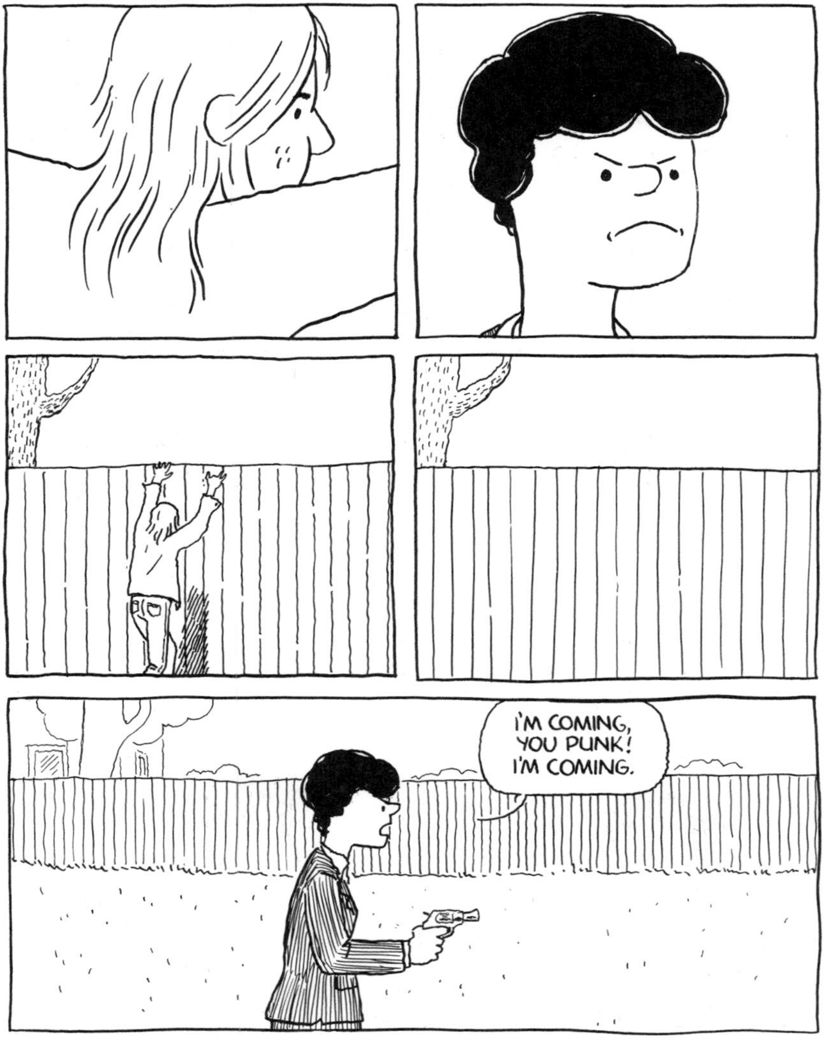
I'M COMING, YOU PUNK! I'M COMING.

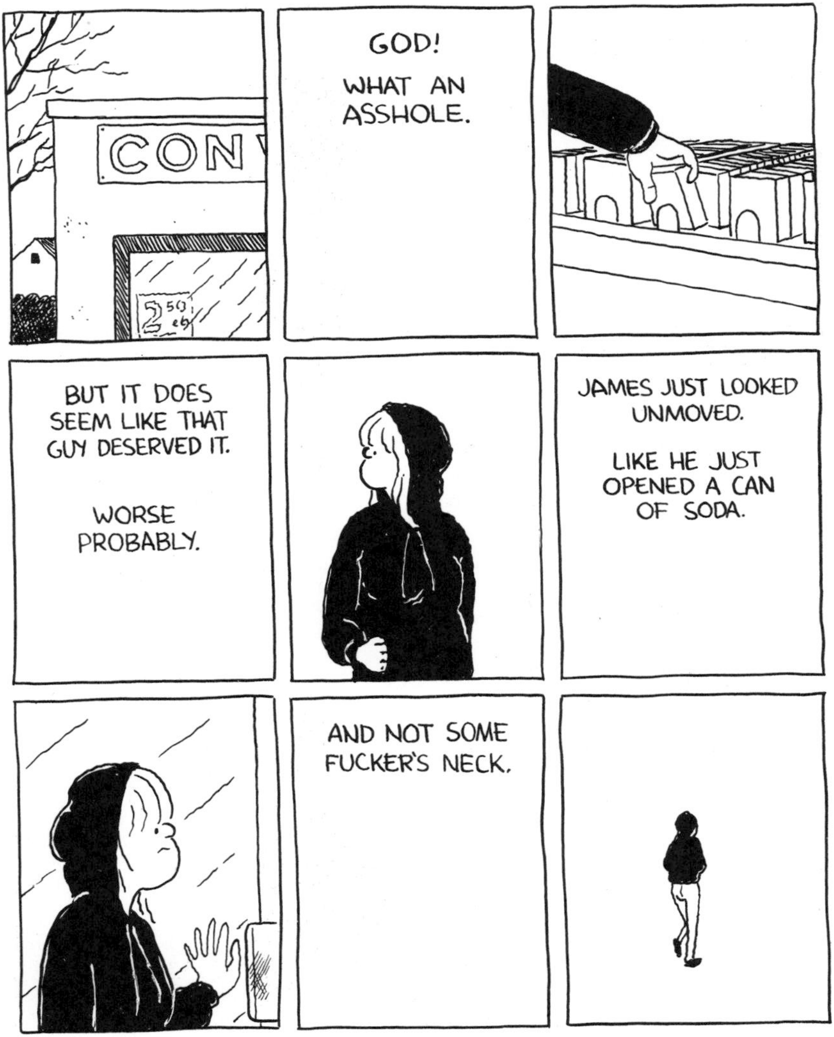
CON
GOD!
WHAT AN ASSHOLE.
BUT IT DOES SEEM LIKE THAT GUY DESERVED IT.
WORSE PROBABLY.
JAMES JUST LOOKED UNMOVED.
LIKE HE JUST OPENED A CAN OF SODA.
AND NOT SOME FUCKER'S NECK.

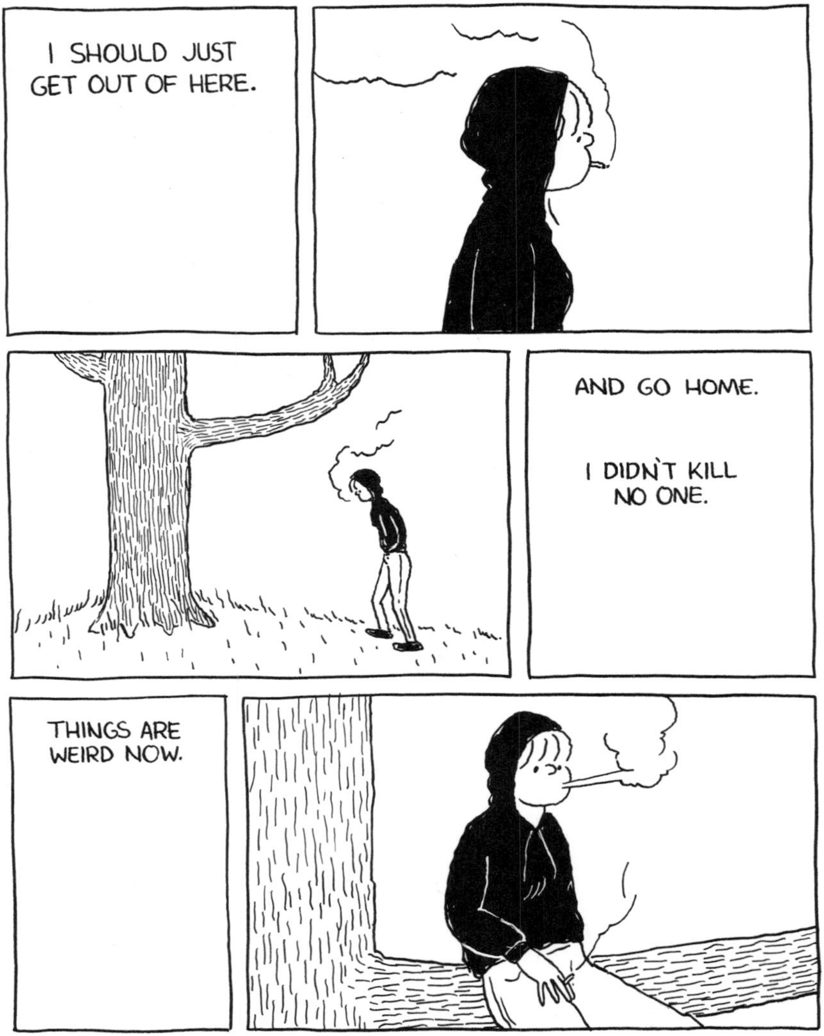
I SHOULD JUST GET OUT OF HERE.
AND GO HOME.
I DIDN'T KILL NO ONE.
THINGS ARE WEIRD NOW.

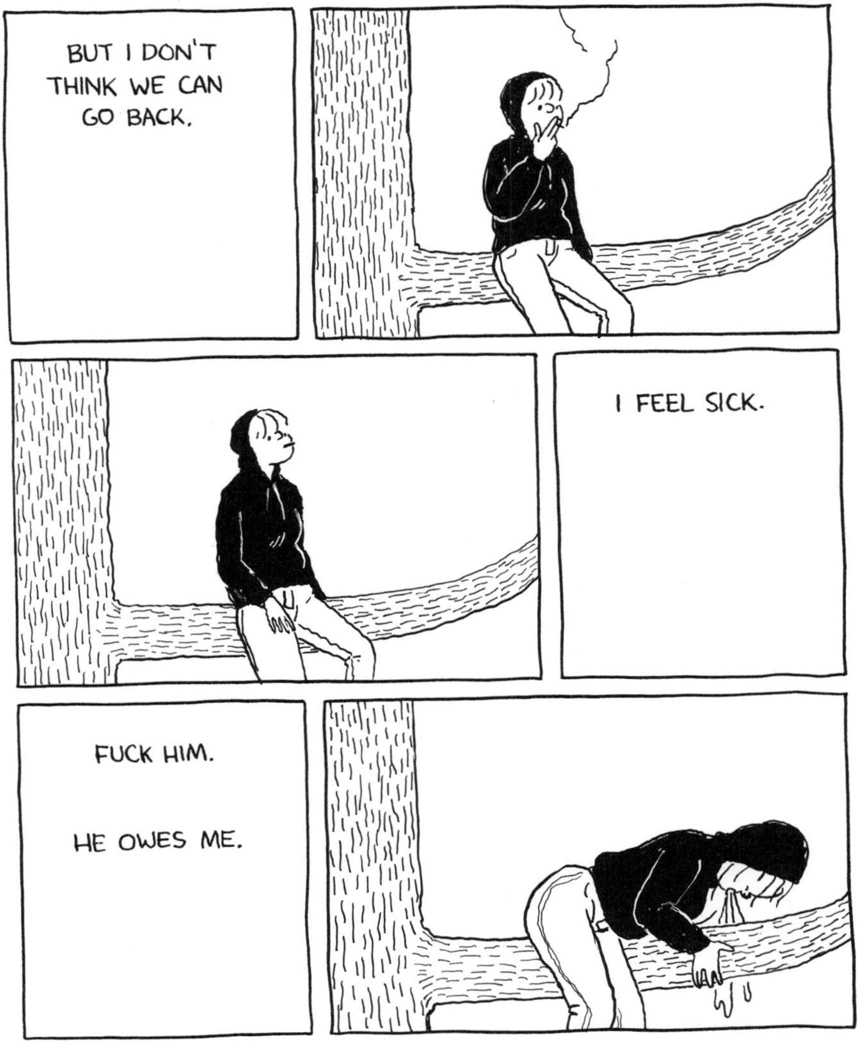
BUT I DON'T THINK WE CAN GO BACK.
I FEEL SICK.
FUCK HIM.
HE OWES ME.

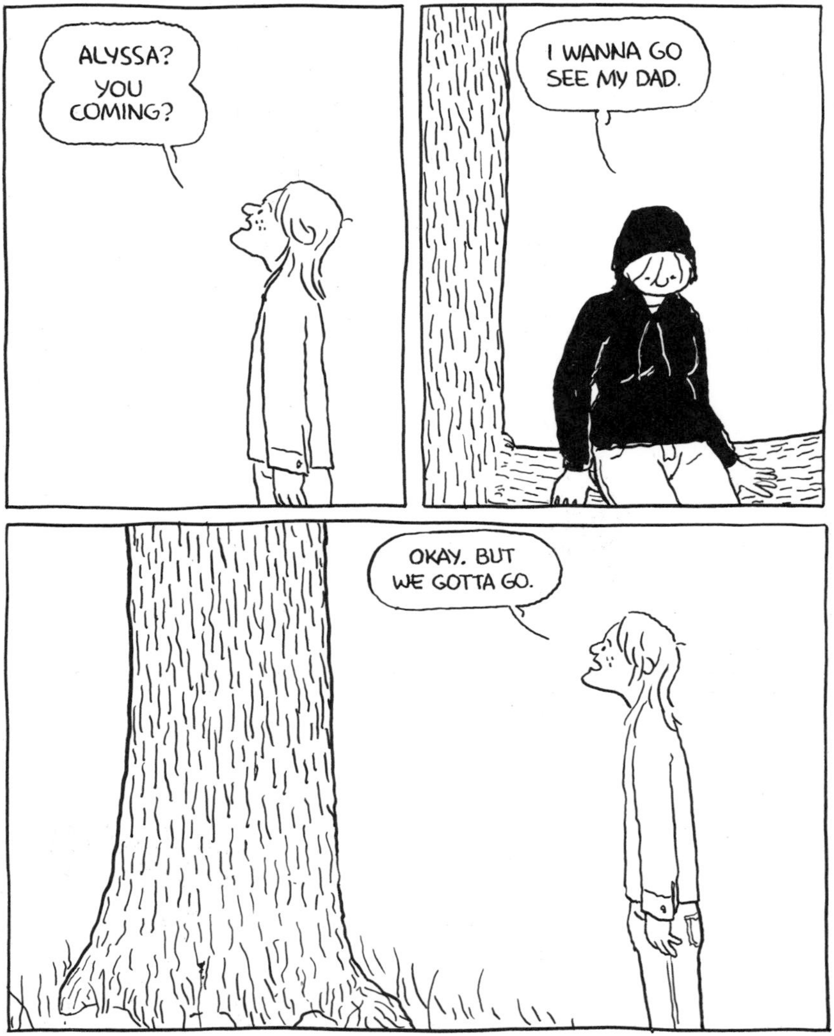
ALYSSA? YOU COMING?
I WANNA GO SEE MY DAD.
OKAY. BUT WE GOTTA GO.

MOTHER

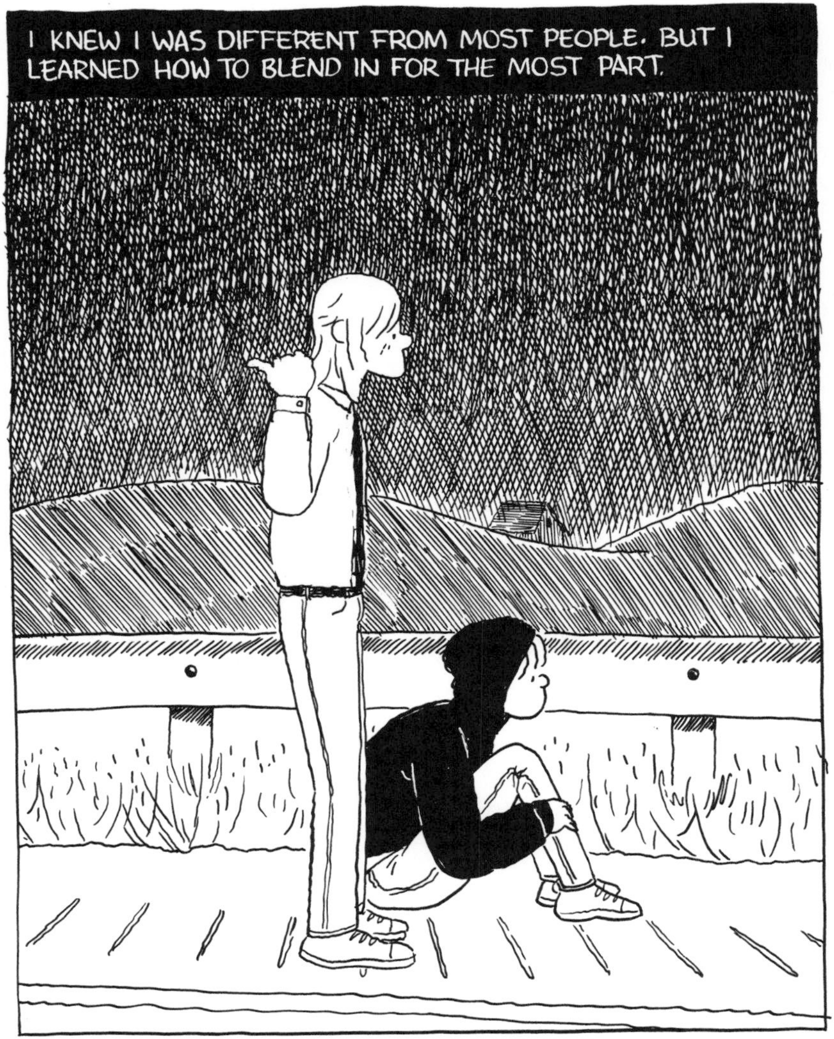
I KNEW I WAS DIFFERENT FROM MOST PEOPLE. BUT I LEARNED HOW TO BLEND IN FOR THE MOST PART.

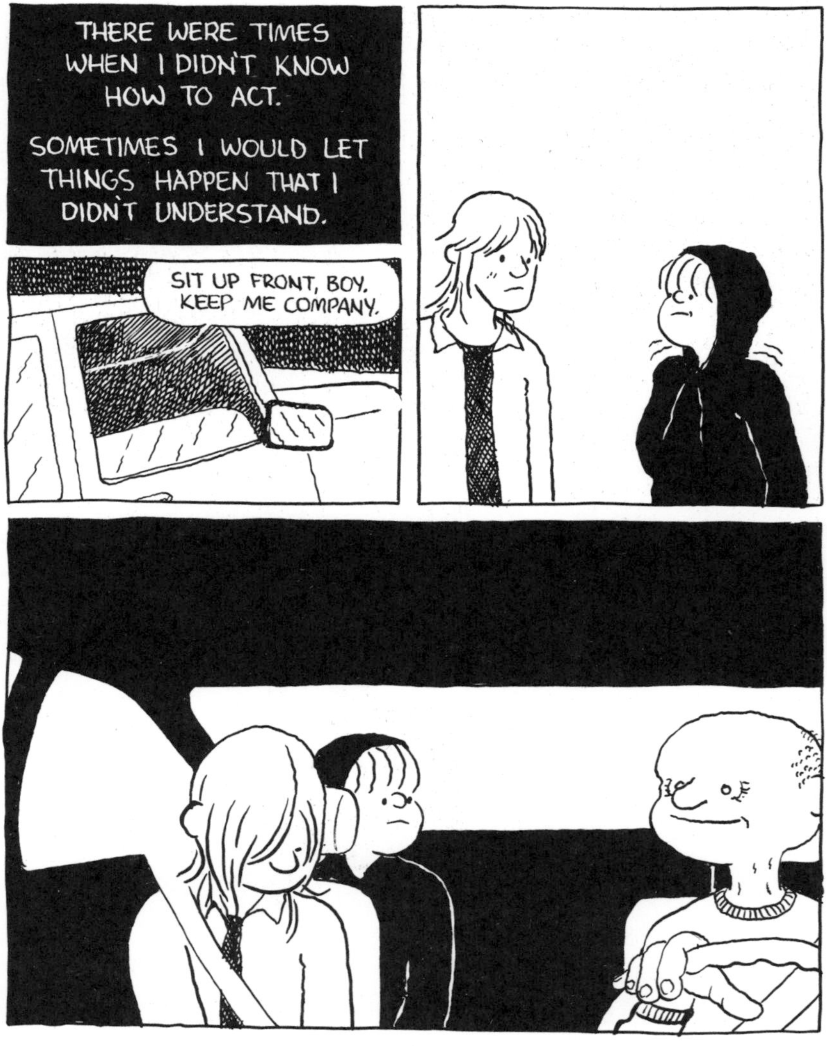
THERE WERE TIMES WHEN I DIDN'T KNOW HOW TO ACT.
SOMETIMES I WOULD LET THINGS HAPPEN THAT I DIDN'T UNDERSTAND.
SIT UP FRONT, BOY. KEEP ME COMPANY.

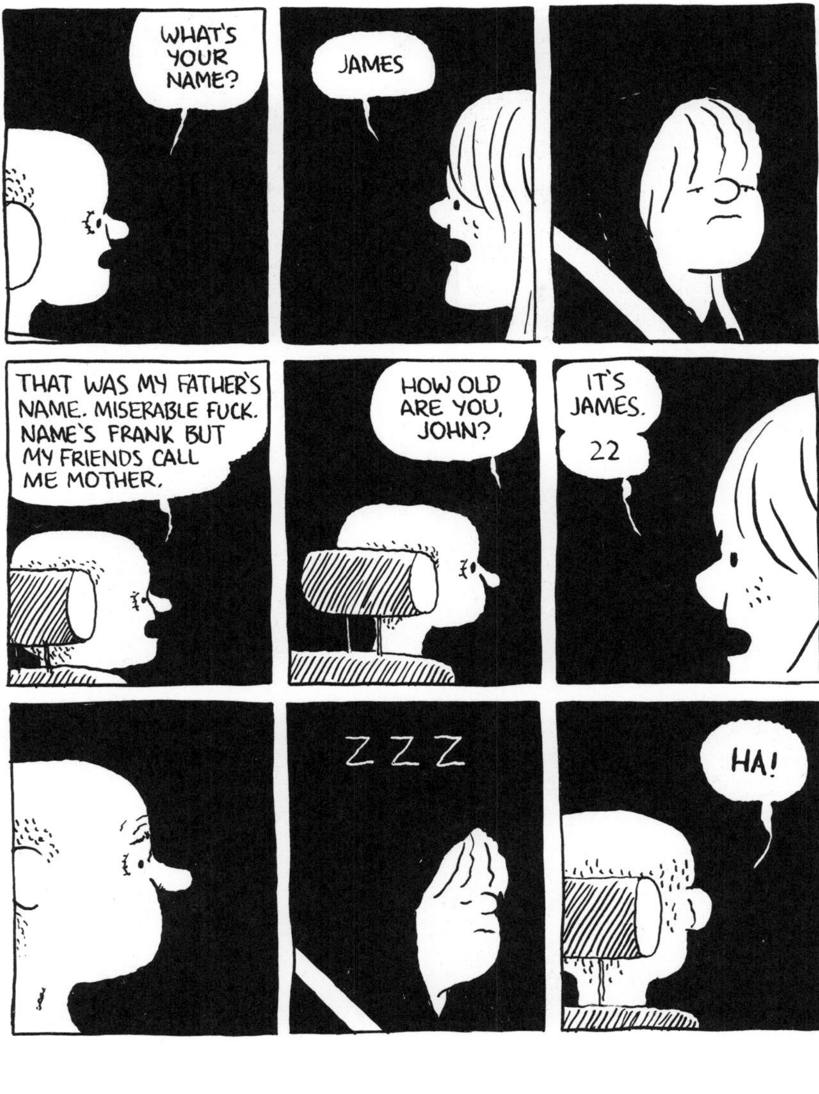

WHAT'S YOUR NAME?
JAMES
THAT WAS MY FATHER'S NAME. MISERABLE FUCK. NAME'S FRANK BUT MY FRIENDS CALL ME MOTHER.
HOW OLD ARE YOU, JOHN?
IT'S JAMES.
22
Z Z Z
HA!

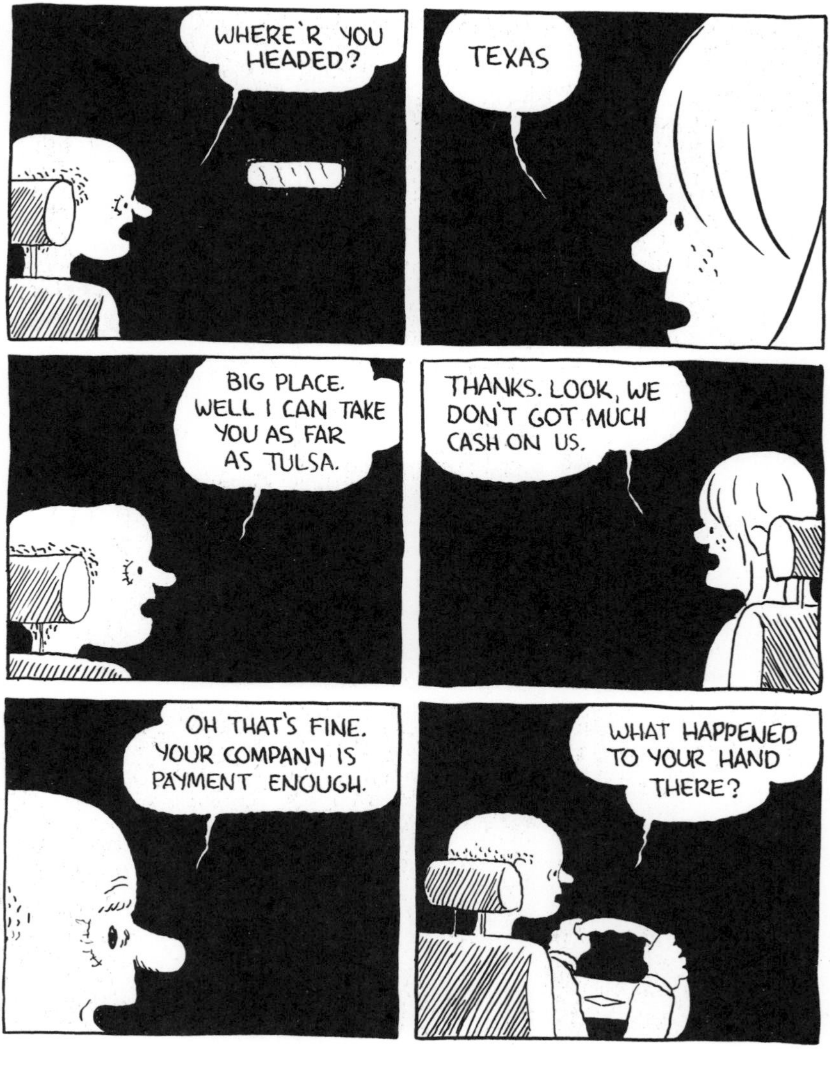
WHERE'R YOU HEADED?
TEXAS
BIG PLACE. WELL I CAN TAKE YOU AS FAR AS TULSA.
THANKS. LOOK, WE DON'T GOT MUCH CASH ON US.
OH THAT'S FINE. YOUR COMPANY IS PAYMENT ENOUGH.
WHAT HAPPENED TO YOUR HAND THERE?

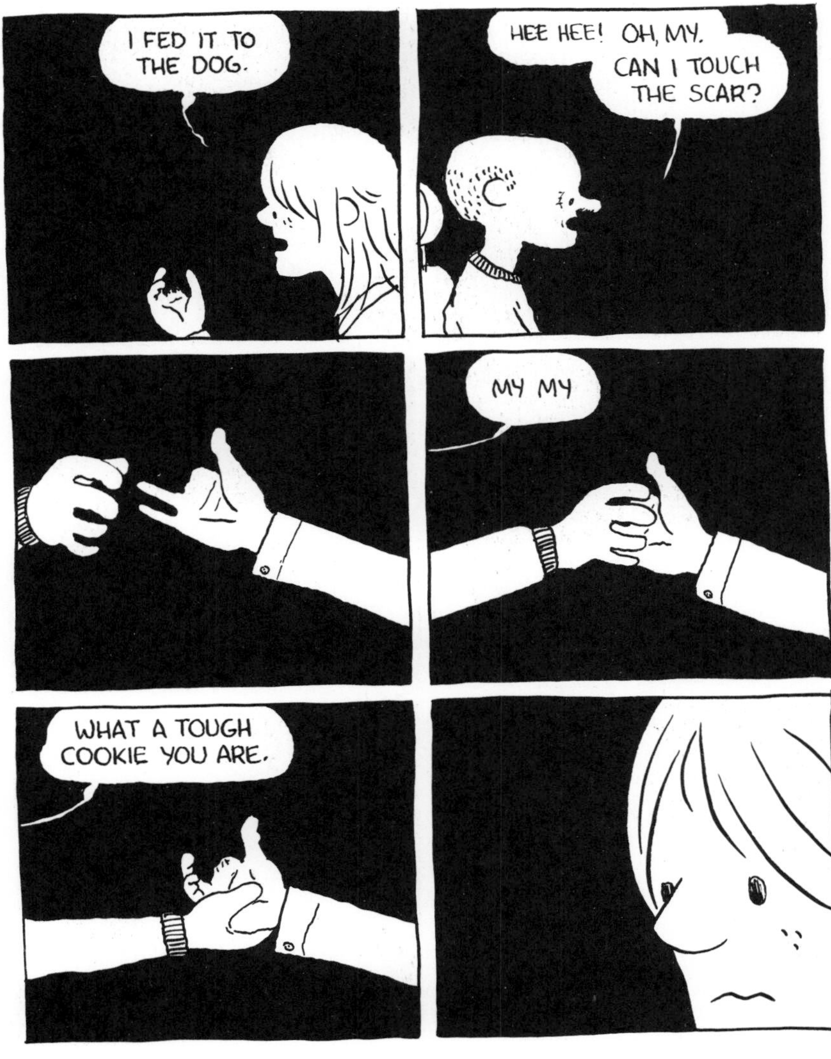
I FED IT TO THE DOG.
HEE HEE! OH, MY.
CAN I TOUCH THE SCAR?
MY MY
WHAT A TOUGH COOKIE YOU ARE.

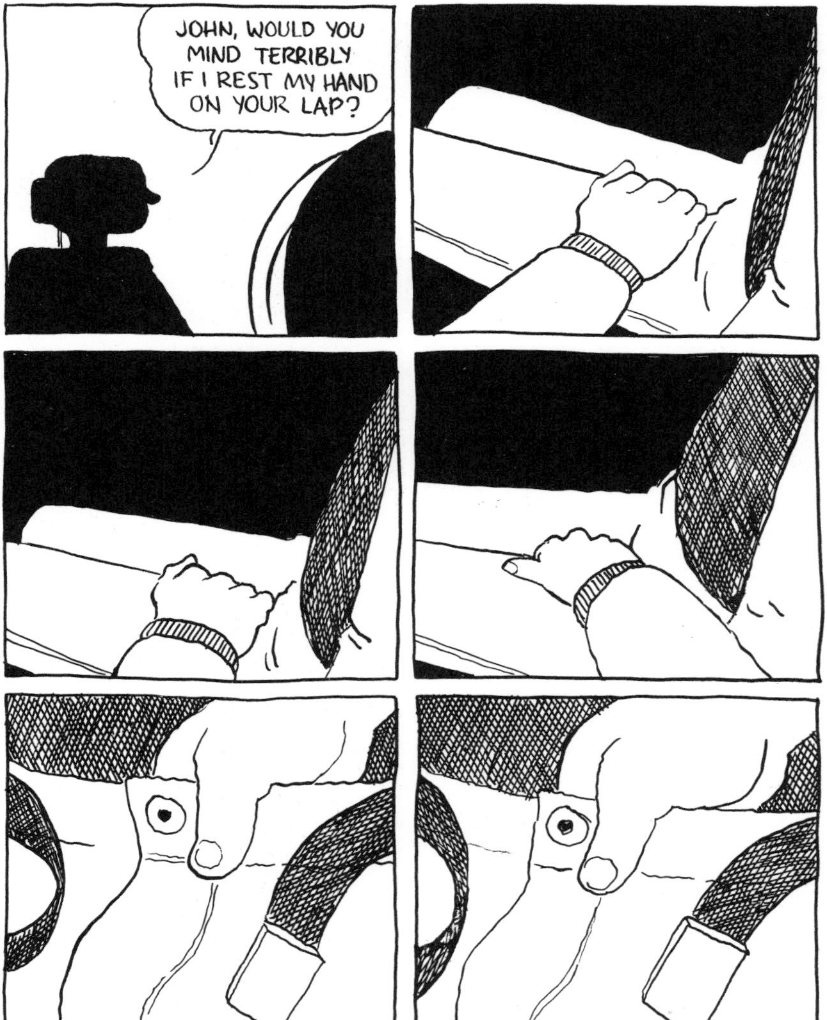
JOHN, WOULD YOU MIND TERRIBLY IF I REST MY HAND ON YOUR LAP?

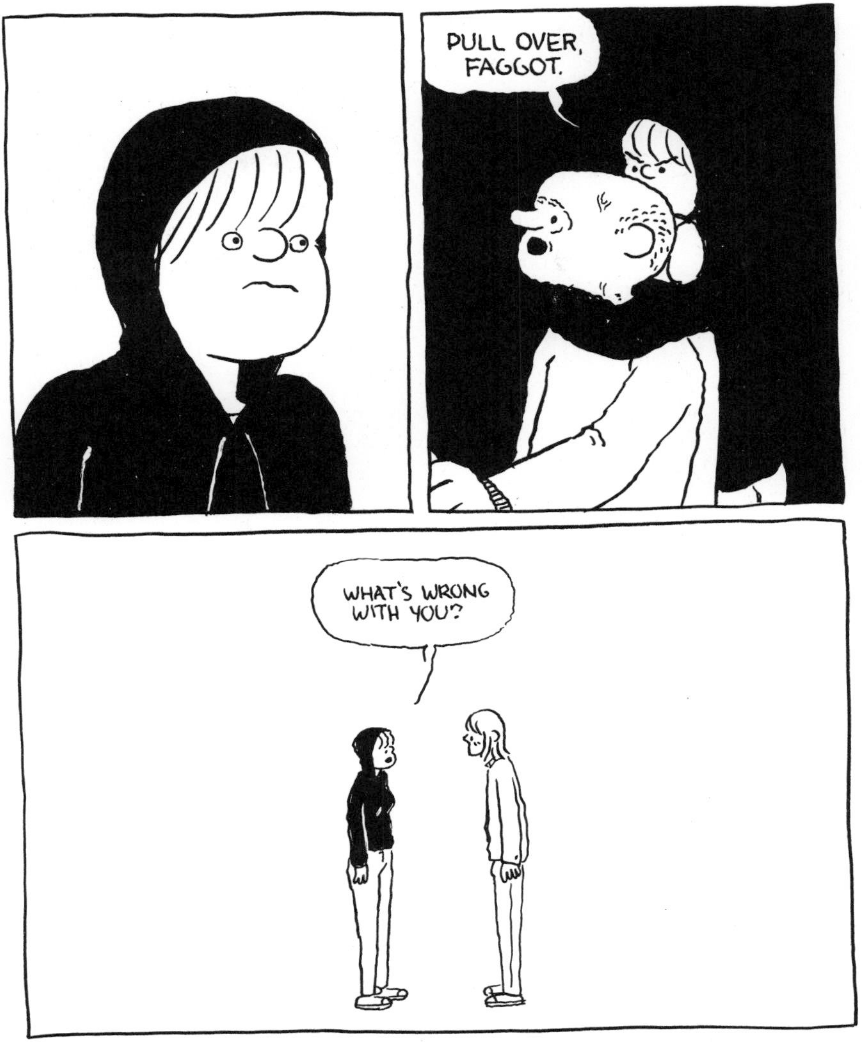
PULL OVER, FAGGOT.
WHAT'S WRONG WITH YOU?

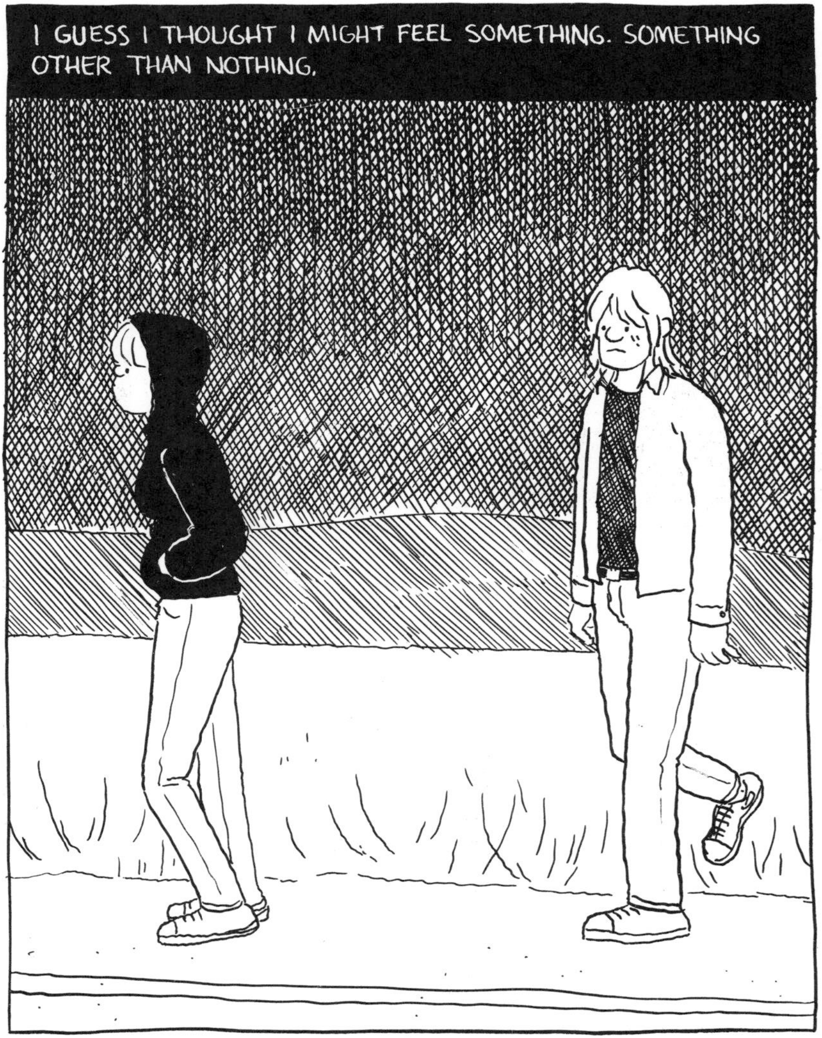
I GUESS I THOUGHT I MIGHT FEEL SOMETHING. SOMETHING OTHER THAN NOTHING.

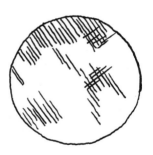

TULSA GOODBYE

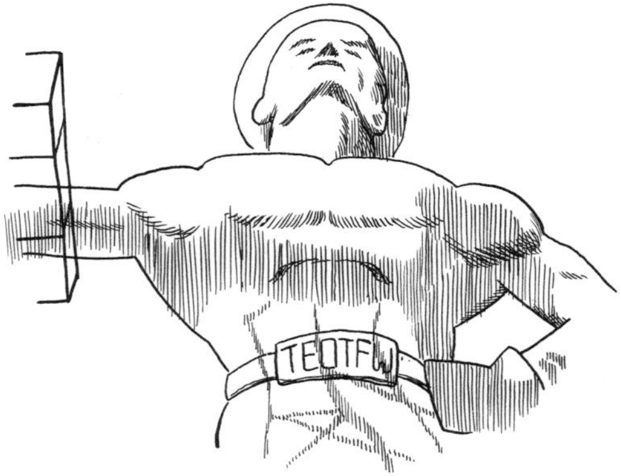
TEOTFW

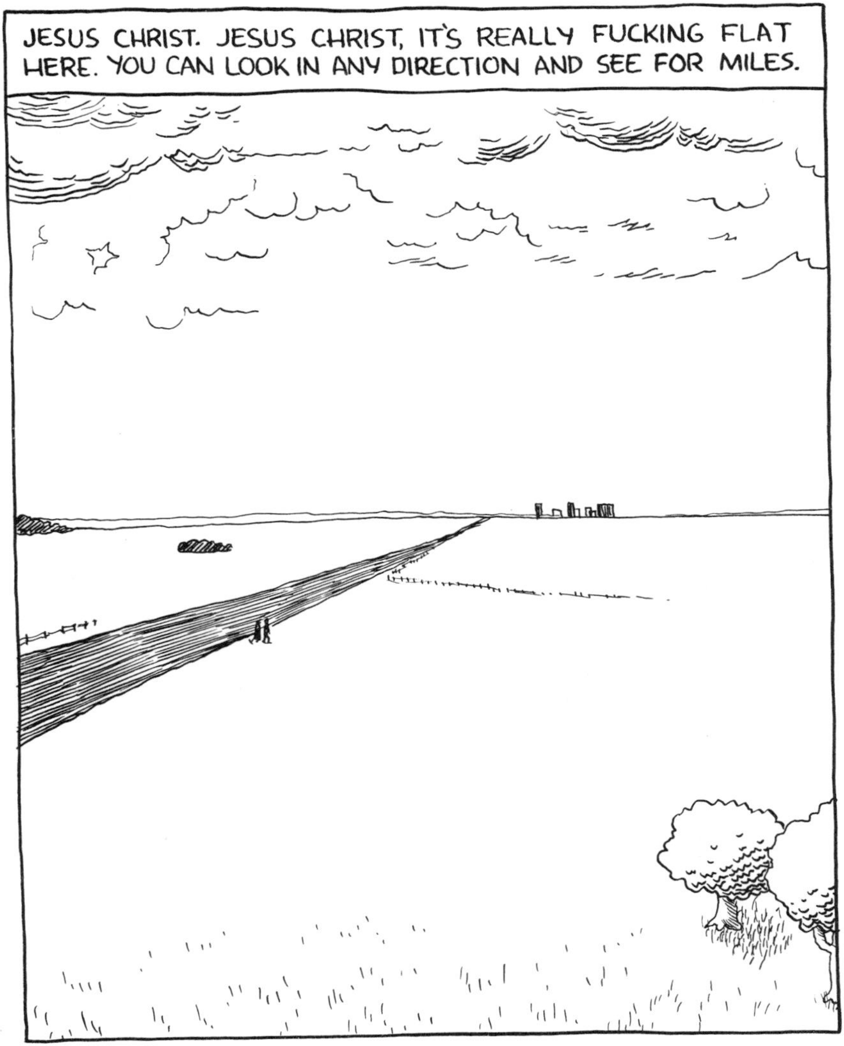
JESUS CHRIST. JESUS CHRIST, IT'S REALLY FUCKING FLAT HERE. YOU CAN LOOK IN ANY DIRECTION AND SEE FOR MILES.

THERE'S JUST
NOTHING TO
LOOK AT.

JAMES.

Suspect on t

sketch released by police of
suspect wanted for murder

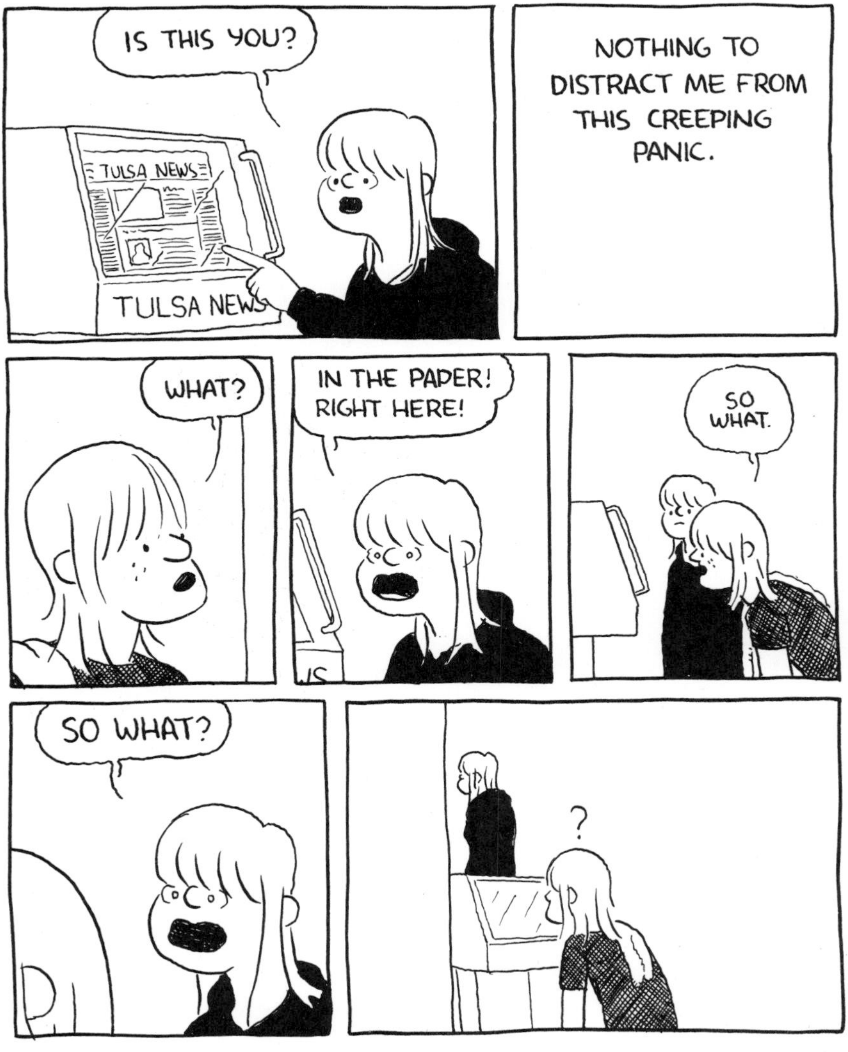
IS THIS YOU?
TULSA NEWS
TULSA NEWS
NOTHING TO DISTRACT ME FROM THIS CREEPING PANIC.
WHAT?
IN THE PAPER! RIGHT HERE!
SO WHAT.
SO WHAT?
?

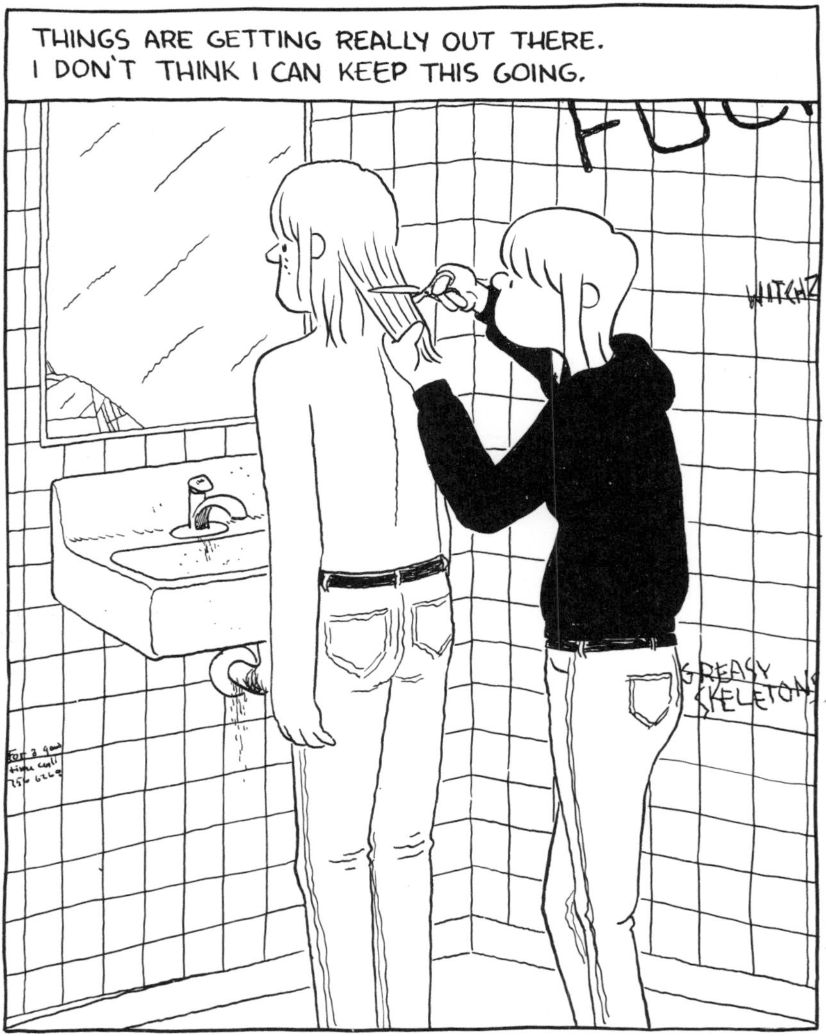
THINGS ARE GETTING REALLY OUT THERE.
I DON'T THINK I CAN KEEP THIS GOING.
FUC
WITCHZ
GREASY SKELETONS
For a good time call 756 6260

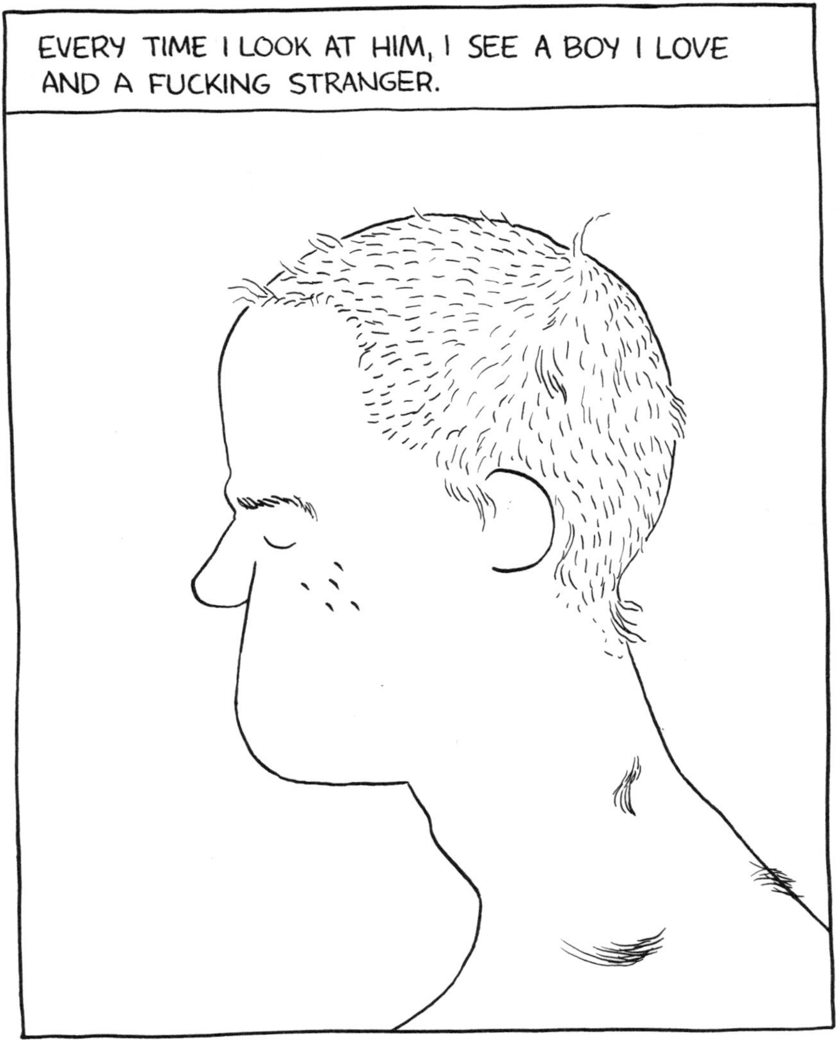
EVERY TIME I LOOK AT HIM, I SEE A BOY I LOVE AND A FUCKING STRANGER.

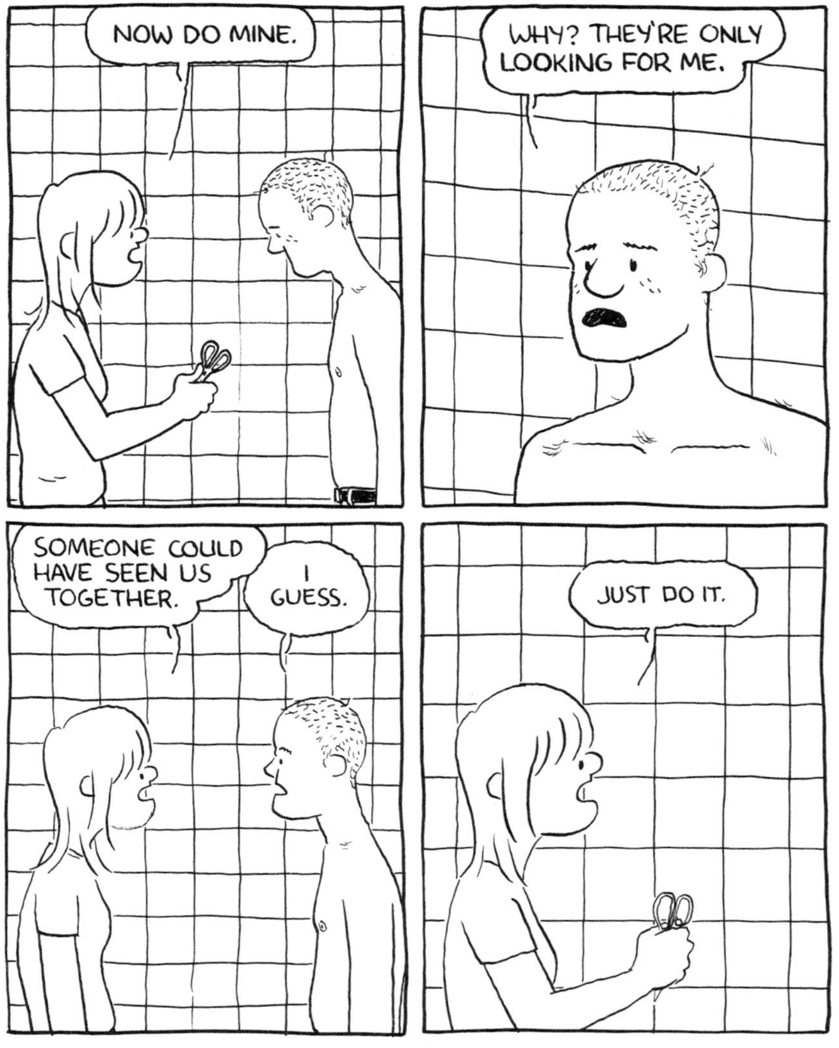
NOW DO MINE.
WHY? THEY'RE ONLY LOOKING FOR ME.
SOMEONE COULD HAVE SEEN US TOGETHER.
I GUESS.
JUST DO IT.

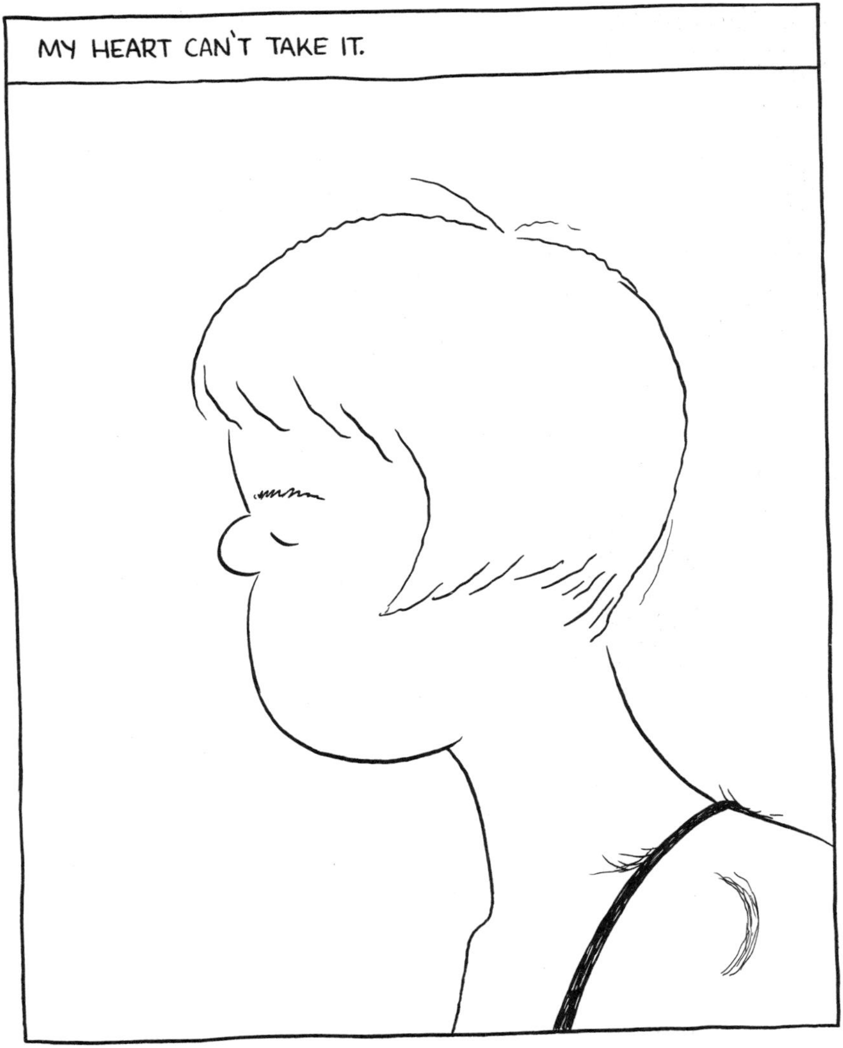
MY HEART CAN'T TAKE IT.

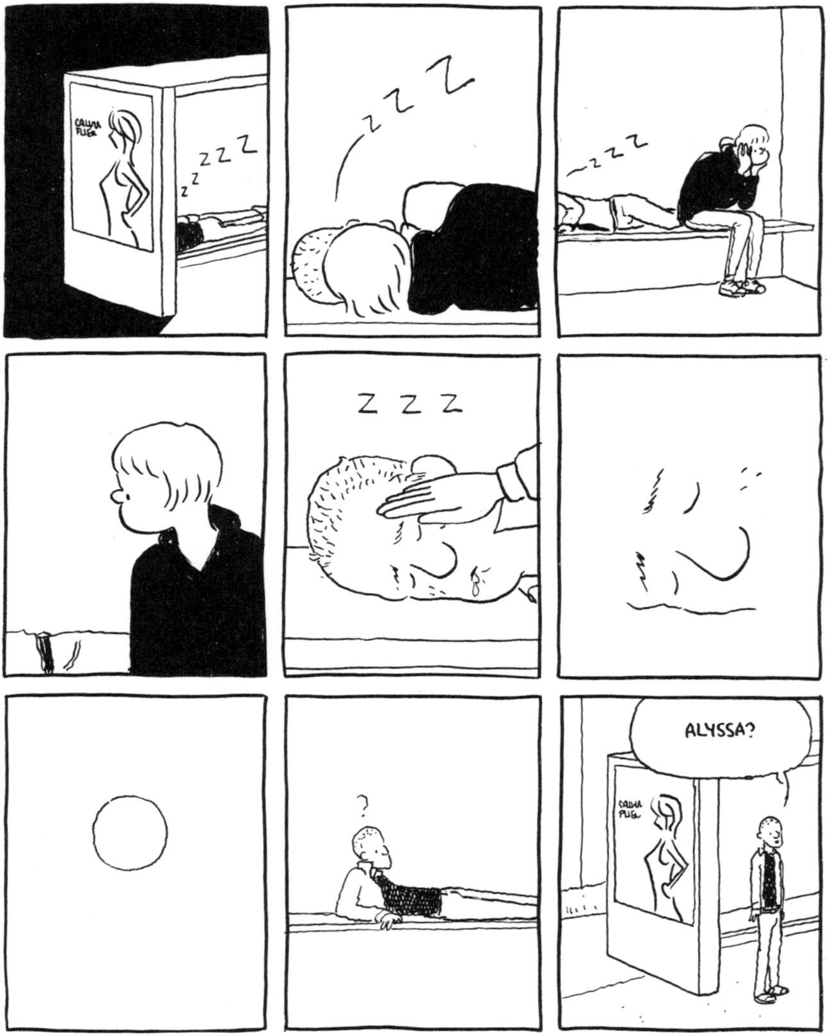
Z Z Z Z Z
Z Z Z
Z Z Z
Z Z Z
?
ALYSSA?

PROTECTOR

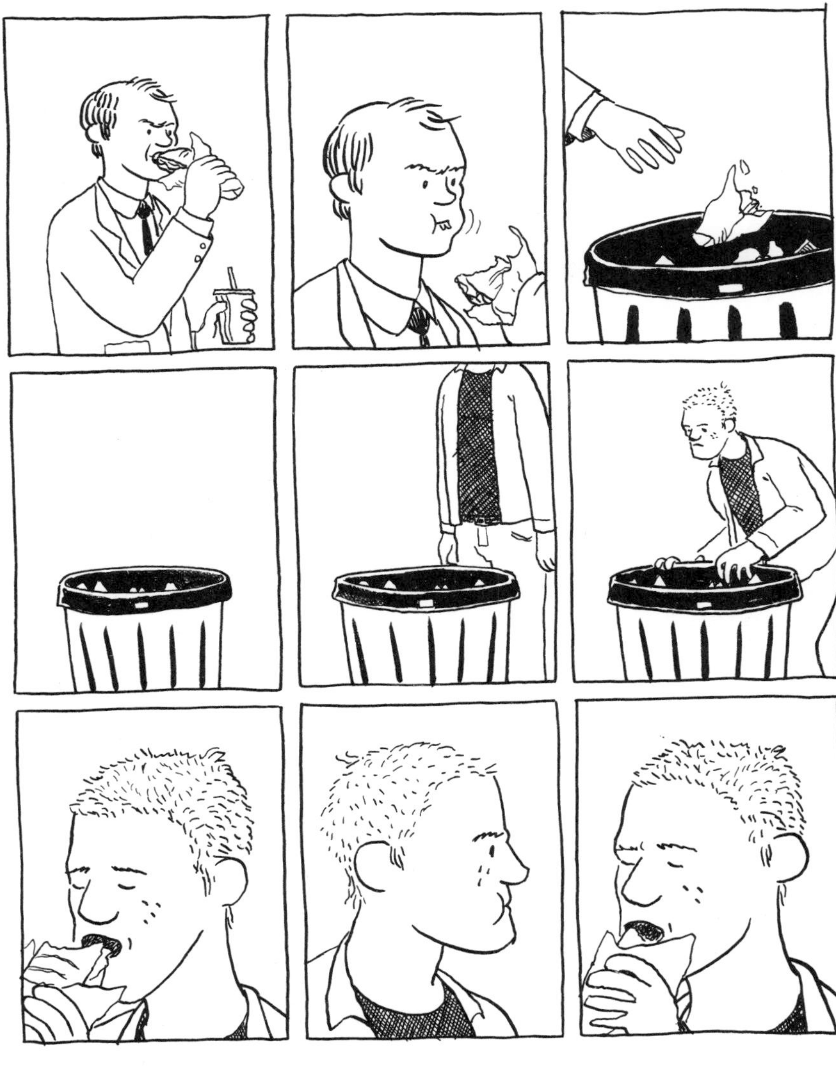

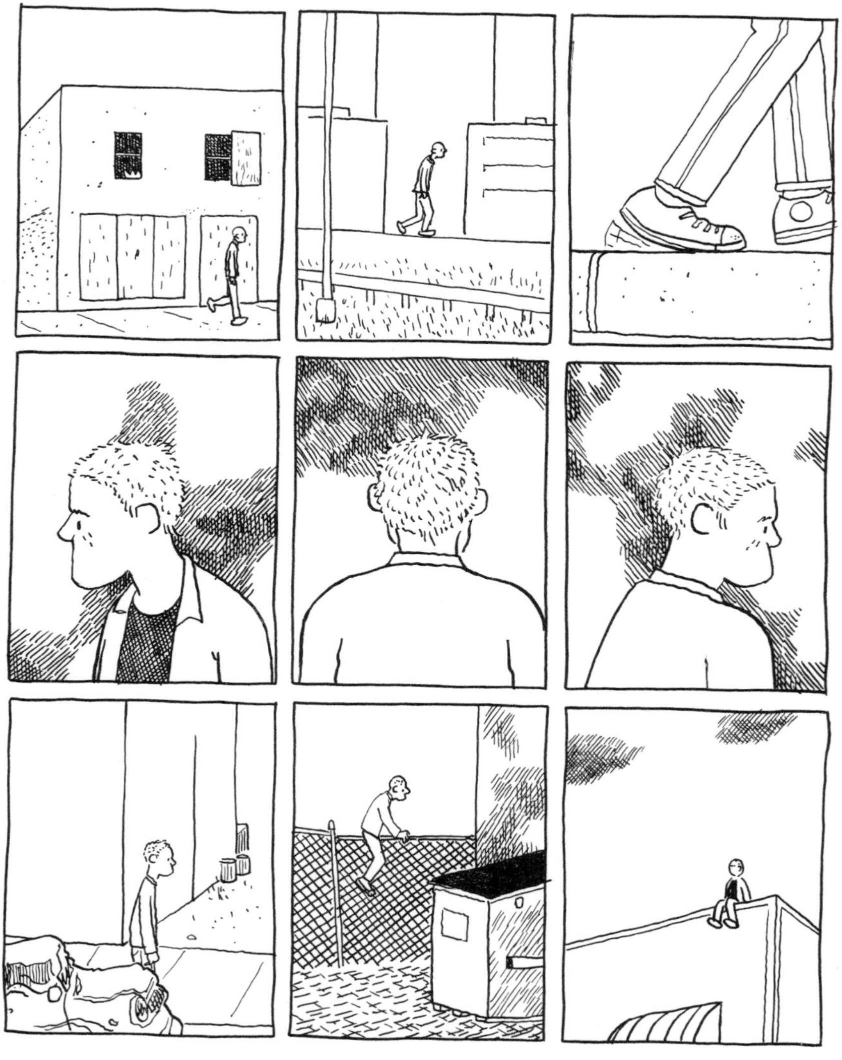

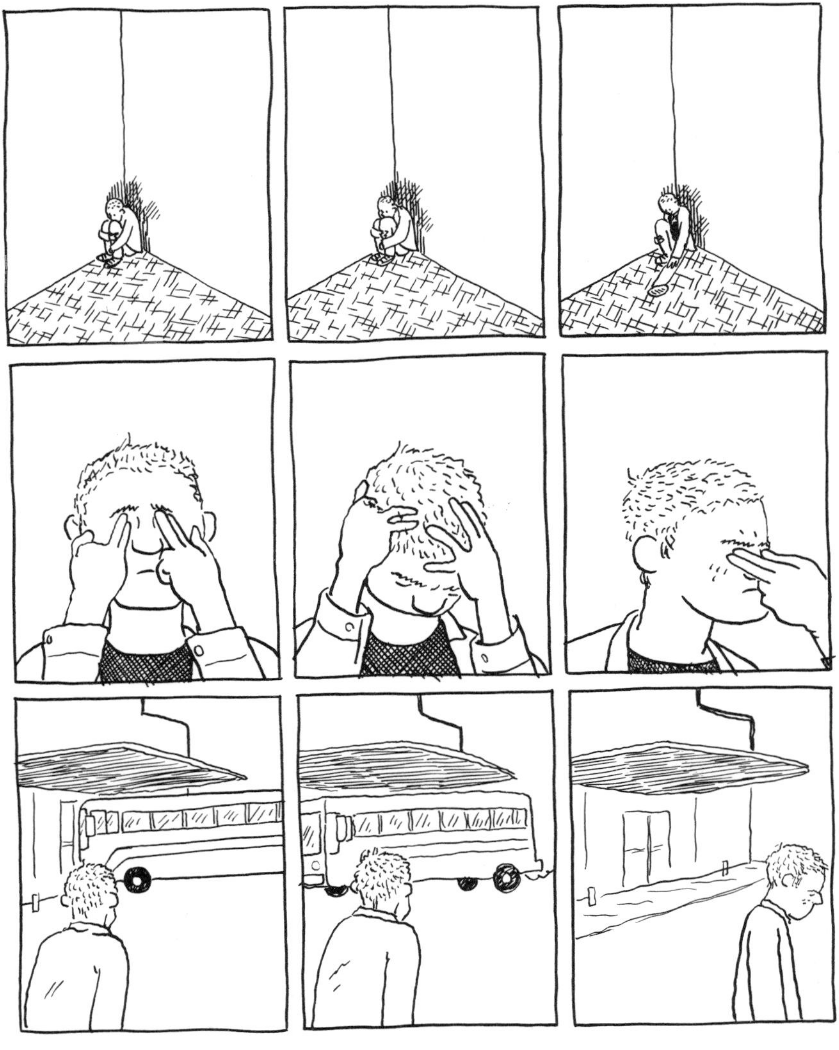

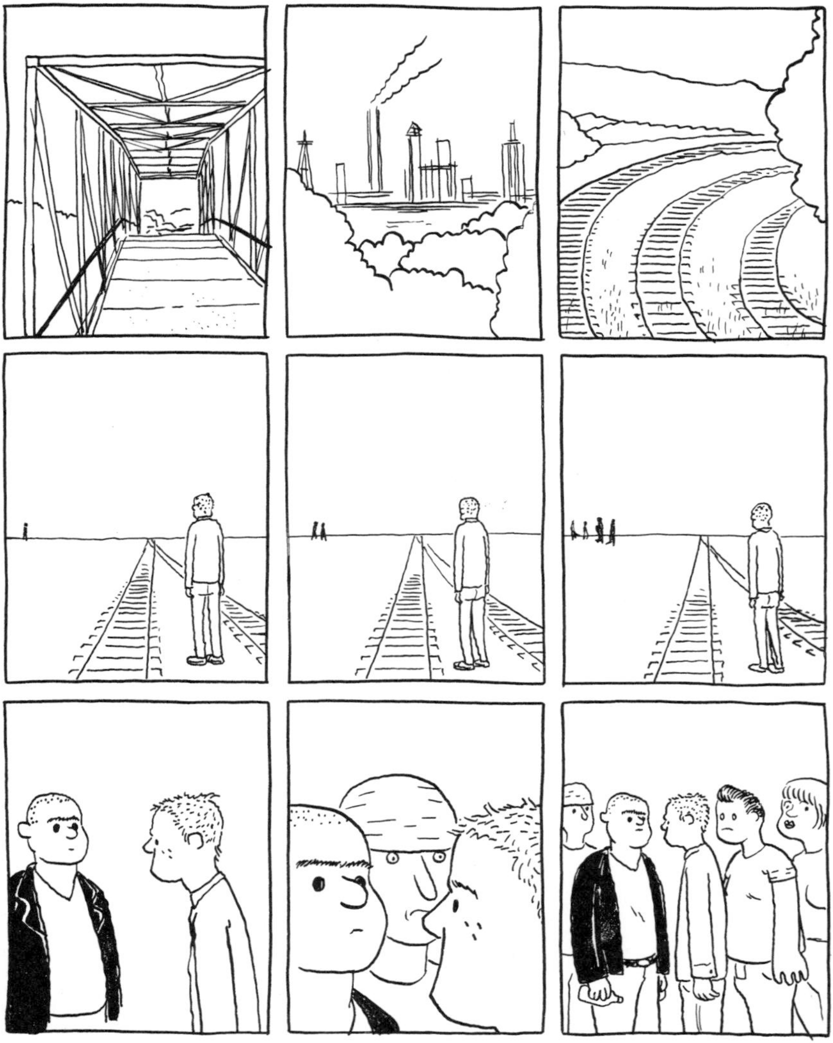

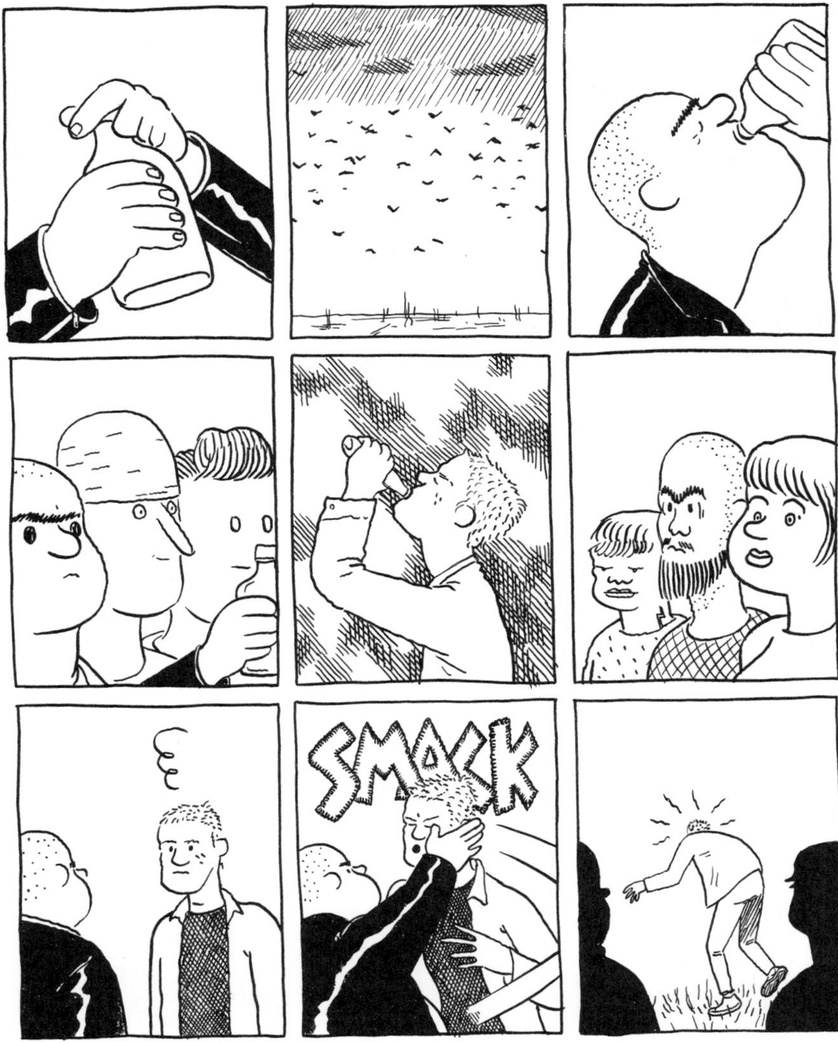
SMACK

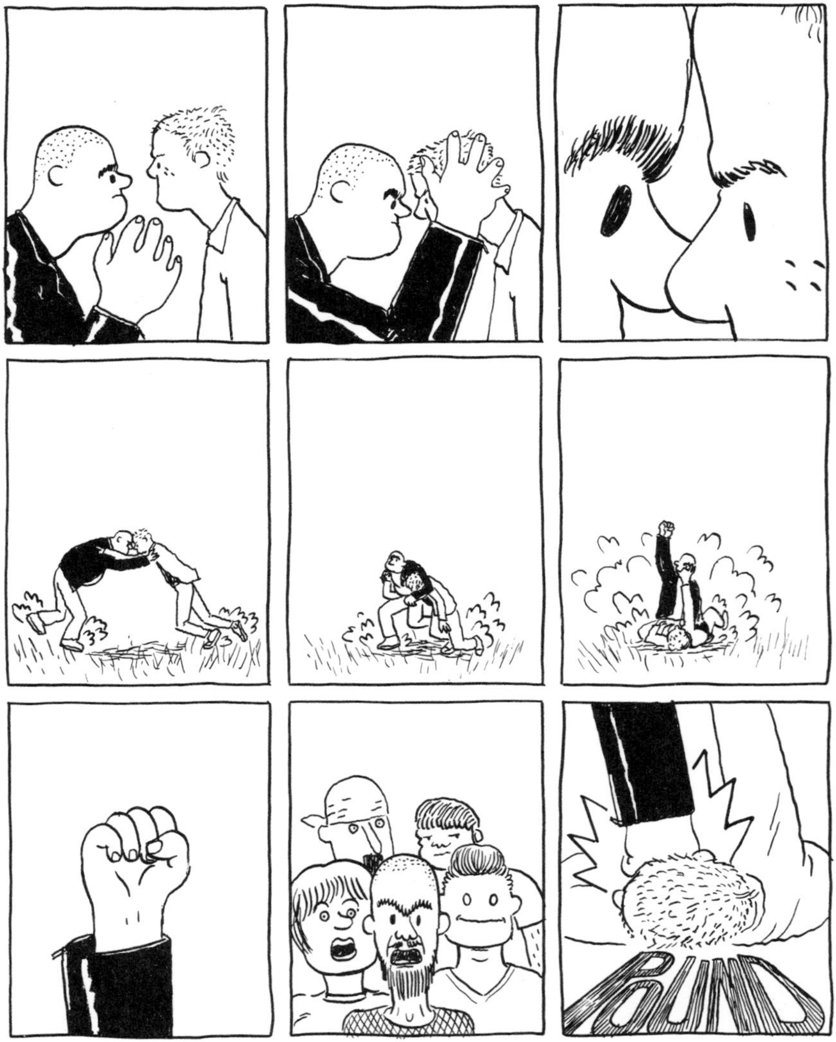
POUND

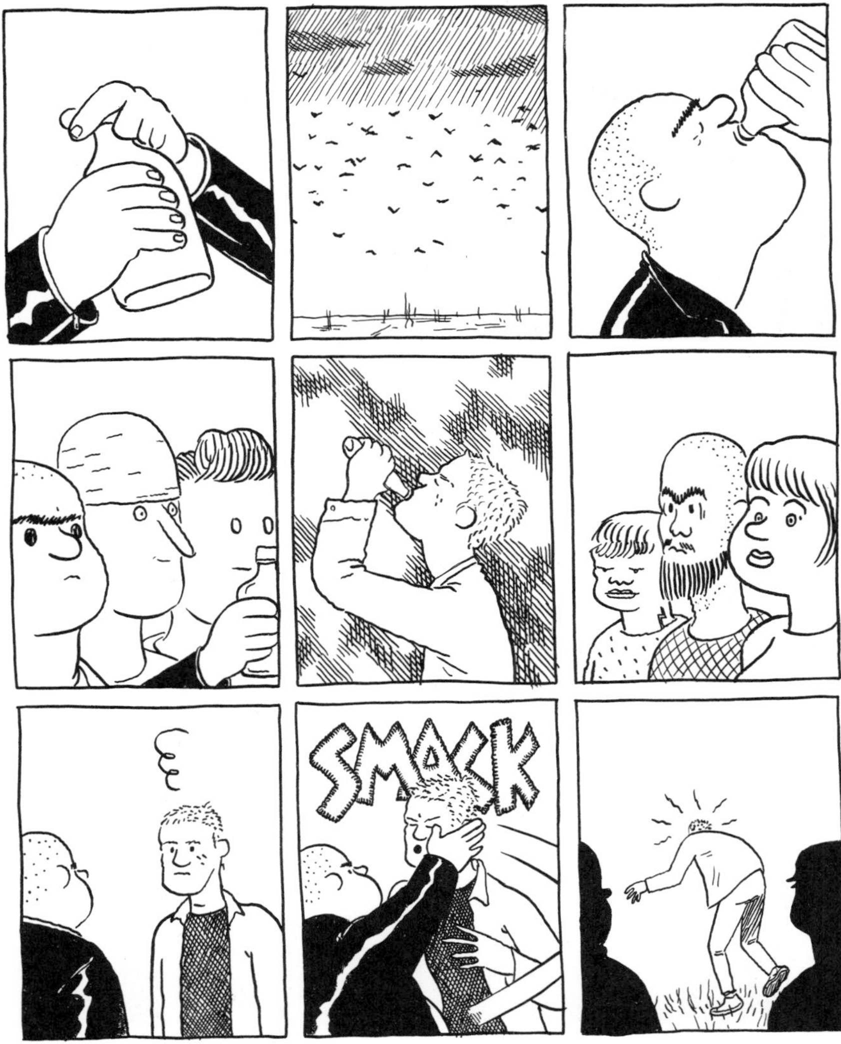
SMACK

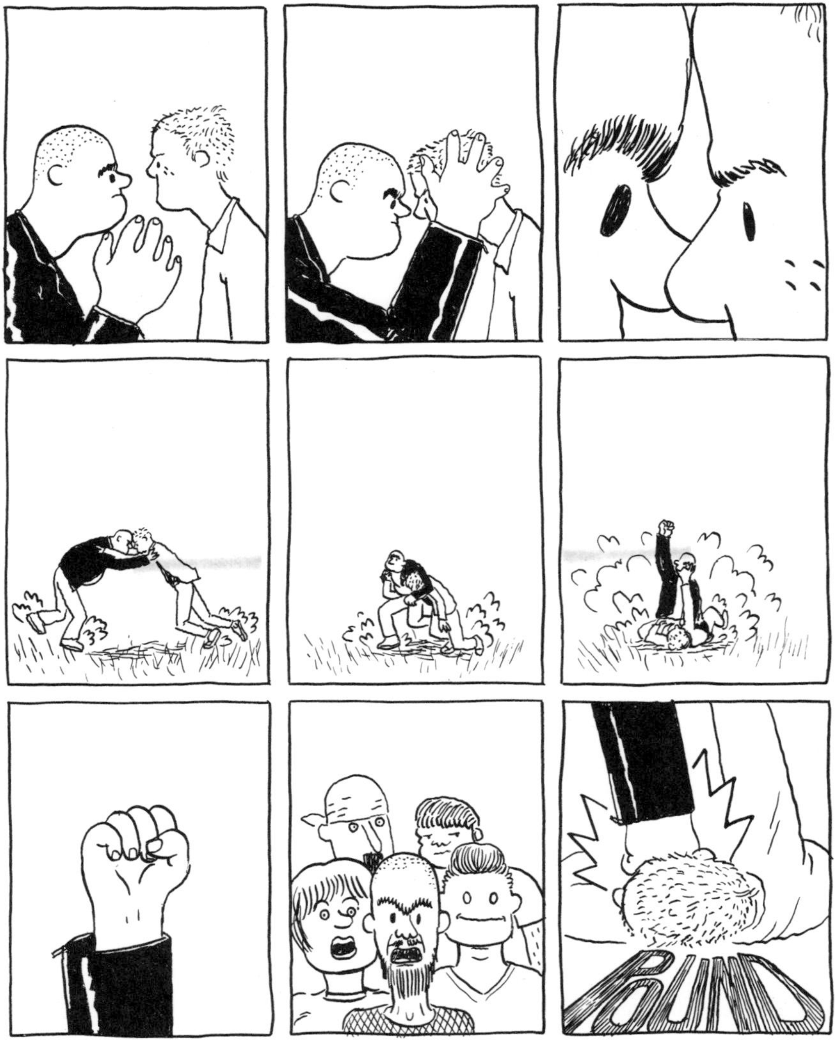
POUND

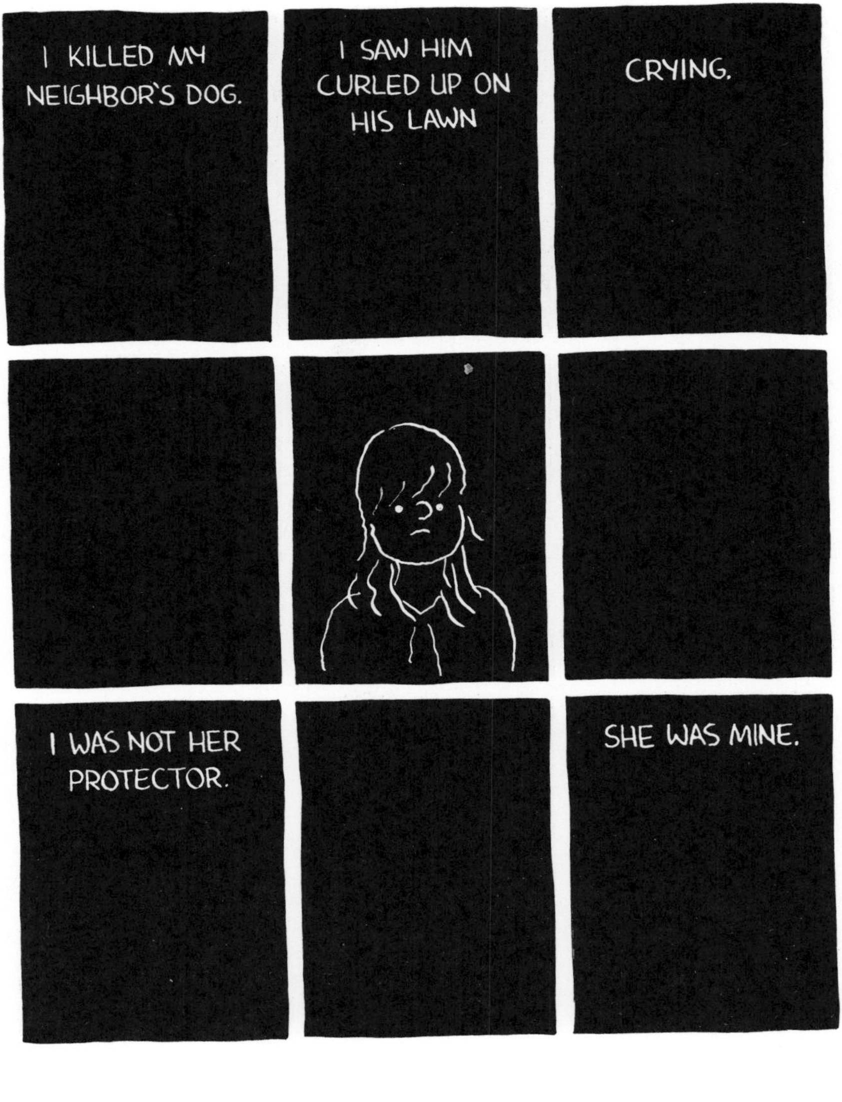
I KILLED MY NEIGHBOR'S DOG.
I SAW HIM CURLED UP ON HIS LAWN
CRYING.
I WAS NOT HER PROTECTOR.
SHE WAS MINE.

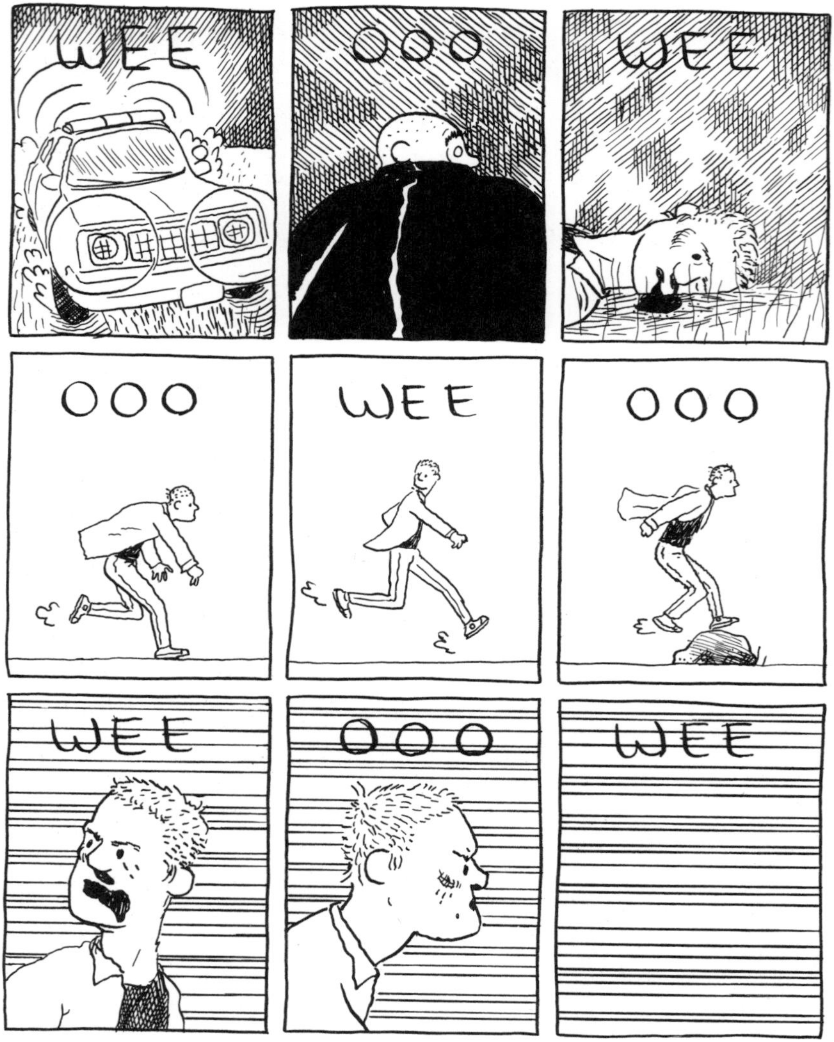
WEE
OOO
WEE
OOO
WEE
OOO
WEE
OOO
WEE

FOREVER

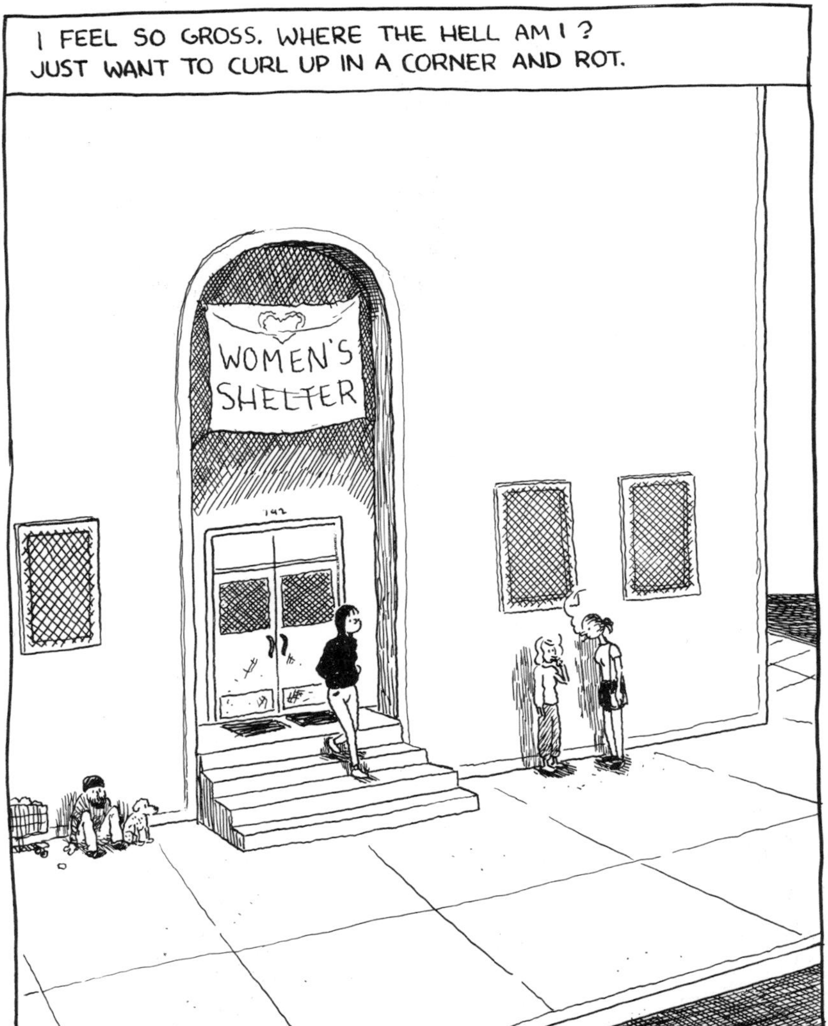
I FEEL SO GROSS. WHERE THE HELL AM I ?
JUST WANT TO CURL UP IN A CORNER AND ROT.
WOMEN'S
SHELTER
142

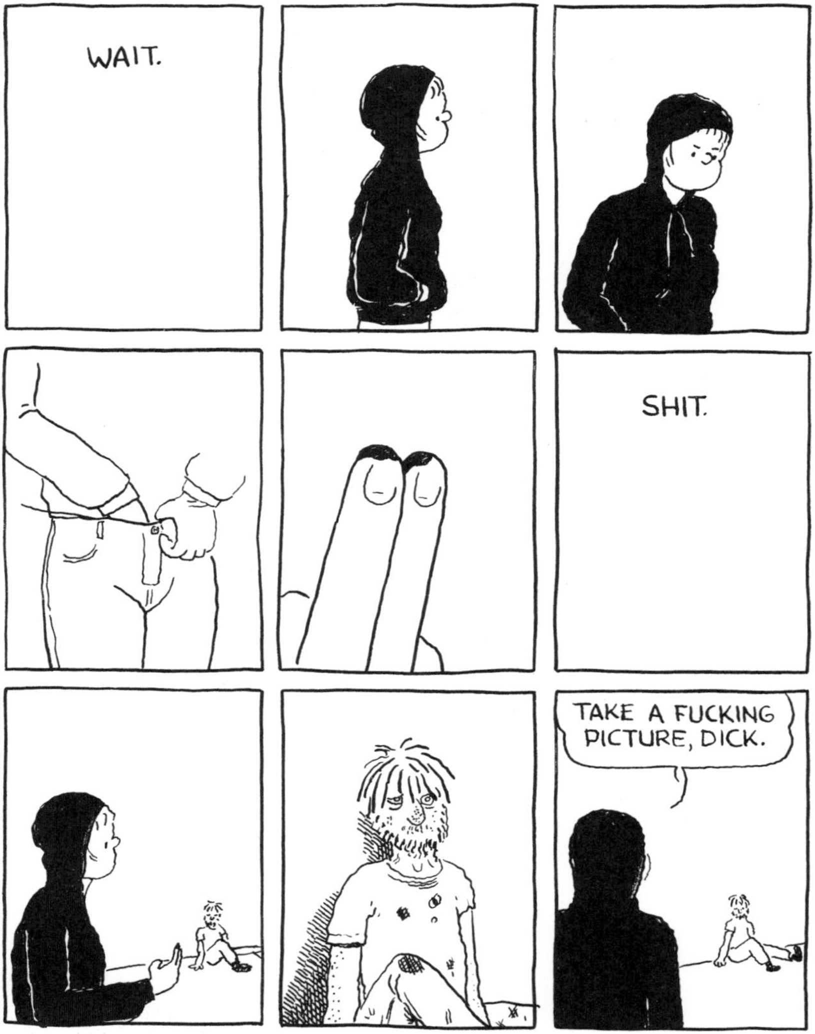
WAIT.
SHIT.
TAKE A FUCKING PICTURE, DICK.

Stern's
DEPARTMENT STORE

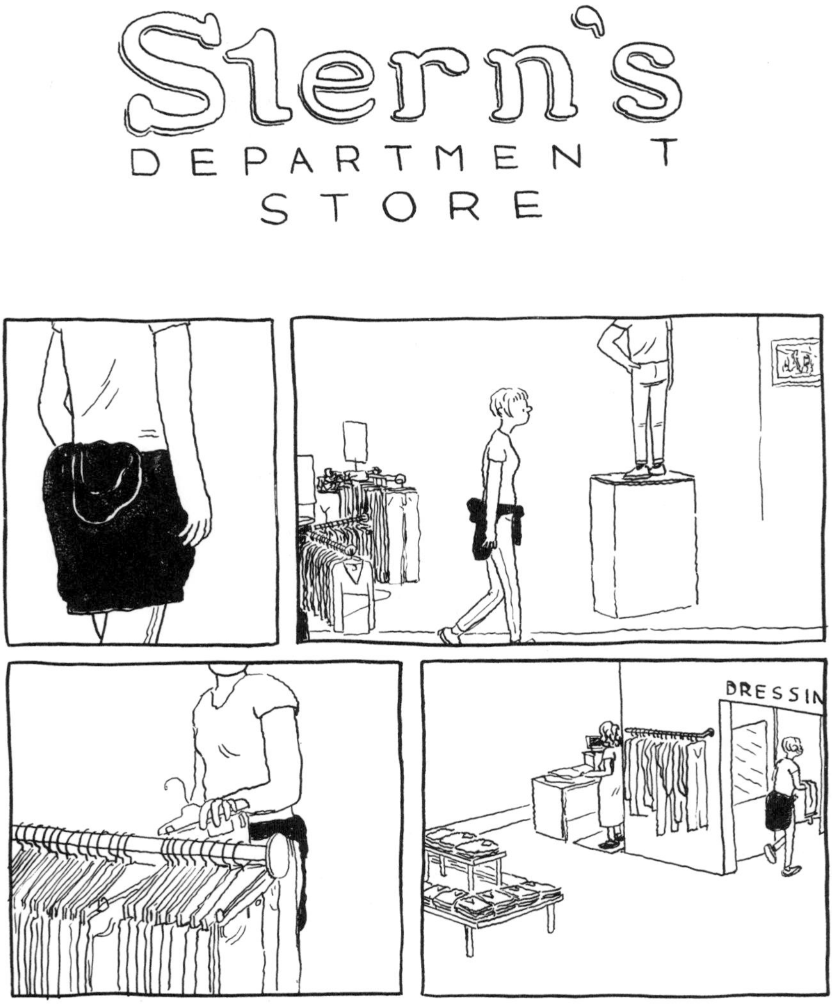
DRESSIN

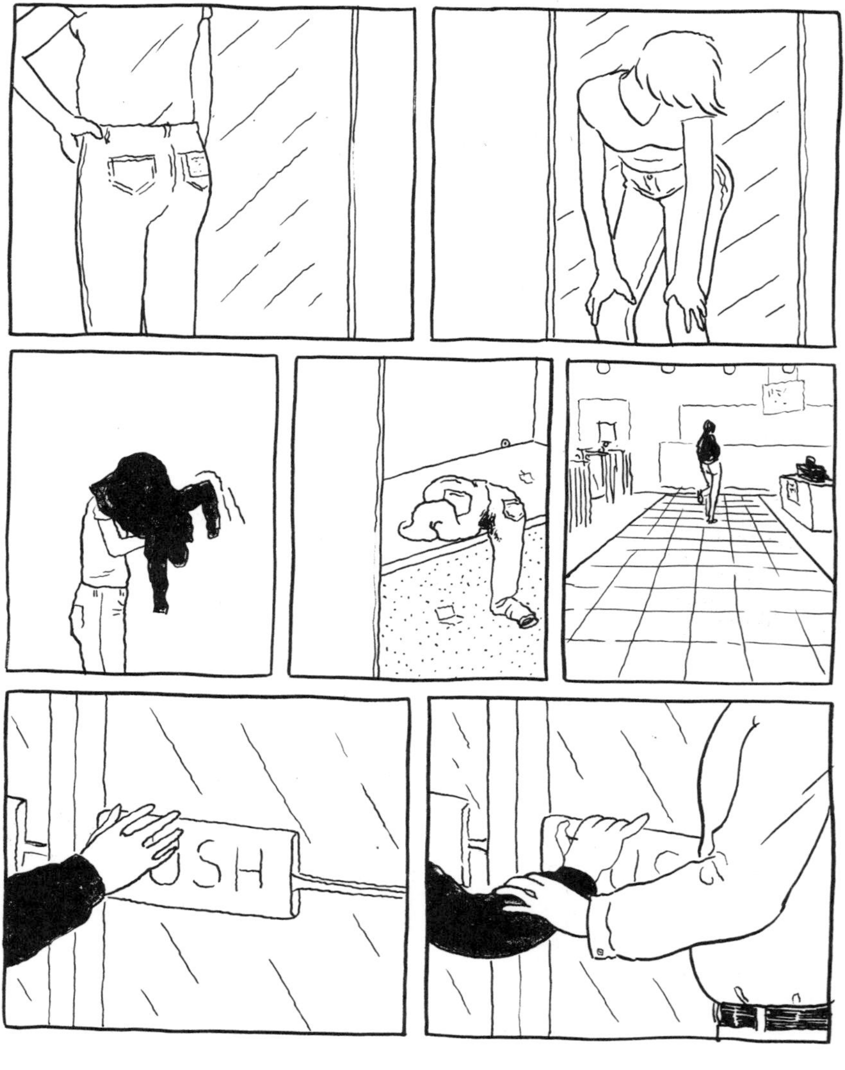

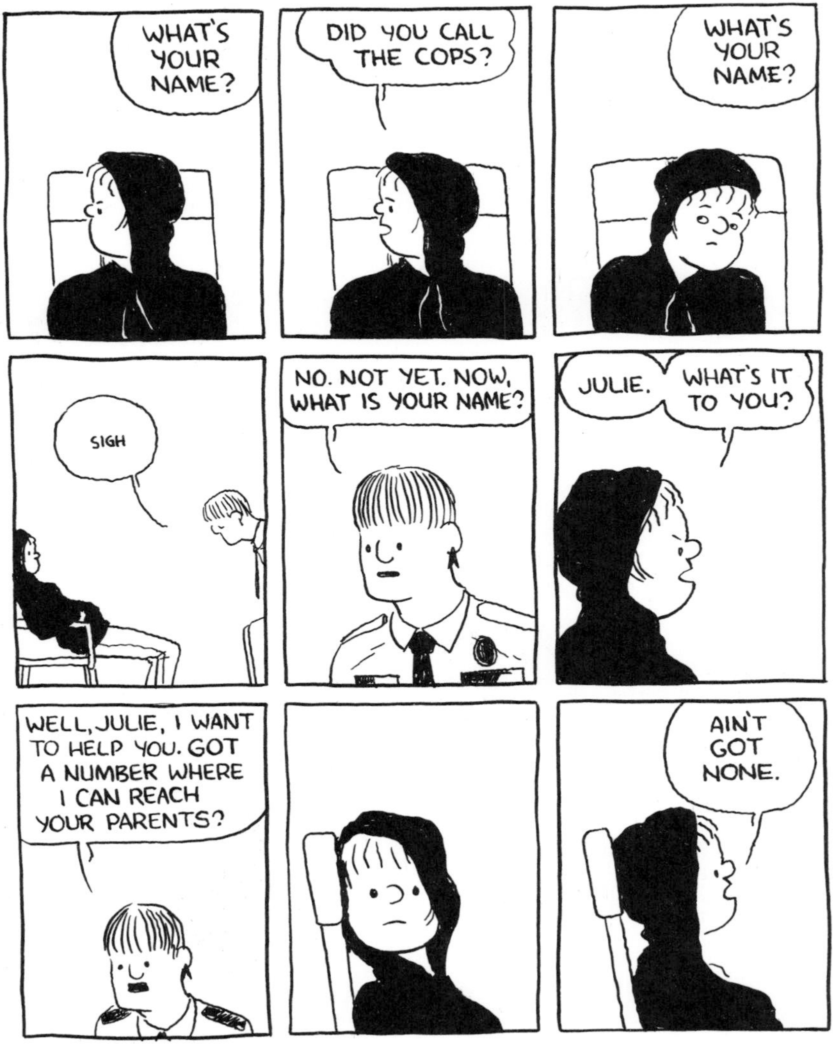
WHAT'S YOUR NAME?
DID YOU CALL THE COPS?
WHAT'S YOUR NAME?
SIGH
NO. NOT YET. NOW, WHAT IS YOUR NAME?
JULIE.
WHAT'S IT TO YOU?
WELL, JULIE, I WANT TO HELP YOU. GOT A NUMBER WHERE I CAN REACH YOUR PARENTS?
AIN'T GOT NONE.

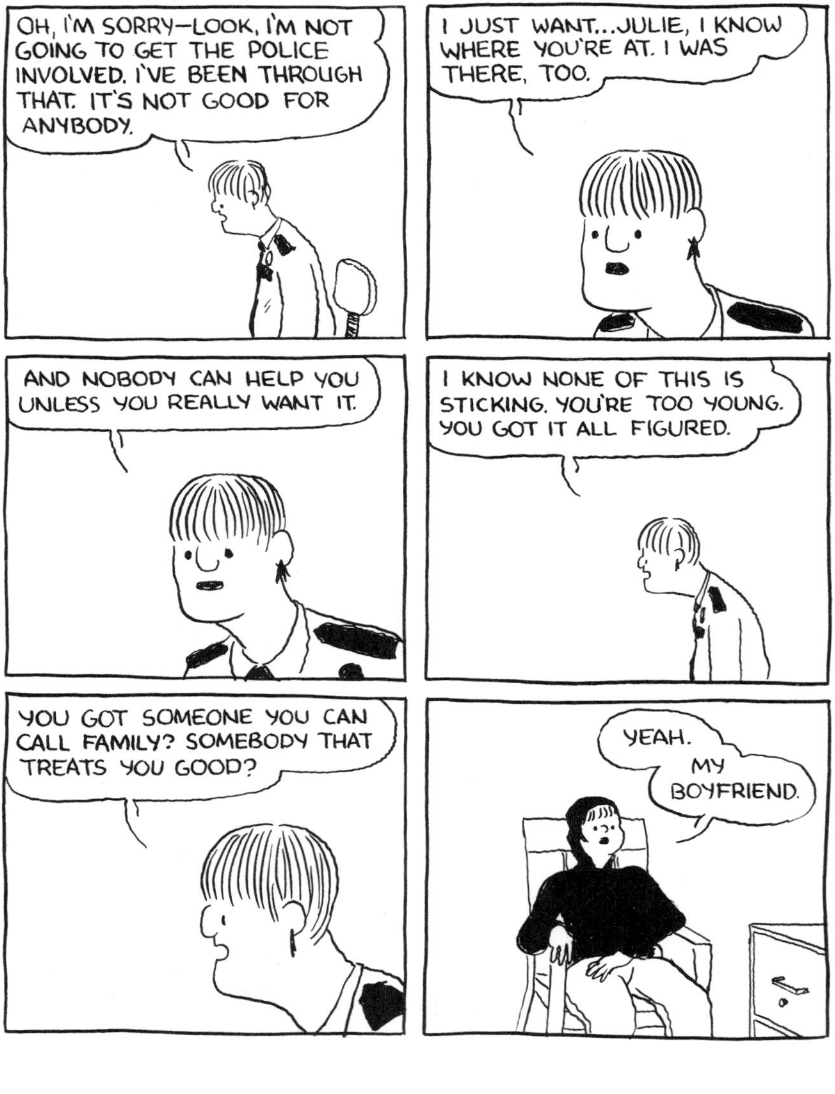
OH, I'M SORRY—LOOK, I'M NOT GOING TO GET THE POLICE INVOLVED. I'VE BEEN THROUGH THAT. IT'S NOT GOOD FOR ANYBODY.
I JUST WANT...JULIE, I KNOW WHERE YOU'RE AT. I WAS THERE, TOO.
AND NOBODY CAN HELP YOU UNLESS YOU REALLY WANT IT.
I KNOW NONE OF THIS IS STICKING. YOU'RE TOO YOUNG. YOU GOT IT ALL FIGURED.
YOU GOT SOMEONE YOU CAN CALL FAMILY? SOMEBODY THAT TREATS YOU GOOD?
YEAH.
MY BOYFRIEND.

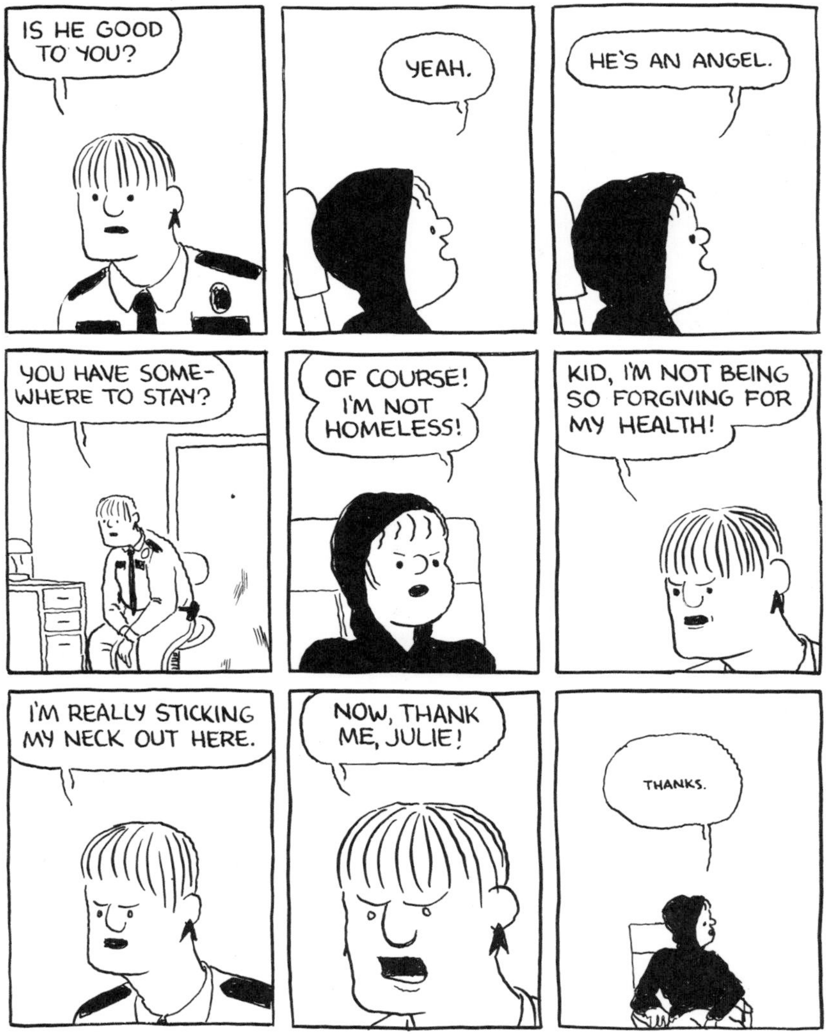
IS HE GOOD TO YOU?
YEAH.
HE'S AN ANGEL.
YOU HAVE SOME-WHERE TO STAY?
OF COURSE! I'M NOT HOMELESS!
KID, I'M NOT BEING SO FORGIVING FOR MY HEALTH!
I'M REALLY STICKING MY NECK OUT HERE.
NOW, THANK ME, JULIE!
THANKS.

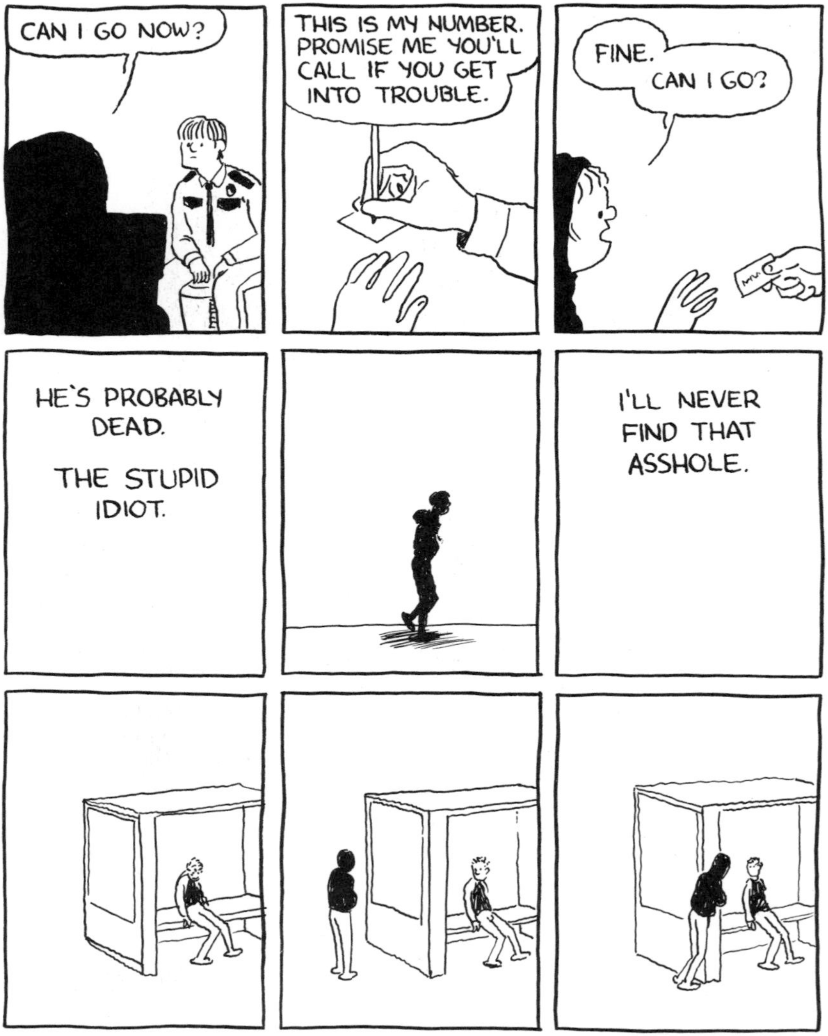
CAN I GO NOW?
THIS IS MY NUMBER. PROMISE ME YOU'LL CALL IF YOU GET INTO TROUBLE.
FINE.
CAN I GO?
HE'S PROBABLY DEAD.
THE STUPID IDIOT.
I'LL NEVER FIND THAT ASSHOLE.

DROWNED DEEPER

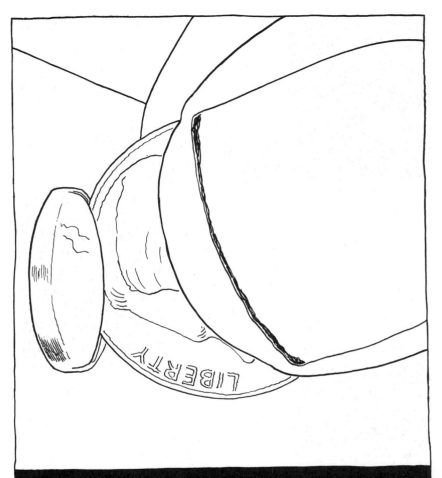

WHEN I WAS 4, MY MOM DROVE ME TO THE LAKE TO FEED THE GEESE WITH THE BUMPY NOSES.

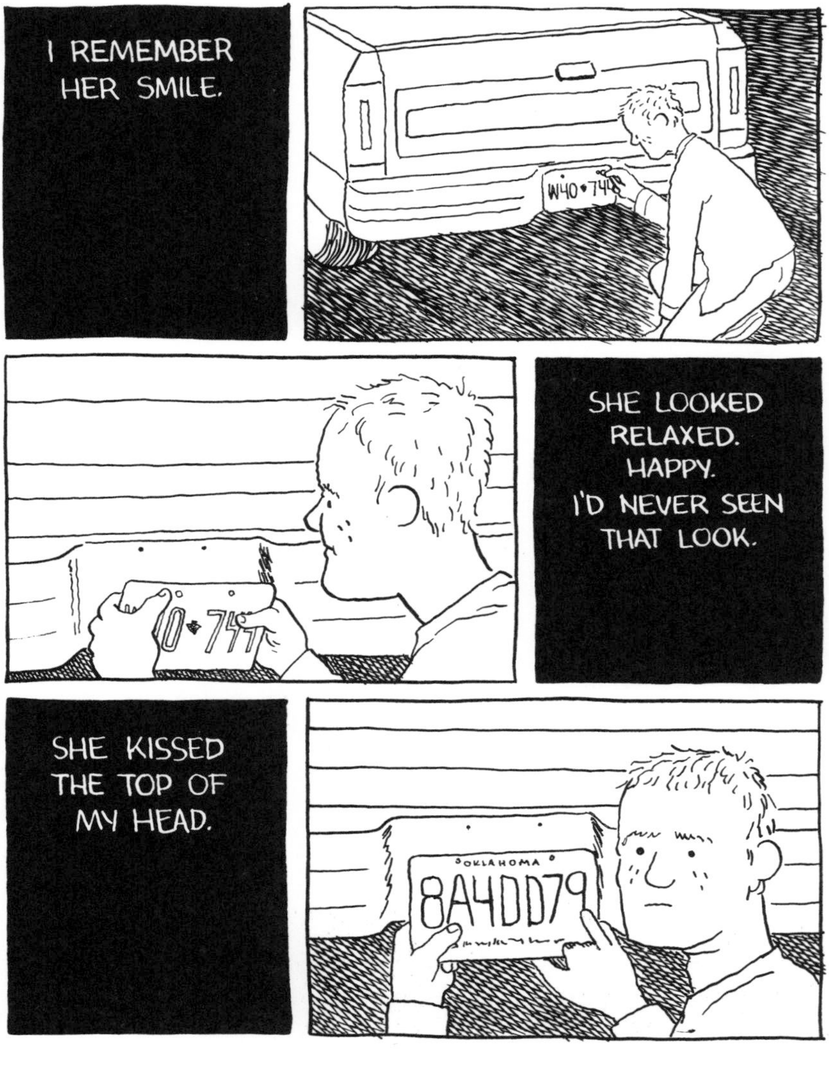
I REMEMBER HER SMILE.
SHE LOOKED RELAXED. HAPPY. I'D NEVER SEEN THAT LOOK.
SHE KISSED THE TOP OF MY HEAD.
OKLAHOMA
8A4DD79

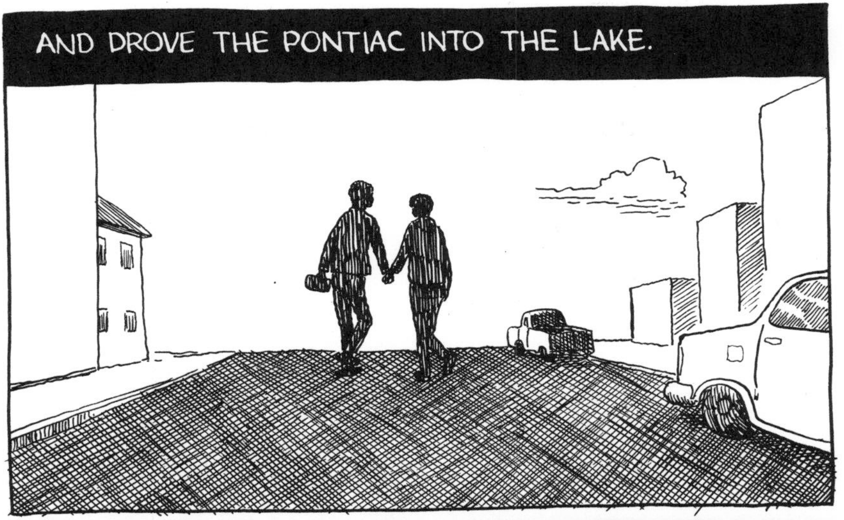
AND DROVE THE PONTIAC INTO THE LAKE.

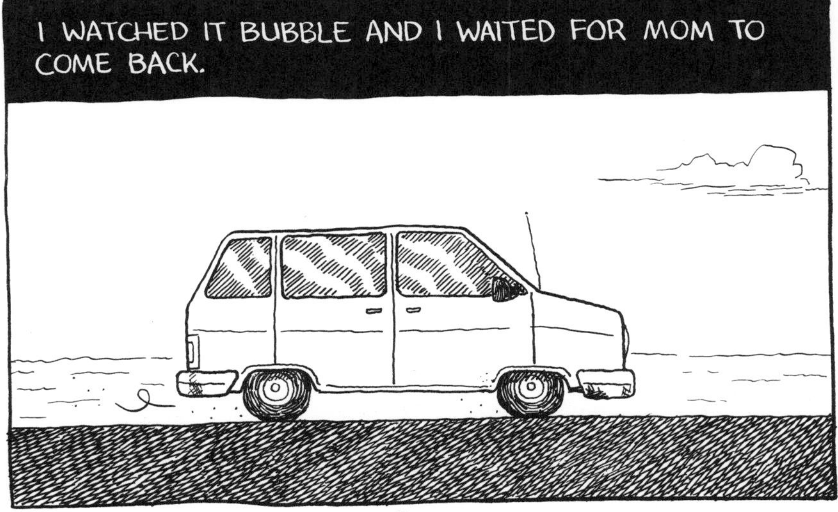
I WATCHED IT BUBBLE AND I WAITED FOR MOM TO COME BACK.

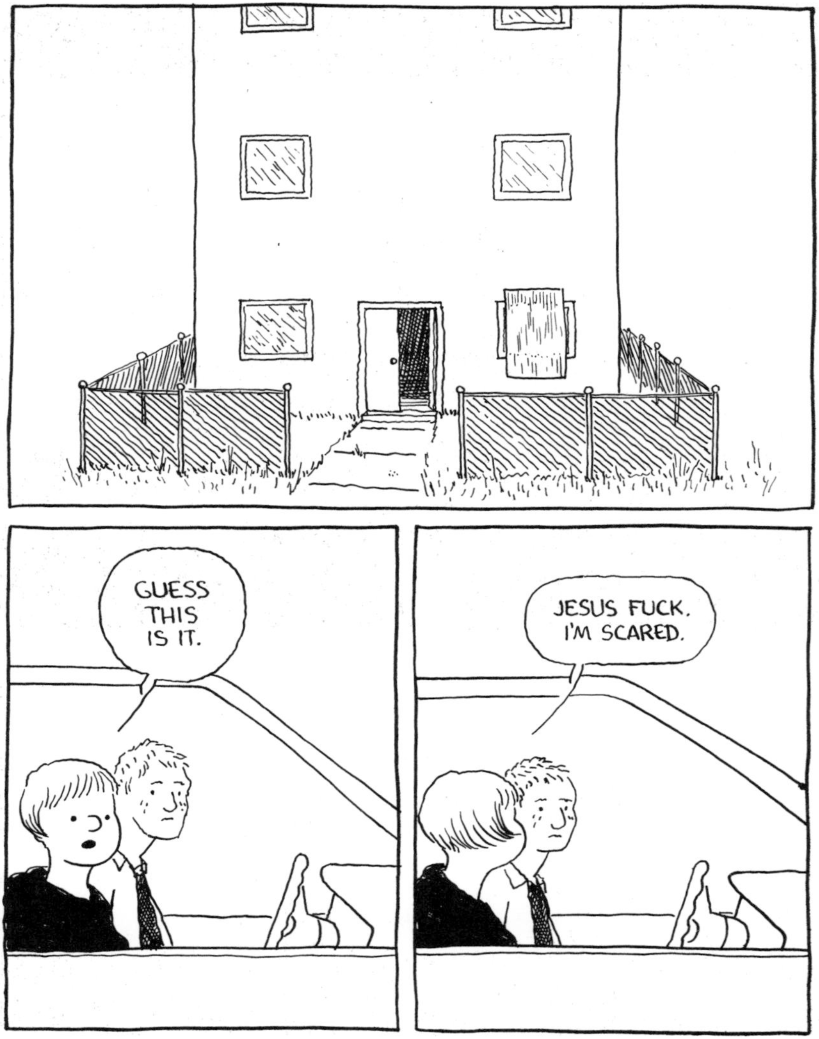
GUESS THIS IS IT.
JESUS FUCK. I'M SCARED.

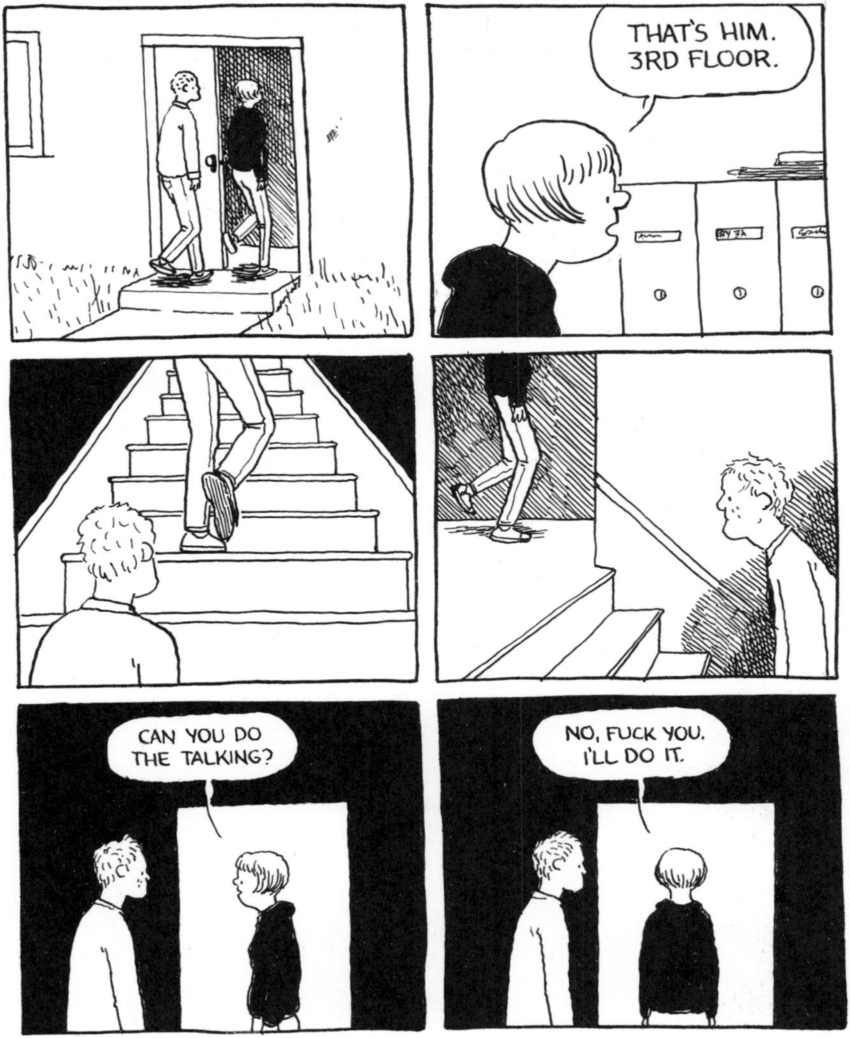
THAT'S HIM. 3RD FLOOR.
CAN YOU DO THE TALKING?
NO, FUCK YOU. I'LL DO IT.

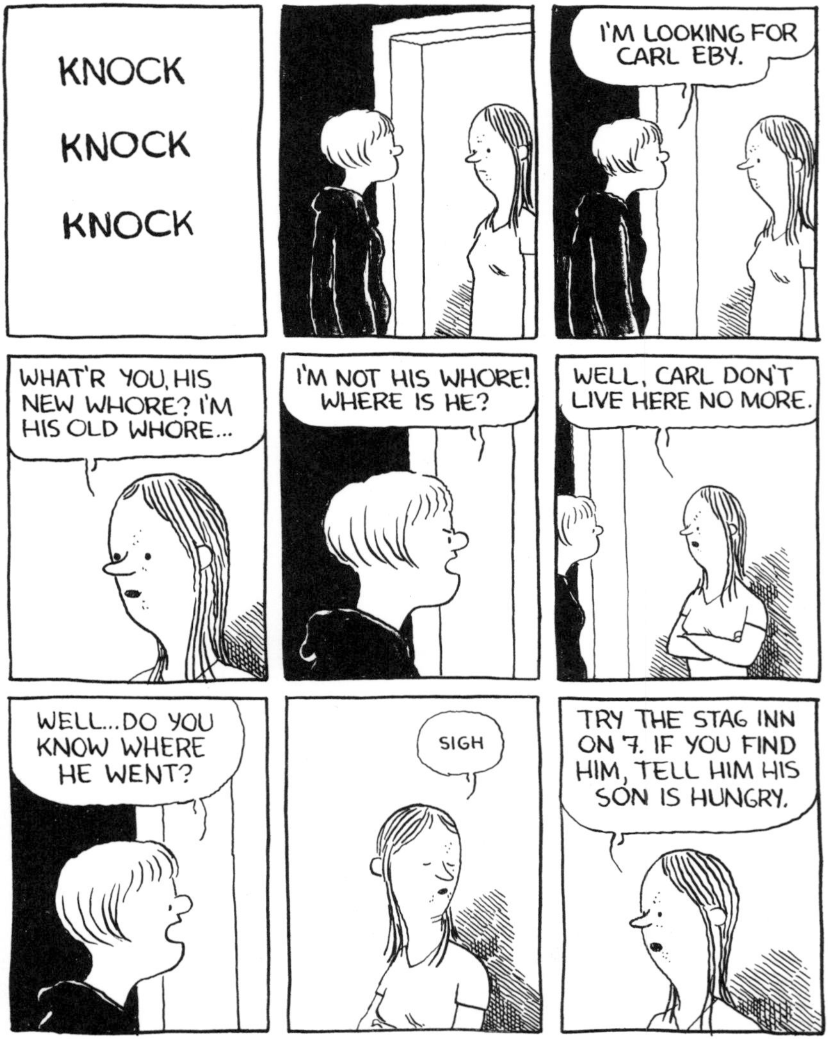
KNOCK
KNOCK
KNOCK
I'M LOOKING FOR CARL EBY.
WHAT'R YOU, HIS NEW WHORE? I'M HIS OLD WHORE...
I'M NOT HIS WHORE! WHERE IS HE?
WELL, CARL DON'T LIVE HERE NO MORE.
WELL...DO YOU KNOW WHERE HE WENT?
SIGH
TRY THE STAG INN ON 7. IF YOU FIND HIM, TELL HIM HIS SON IS HUNGRY.

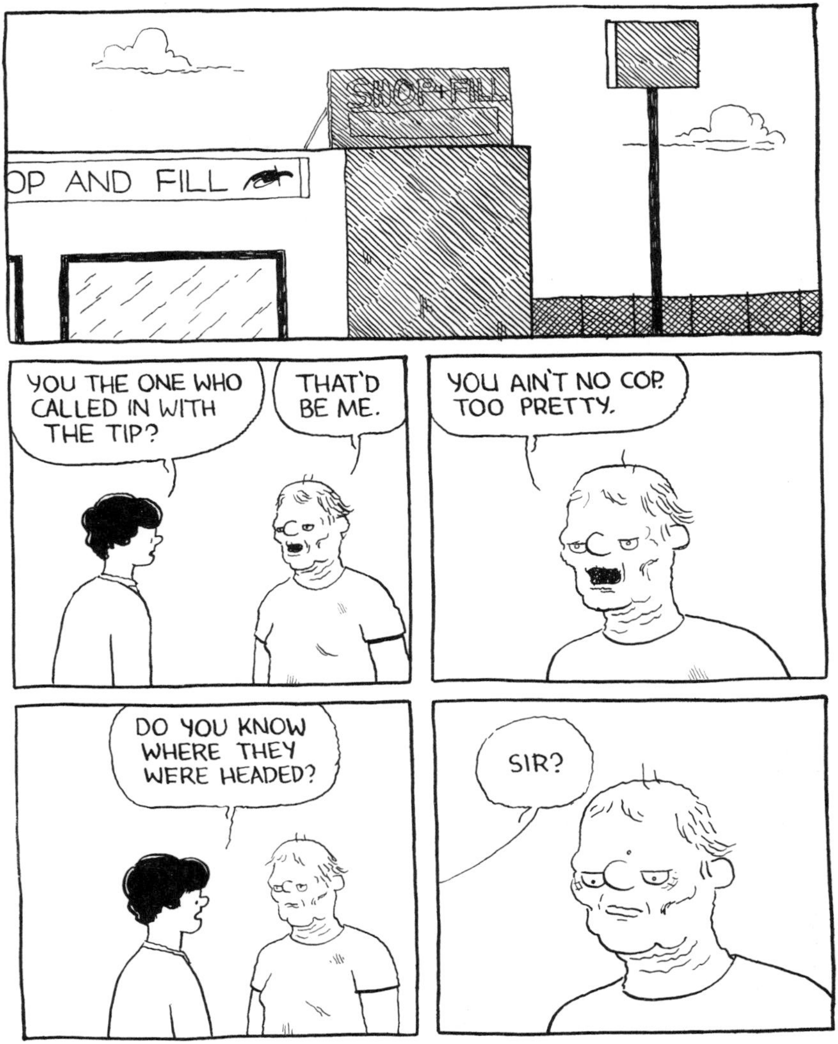
SHOP+FILL
OP AND FILL
YOU THE ONE WHO CALLED IN WITH THE TIP?
THAT'D BE ME.
YOU AIN'T NO COP. TOO PRETTY.
DO YOU KNOW WHERE THEY WERE HEADED?
SIR?

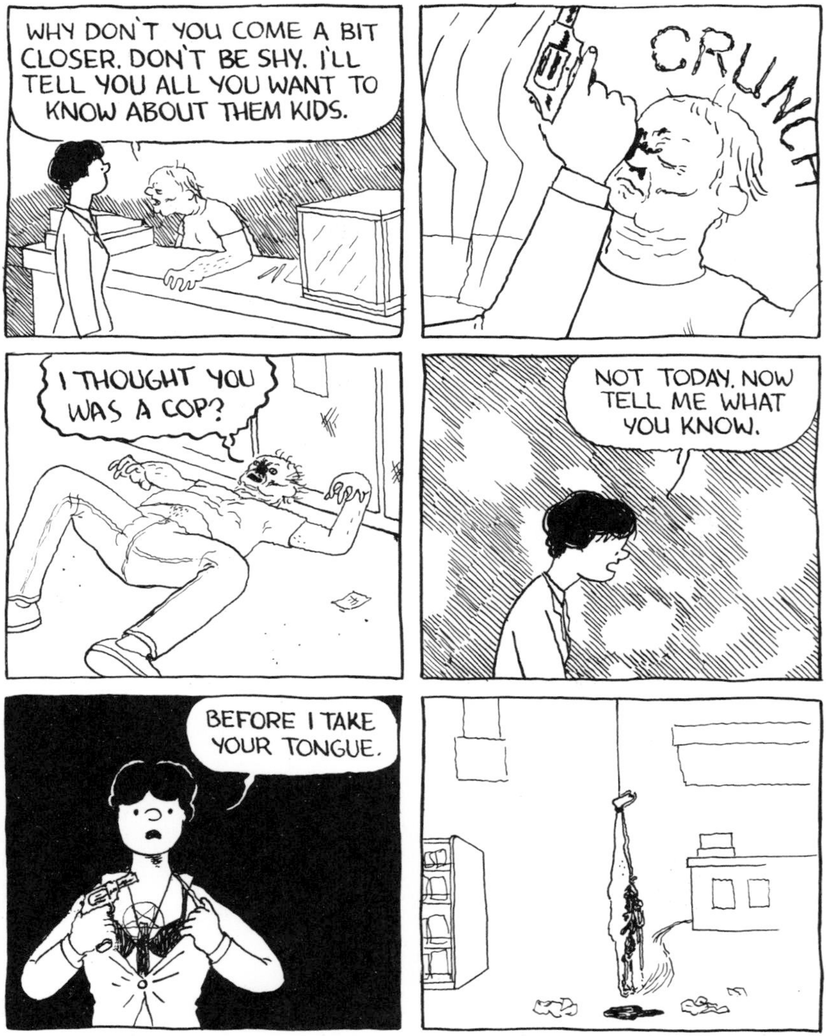
WHY DON'T YOU COME A BIT CLOSER. DON'T BE SHY. I'LL TELL YOU ALL YOU WANT TO KNOW ABOUT THEM KIDS.
CRUNCH
I THOUGHT YOU WAS A COP?
NOT TODAY. NOW TELL ME WHAT YOU KNOW.
BEFORE I TAKE YOUR TONGUE.

DAD, FATHER

I HAVE A LOT OF CRAPPY MEMORIES OF MY DAD. SCREAMING MOSTLY.
GRRR

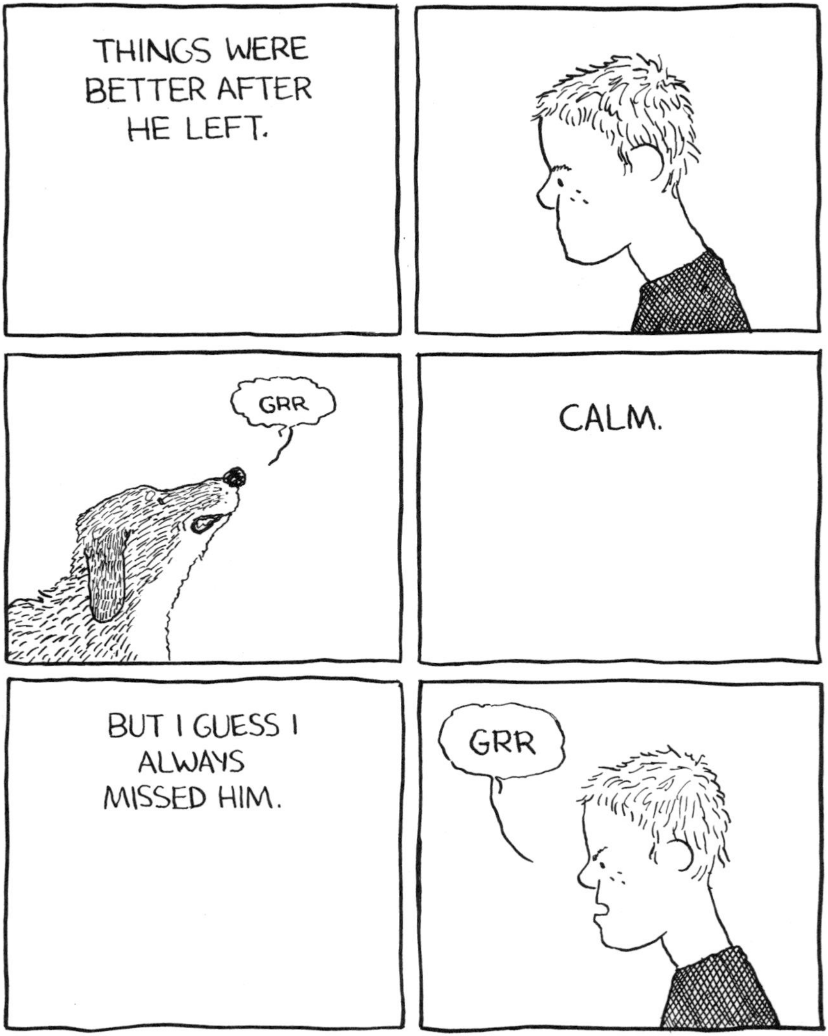
THINGS WERE BETTER AFTER HE LEFT.
GRR
CALM.
BUT I GUESS I ALWAYS MISSED HIM.
GRR

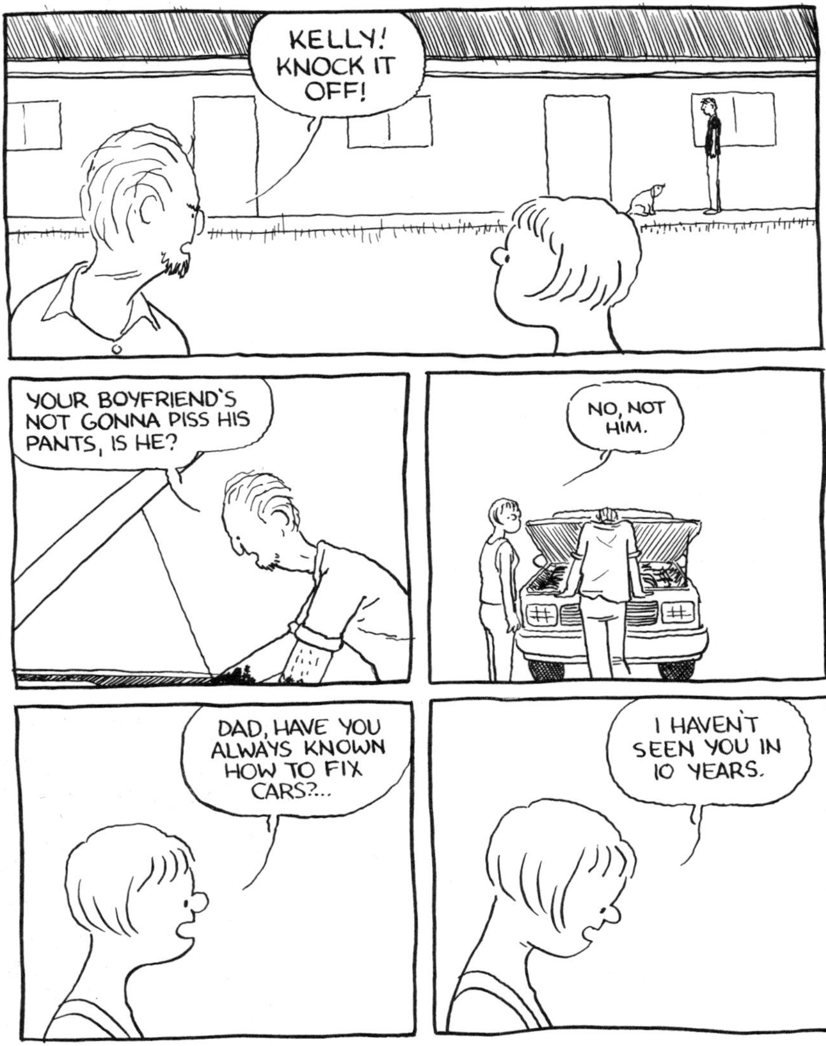
KELLY! KNOCK IT OFF!
YOUR BOYFRIEND'S NOT GONNA PISS HIS PANTS, IS HE?
NO, NOT HIM.
DAD, HAVE YOU ALWAYS KNOWN HOW TO FIX CARS?...
I HAVEN'T SEEN YOU IN 10 YEARS.

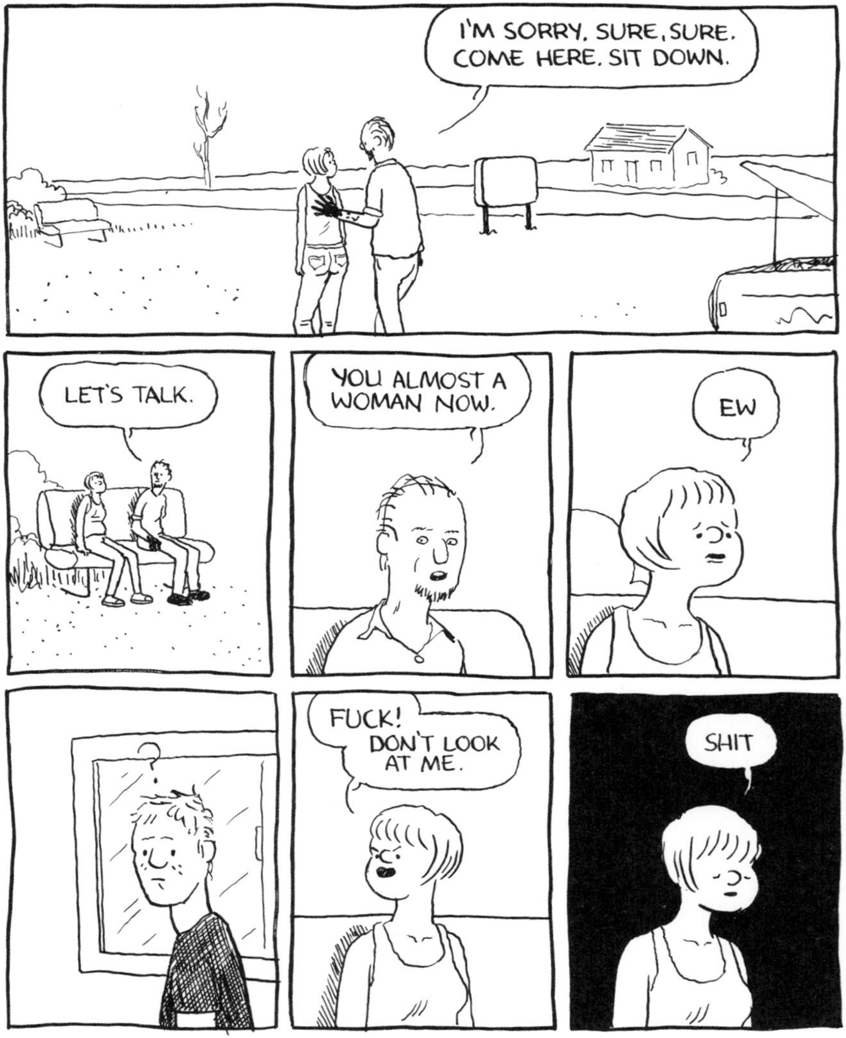
I'M SORRY. SURE, SURE. COME HERE. SIT DOWN.
LET'S TALK.
YOU ALMOST A WOMAN NOW.
EW
?
FUCK! DON'T LOOK AT ME.
SHIT

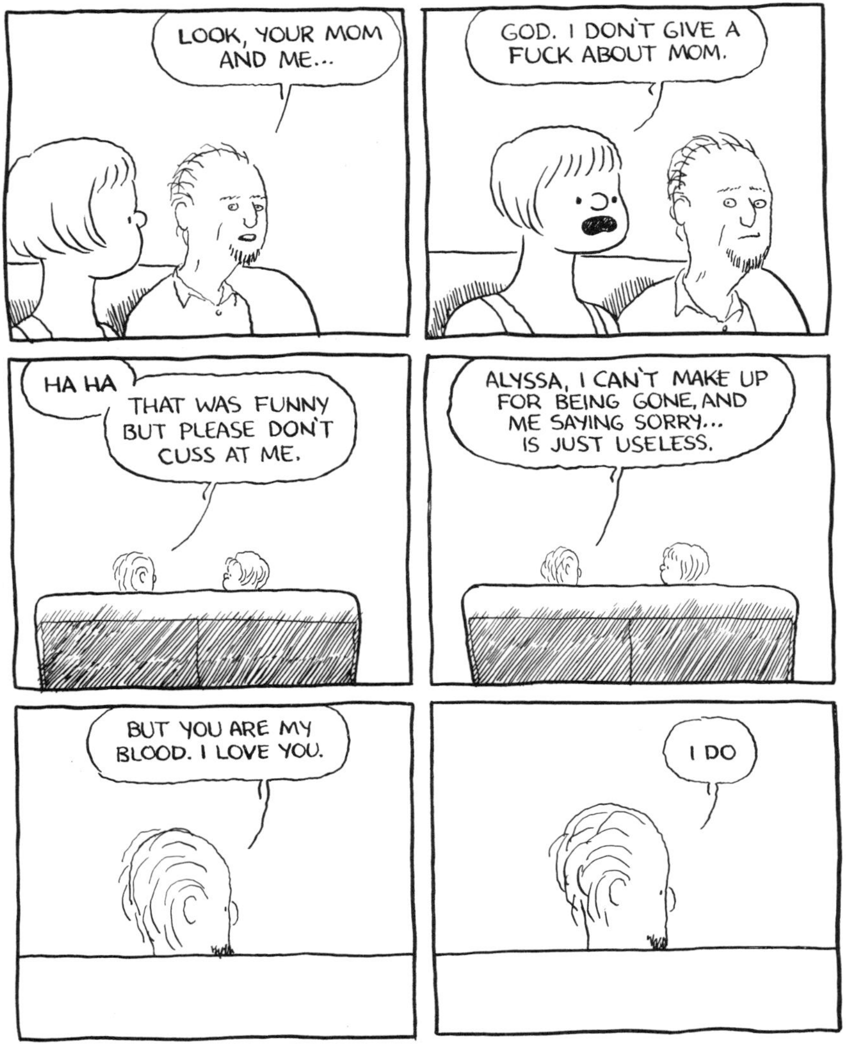
LOOK, YOUR MOM AND ME...
GOD. I DON'T GIVE A FUCK ABOUT MOM.
HA HA
THAT WAS FUNNY BUT PLEASE DON'T CUSS AT ME.
ALYSSA, I CAN'T MAKE UP FOR BEING GONE, AND ME SAYING SORRY... IS JUST USELESS.
BUT YOU ARE MY BLOOD. I LOVE YOU.
I DO

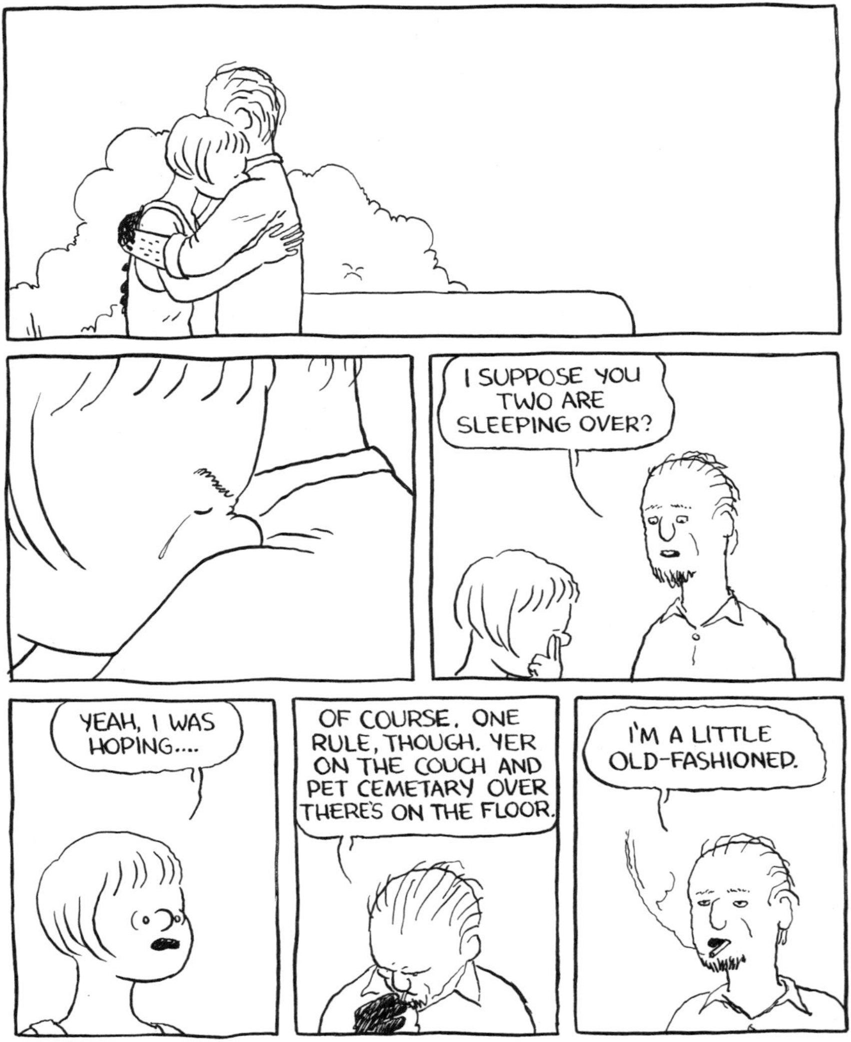
I SUPPOSE YOU TWO ARE SLEEPING OVER?
YEAH, I WAS HOPING....
OF COURSE. ONE RULE, THOUGH. YER ON THE COUCH AND PET CEMETARY OVER THERE'S ON THE FLOOR.
I'M A LITTLE OLD-FASHIONED.

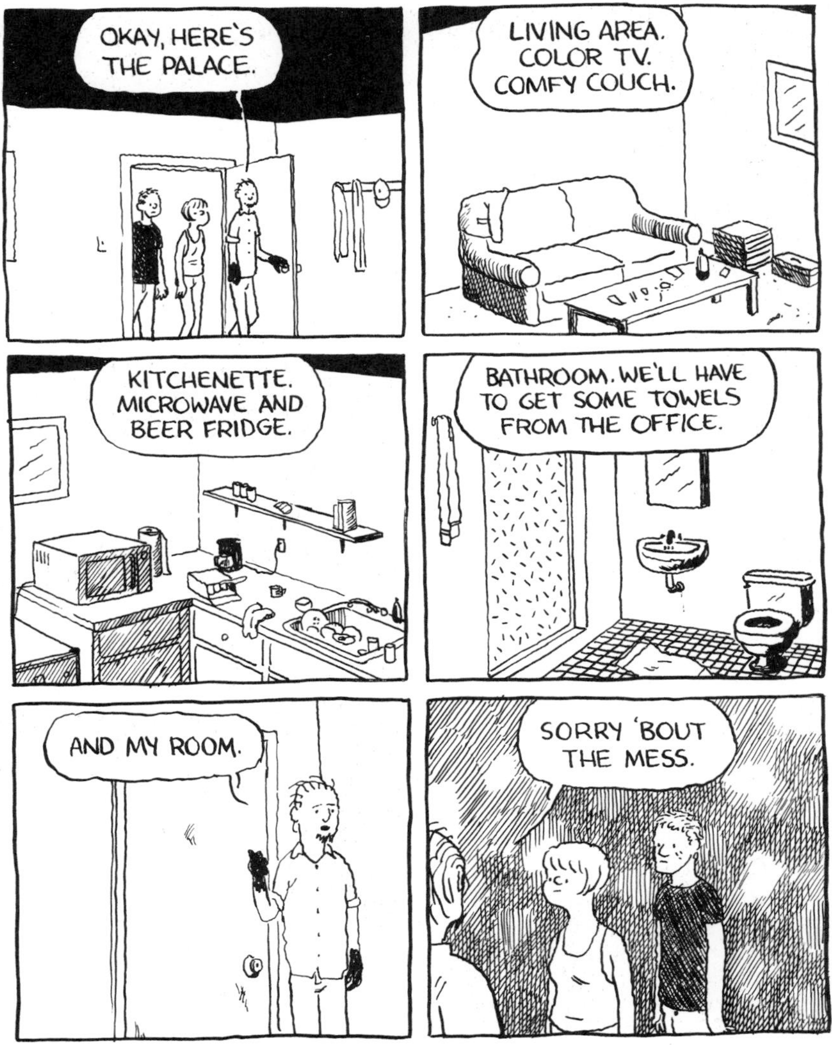
OKAY, HERE'S THE PALACE.
LIVING AREA. COLOR TV. COMFY COUCH.
KITCHENETTE. MICROWAVE AND BEER FRIDGE.
BATHROOM. WE'LL HAVE TO GET SOME TOWELS FROM THE OFFICE.
AND MY ROOM.
SORRY 'BOUT THE MESS.

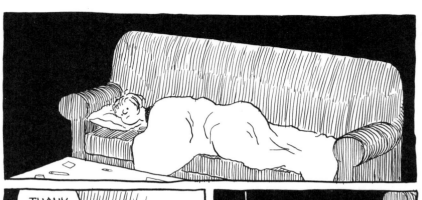

THANK YOU.

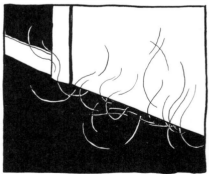

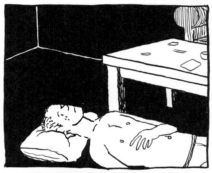

WHAT'S THAT SMELL?

LIVING WITH DAD

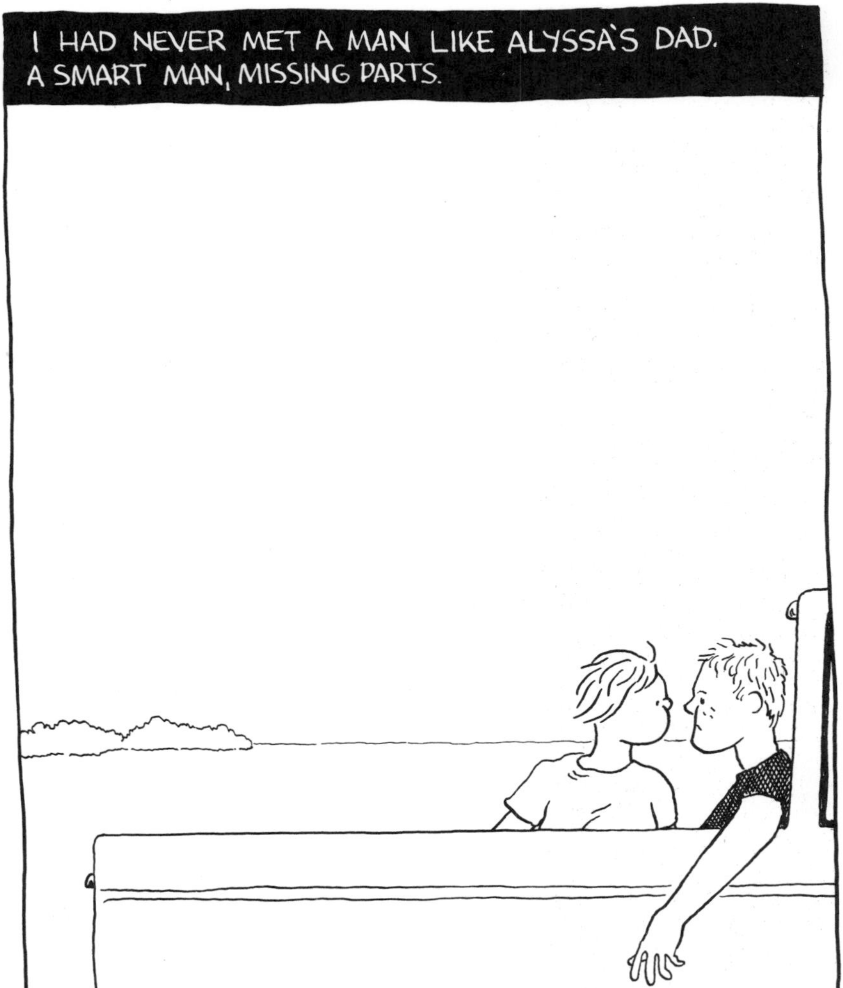
I HAD NEVER MET A MAN LIKE ALYSSA'S DAD.
A SMART MAN, MISSING PARTS.

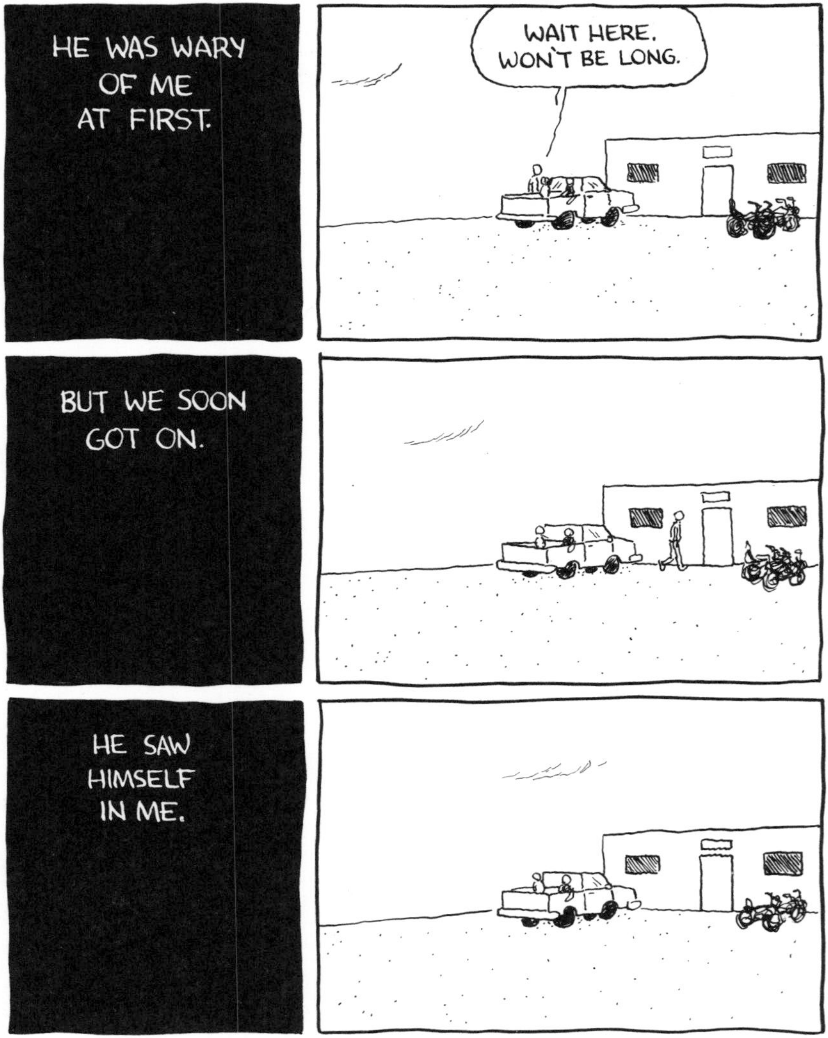
HE WAS WARY OF ME AT FIRST.
WAIT HERE. WON'T BE LONG.
BUT WE SOON GOT ON.
HE SAW HIMSELF IN ME.

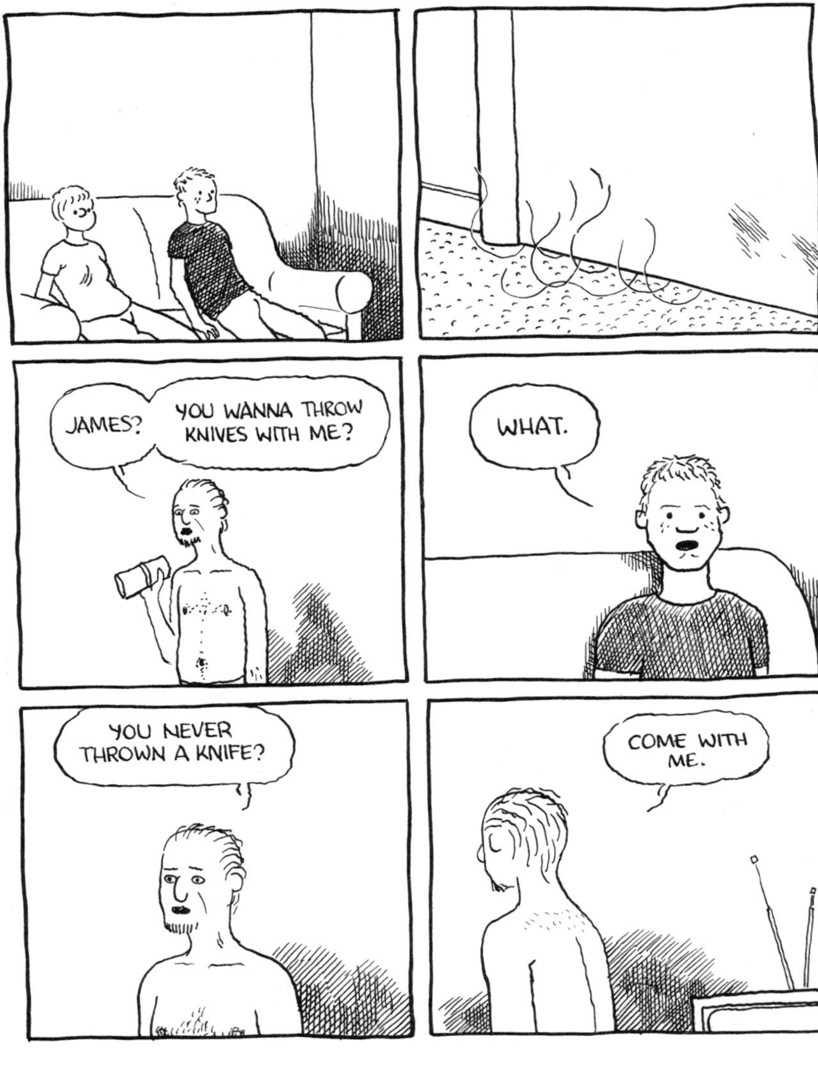
JAMES?
YOU WANNA THROW KNIVES WITH ME?
WHAT.
YOU NEVER THROWN A KNIFE?
COME WITH ME.

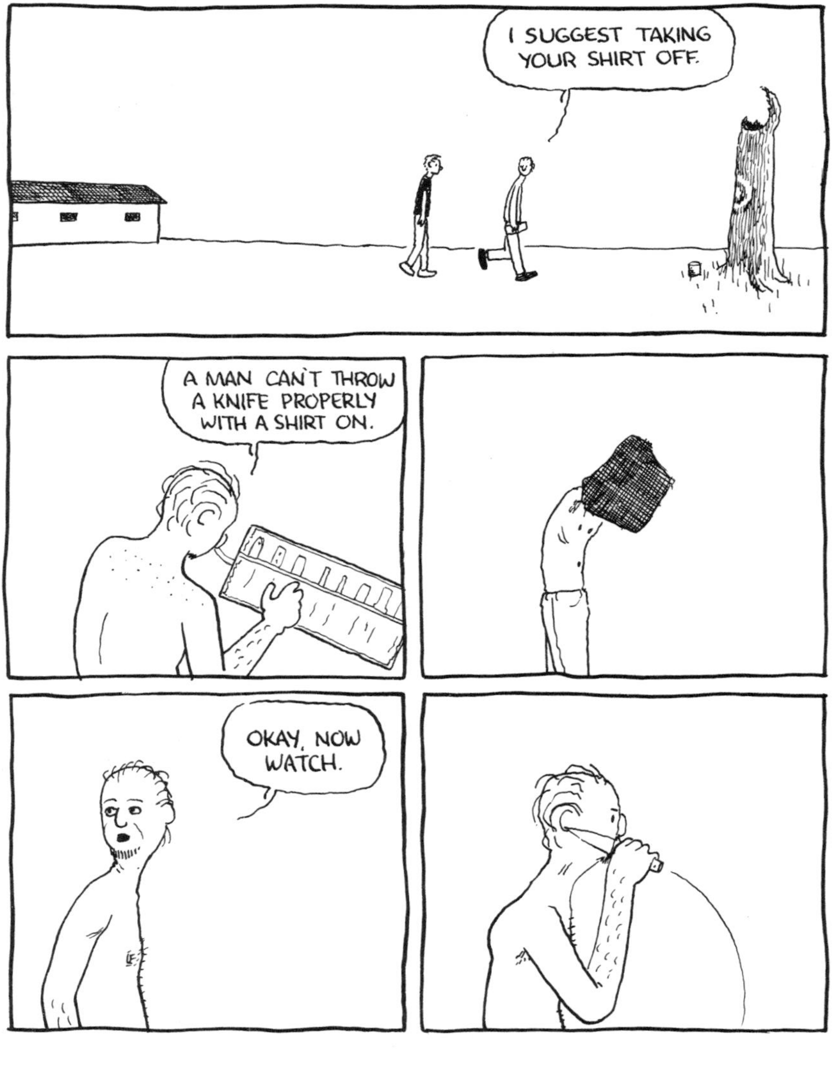
I SUGGEST TAKING YOUR SHIRT OFF.
A MAN CAN'T THROW A KNIFE PROPERLY WITH A SHIRT ON.
OKAY, NOW WATCH.

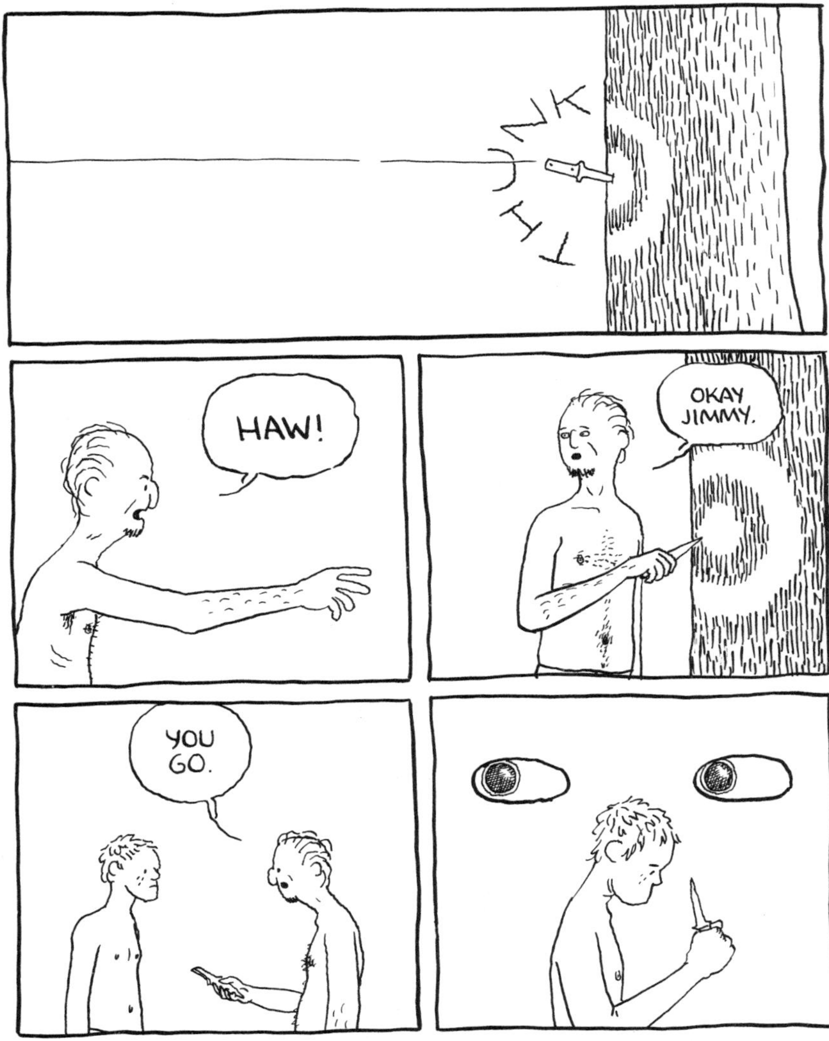
THUNK
HAW!
OKAY JIMMY.
YOU GO.

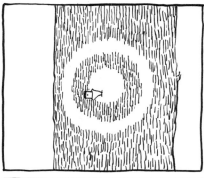

CHRIST

DON'T SIT THERE AND TELL ME YOU NEVER TOSSED A BLADE BEFORE.

DO IT AGAIN.

THUNK

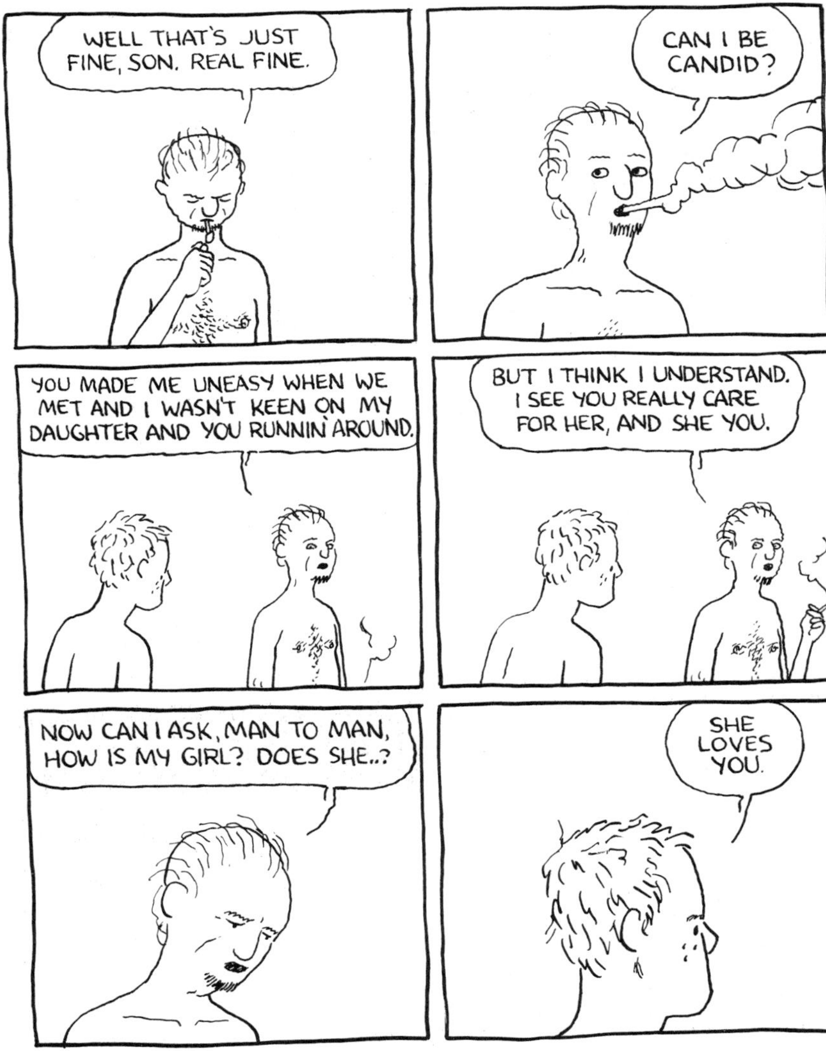
WELL THAT'S JUST FINE, SON. REAL FINE.
CAN I BE CANDID?
YOU MADE ME UNEASY WHEN WE MET AND I WASN'T KEEN ON MY DAUGHTER AND YOU RUNNIN' AROUND.
BUT I THINK I UNDERSTAND. I SEE YOU REALLY CARE FOR HER, AND SHE YOU.
NOW CAN I ASK, MAN TO MAN, HOW IS MY GIRL? DOES SHE..?
SHE LOVES YOU.

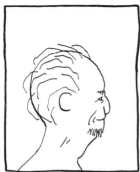

JAMES, DO YOU LIKE COORS?

WHAT'S THAT?

BEER!

I SAW A MAN THAT COULDN'T HELP HIMSELF

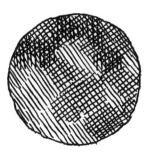

FATHER FUCKER

SOMETIMES I GET THIS FEELING. A FEELING OF NOTHINGNESS.
YEAH. THAT'S THE ADDRESS.

IT'S NOT A
BAD FEELING.

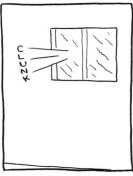

IT'S A CALM
FEELING.

WHEN
EVERYTHING
IS QUIET.

NO
EXPECTATIONS.

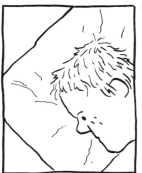

IT DOESN'T
HAPPEN VERY
OFTEN.

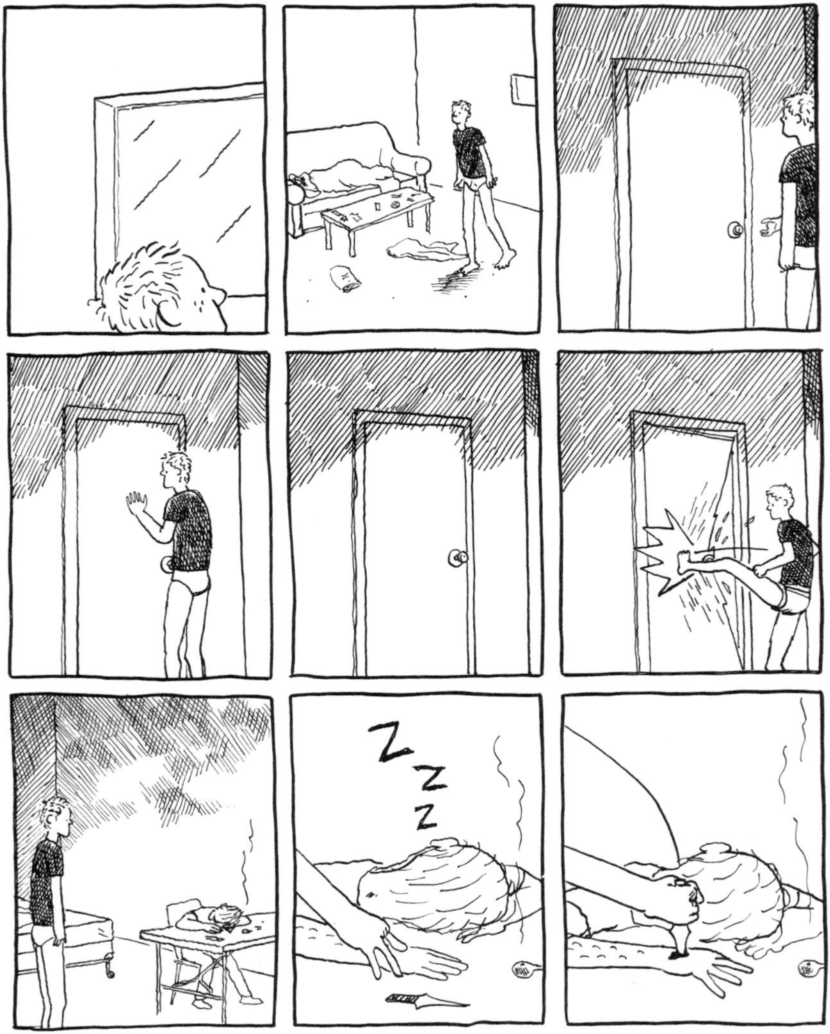
Z Z Z

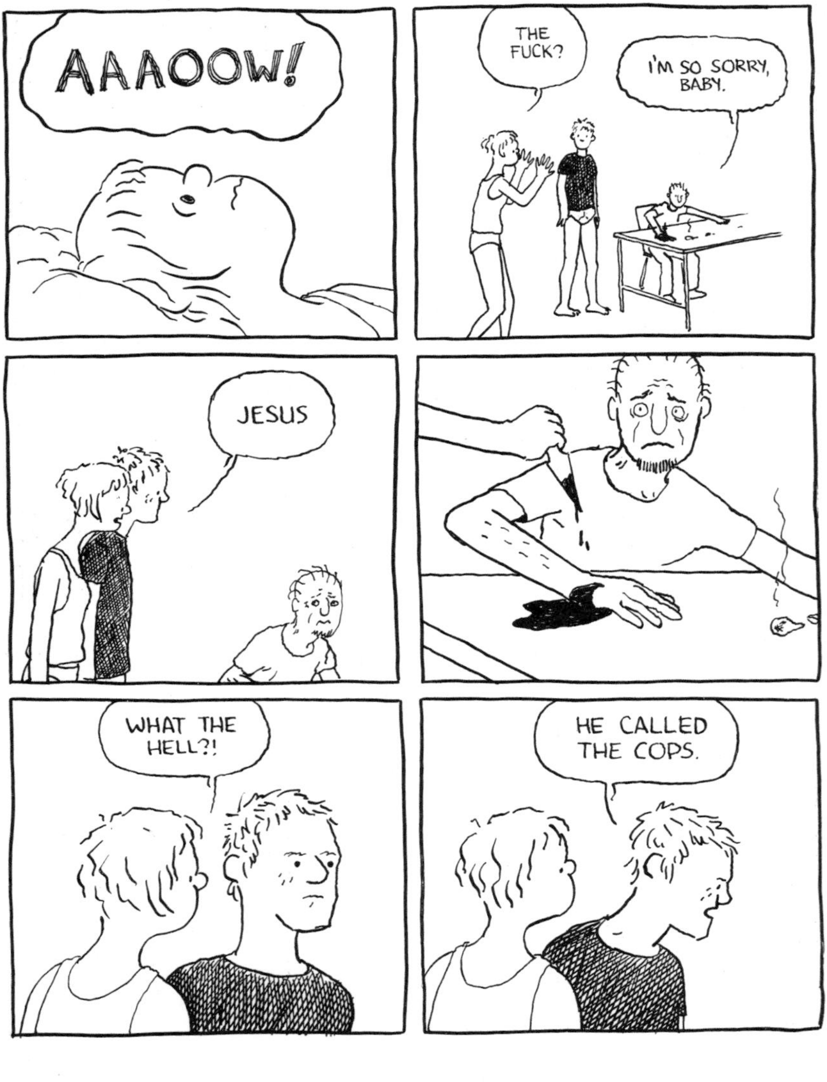
AAAOOW!
THE FUCK?
I'M SO SORRY, BABY.
JESUS
WHAT THE HELL?!
HE CALLED THE COPS.

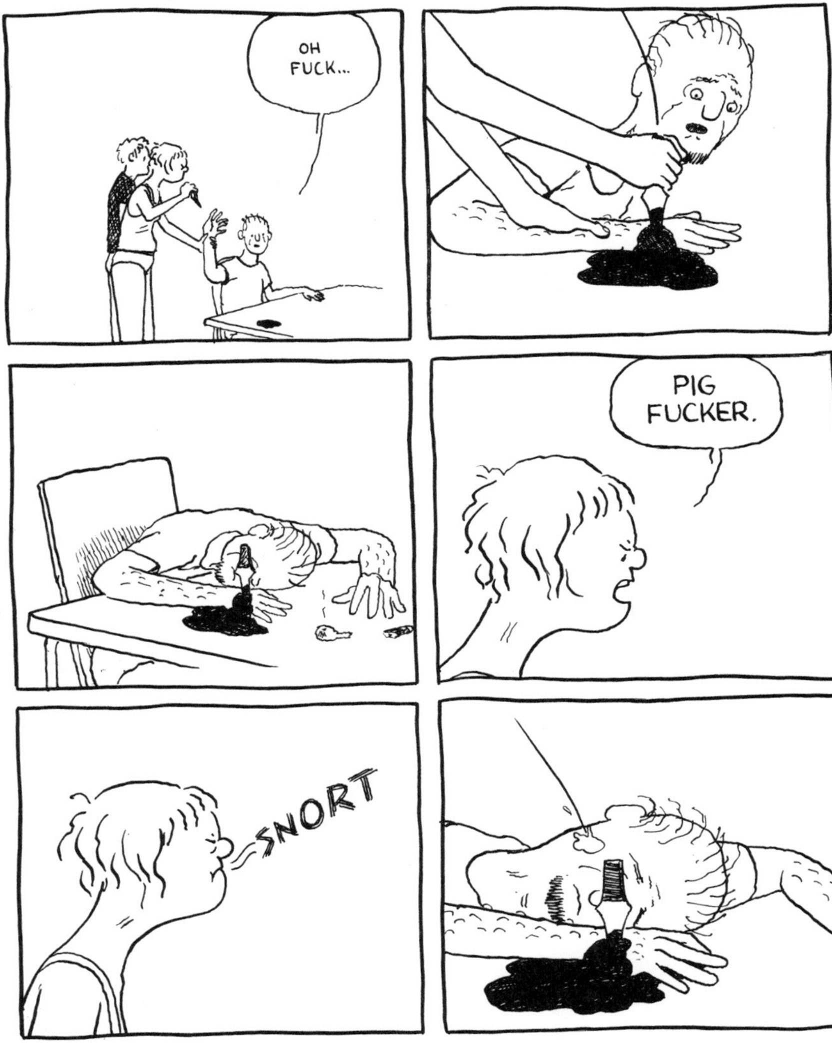
OH FUCK...
PIG FUCKER.
SNORT

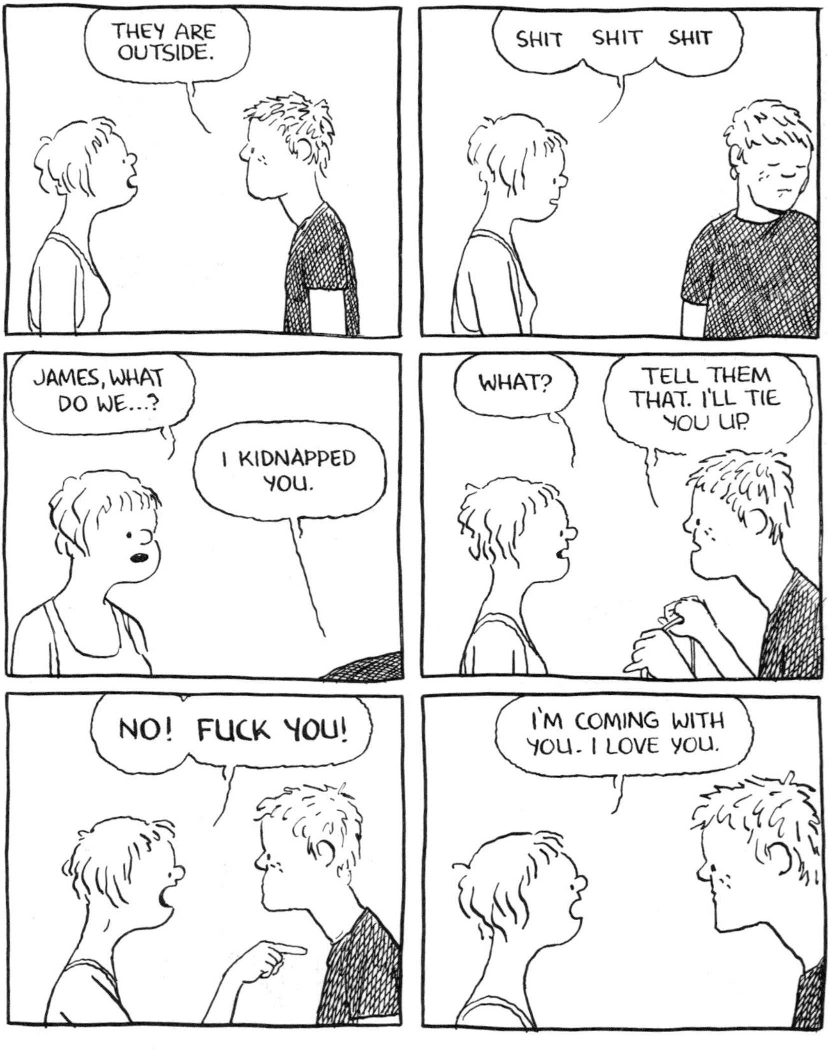

THEY ARE OUTSIDE.
SHIT SHIT SHIT
JAMES, WHAT DO WE...?
I KIDNAPPED YOU.
WHAT?
TELL THEM THAT. I'LL TIE YOU UP.
NO! FUCK YOU!
I'M COMING WITH YOU. I LOVE YOU.

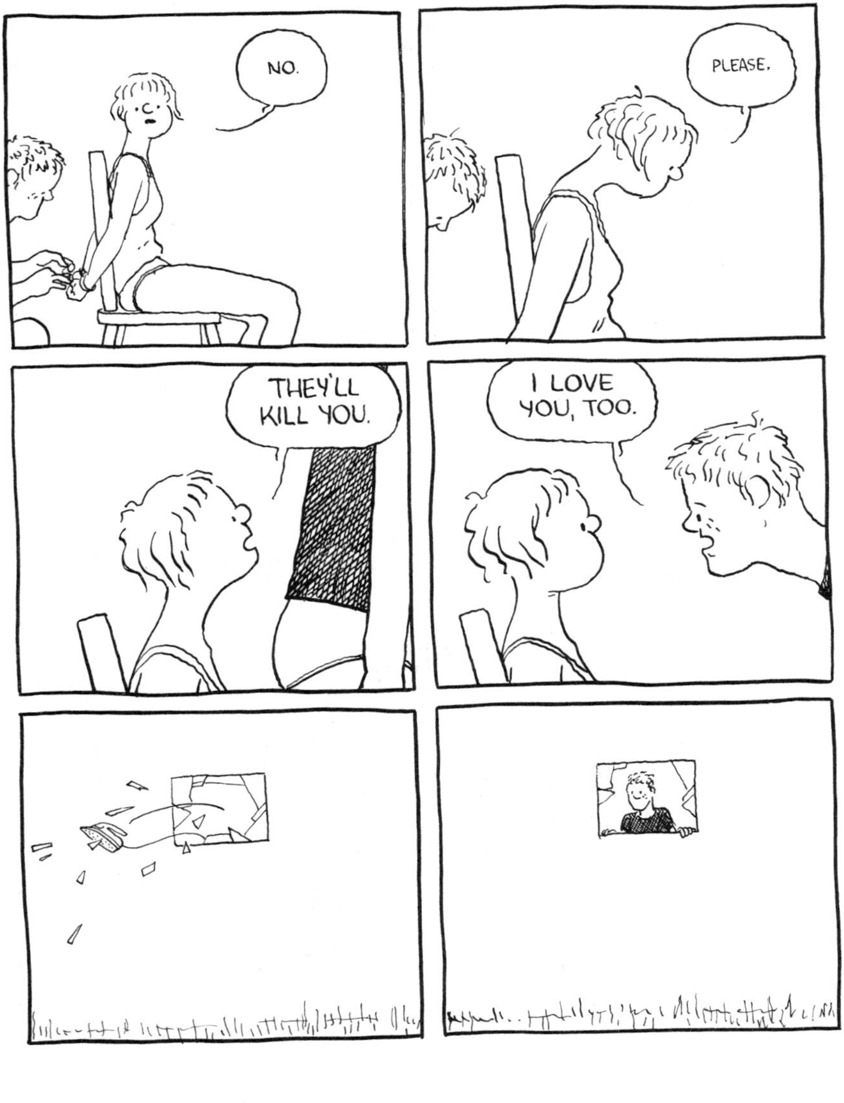
NO.
PLEASE.
THEY'LL KILL YOU.
I LOVE YOU, TOO.

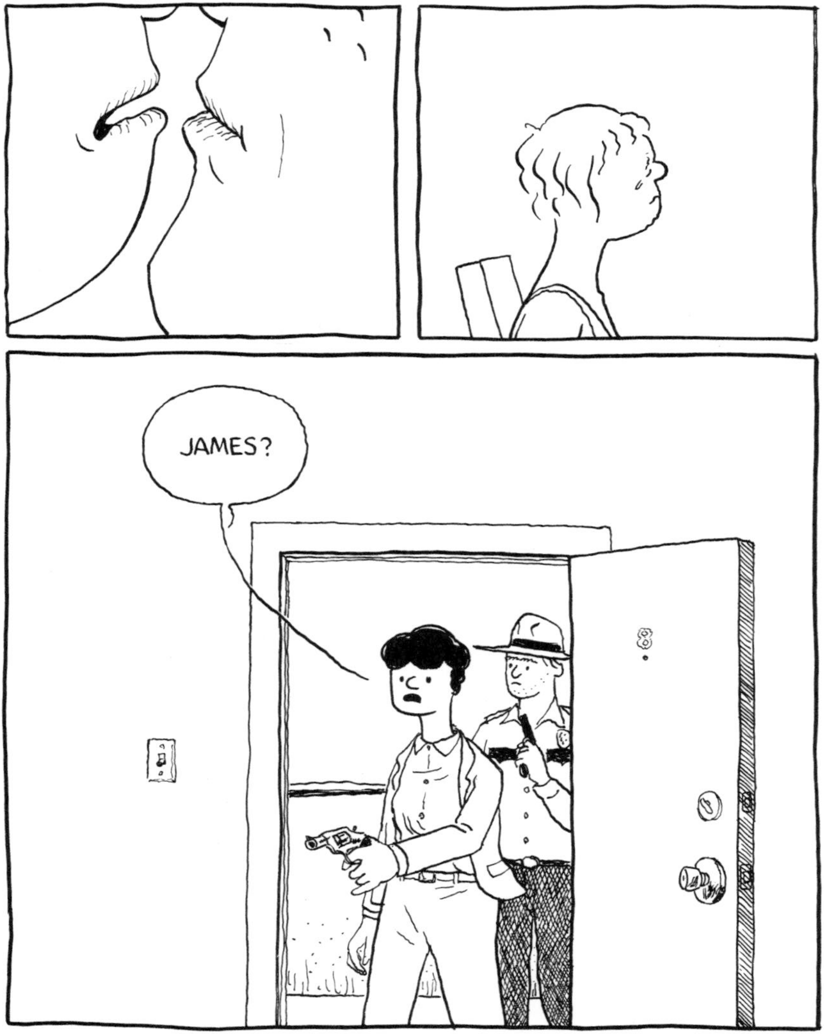
JAMES?

FORCED FEELINGS

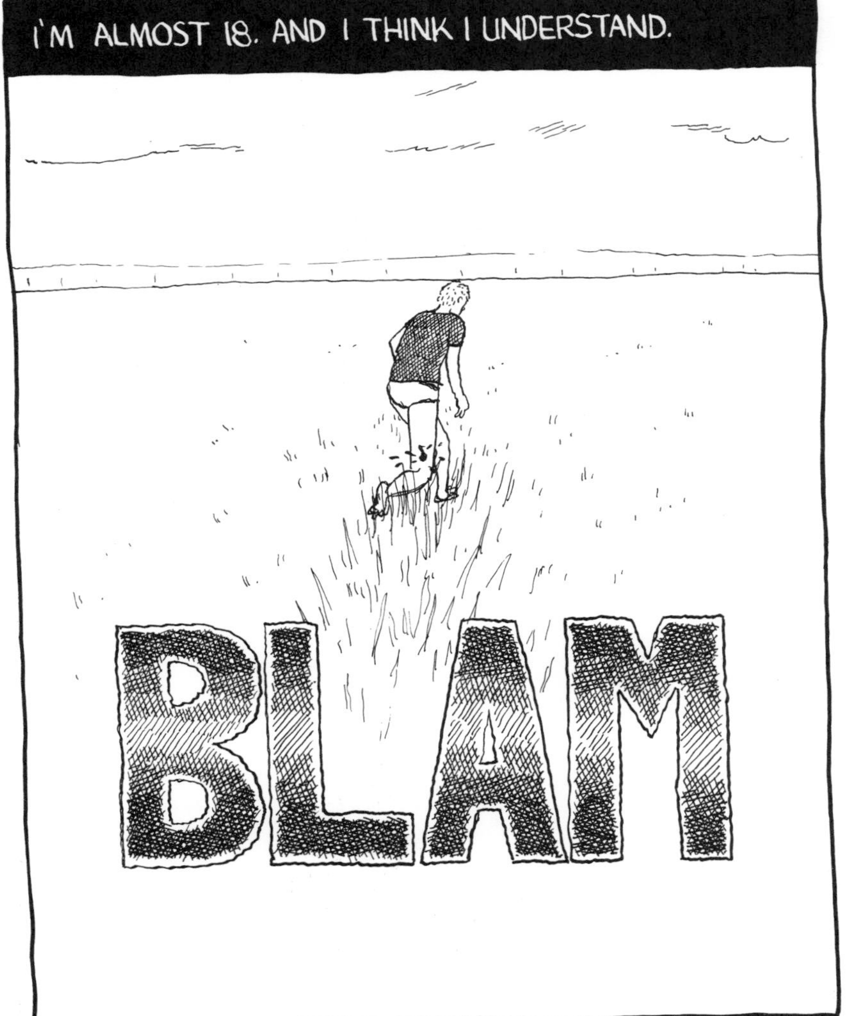
I'M ALMOST 18. AND I THINK I UNDERSTAND.
BLAM

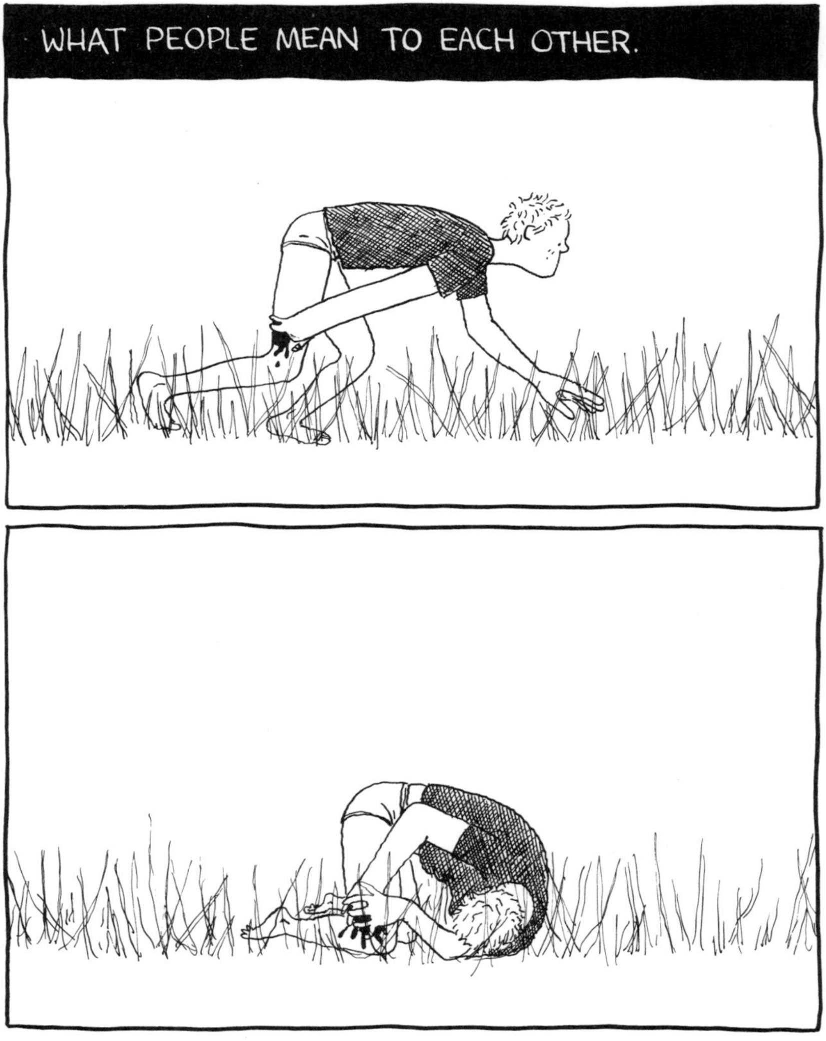
WHAT PEOPLE MEAN TO EACH OTHER.

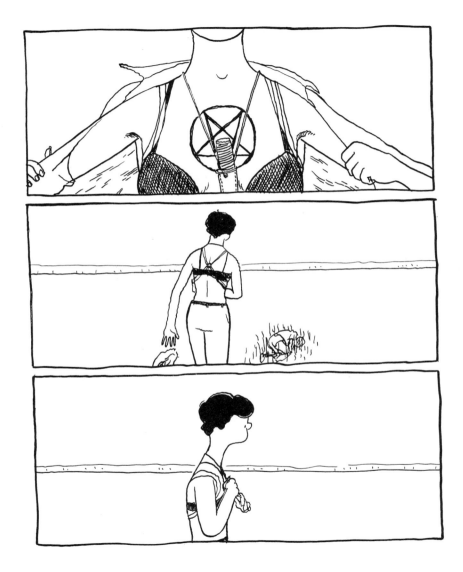

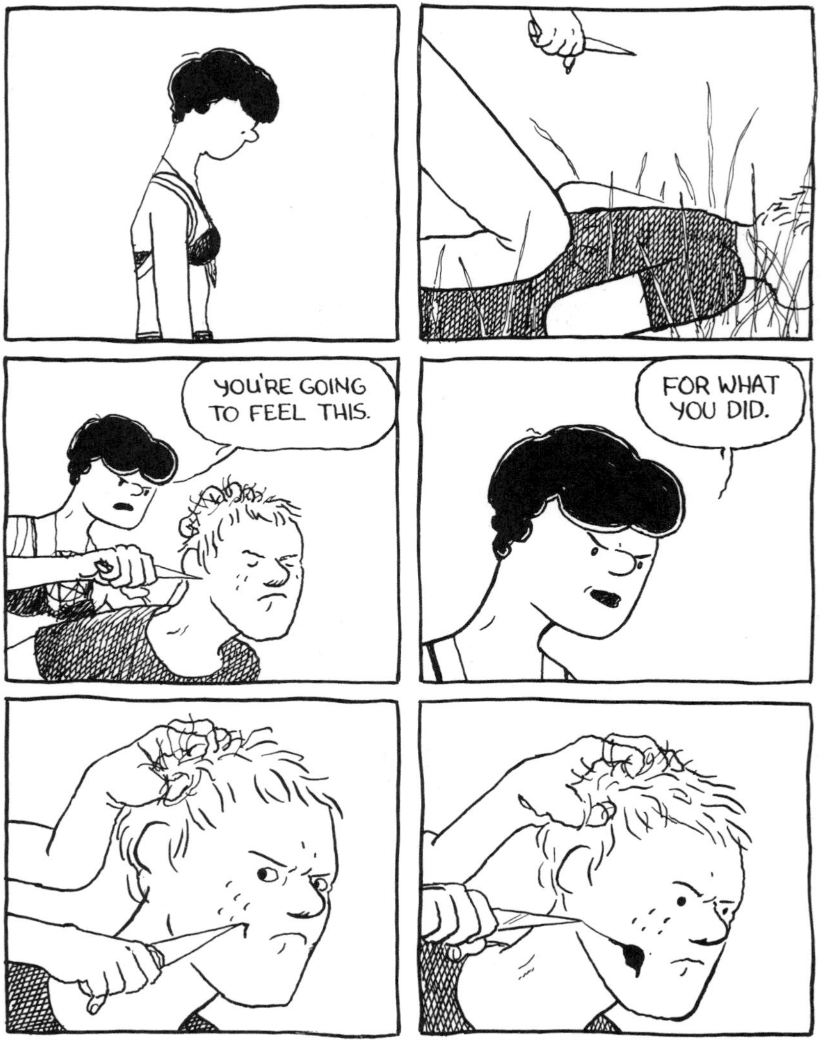
YOU'RE GOING TO FEEL THIS.
FOR WHAT YOU DID.

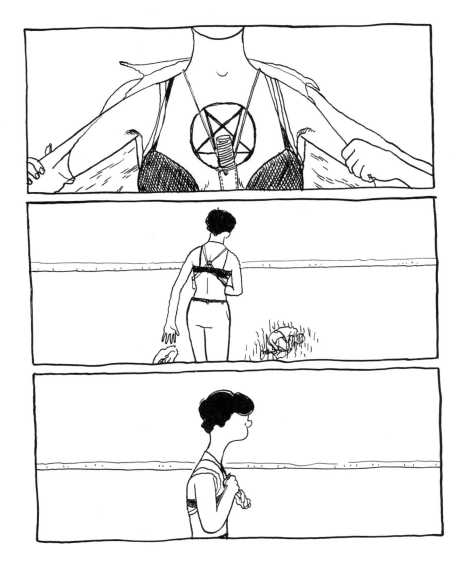

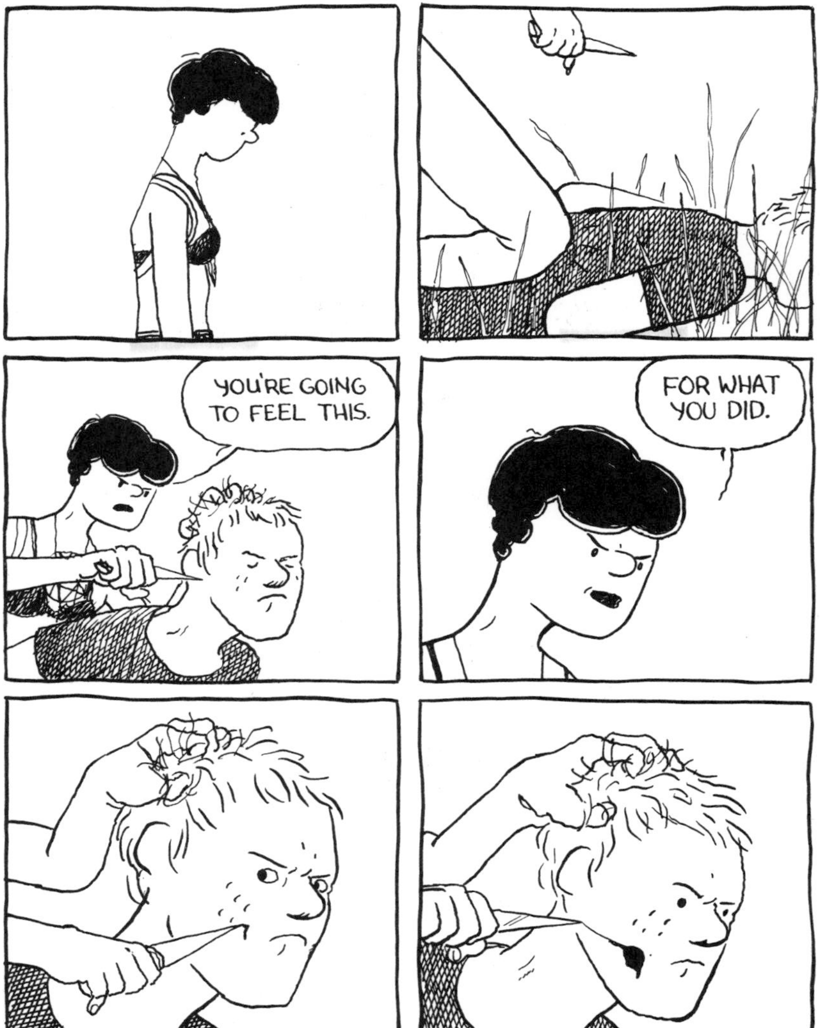
YOU'RE GOING TO FEEL THIS.
FOR WHAT YOU DID.

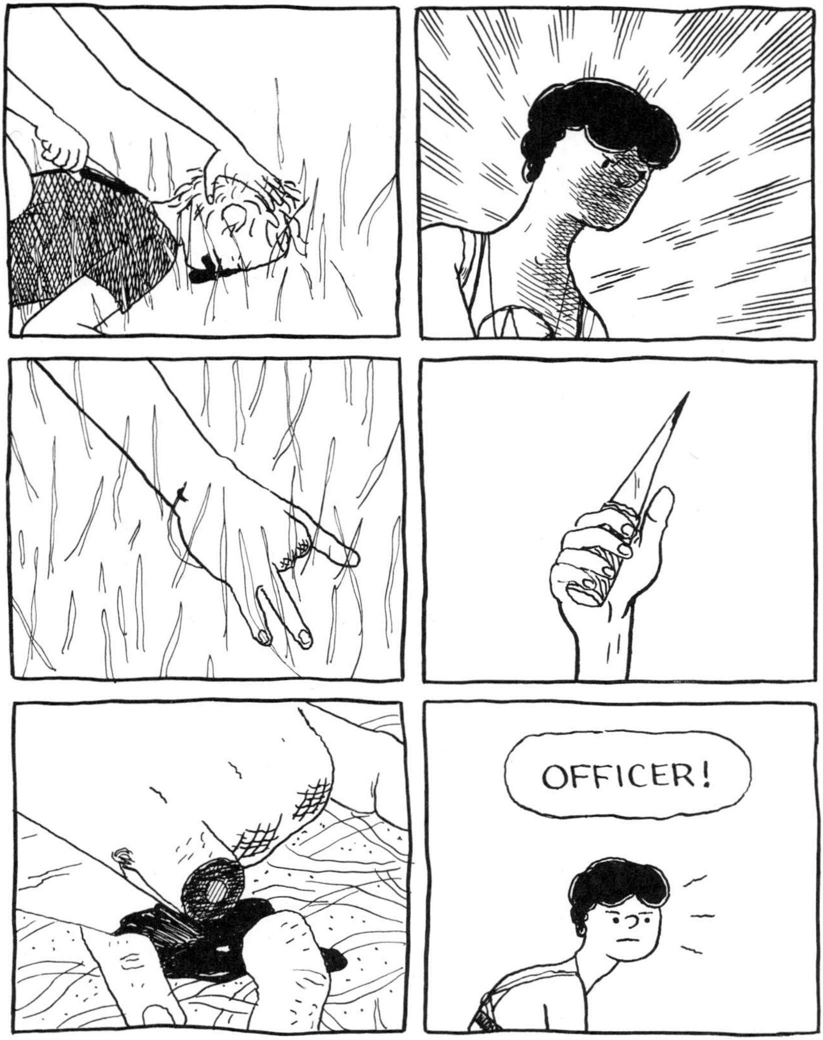
OFFICER!

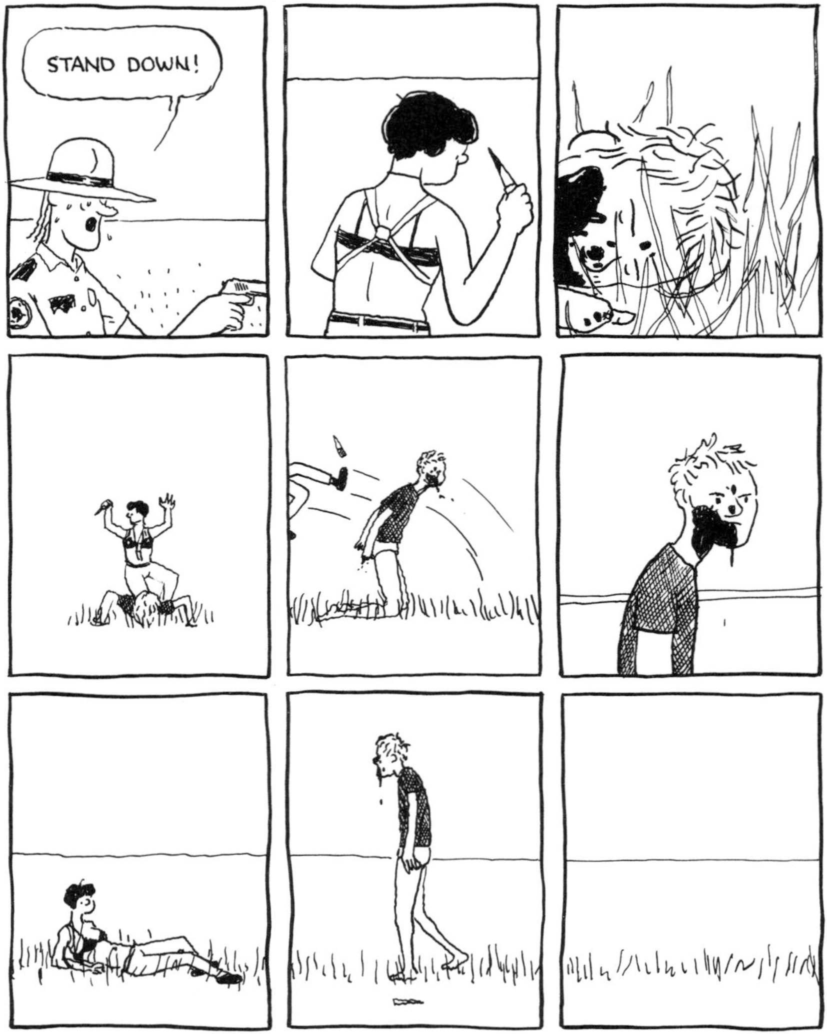
STAND DOWN!

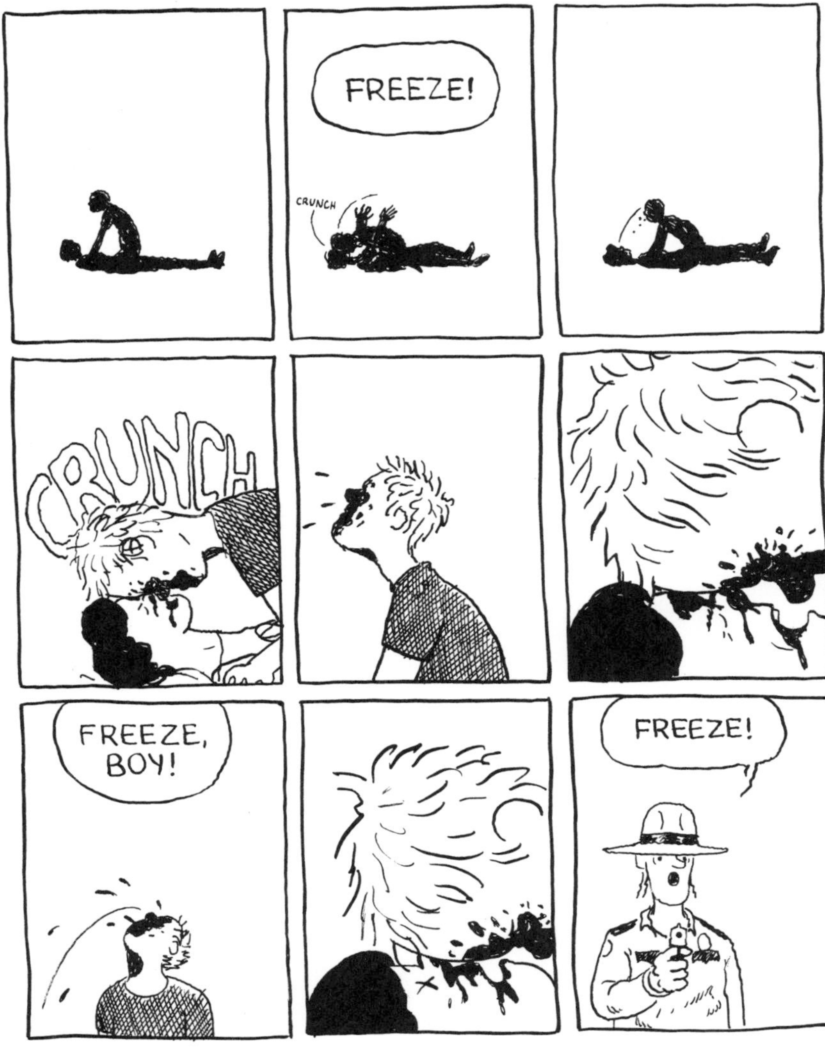
FREEZE!
CRUNCH
CRUNCH
FREEZE, BOY!
FREEZE!

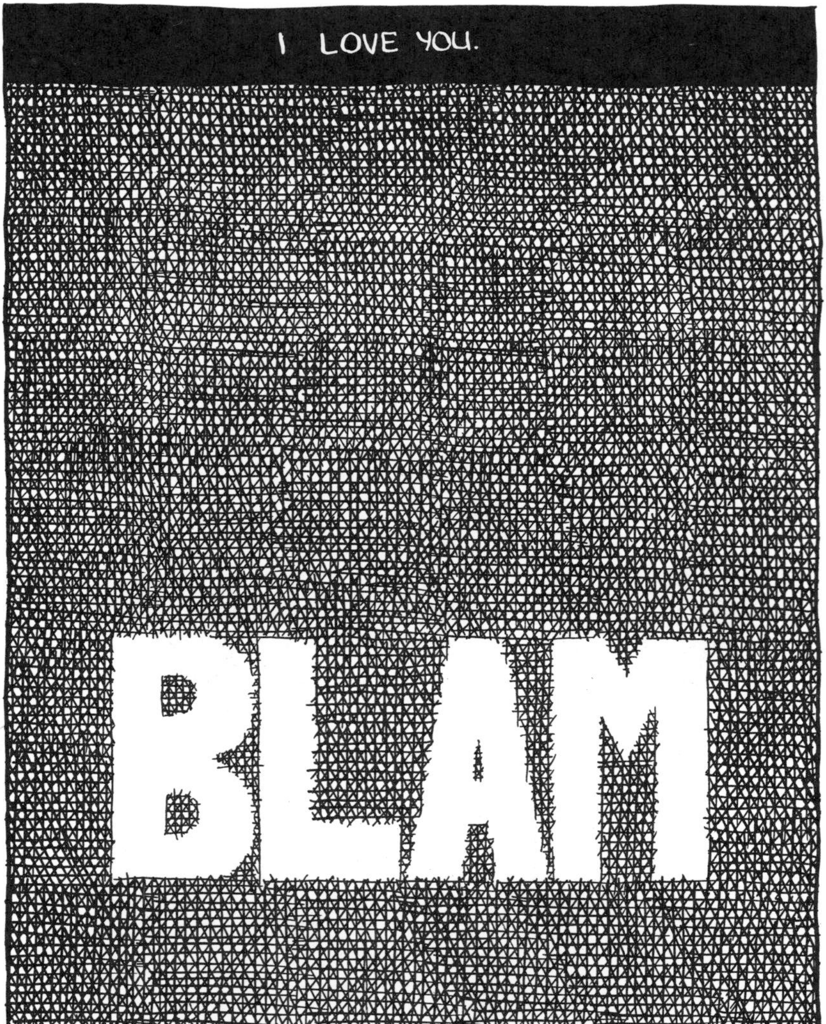
I LOVE YOU.
BLAM

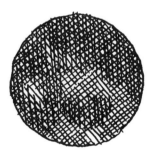

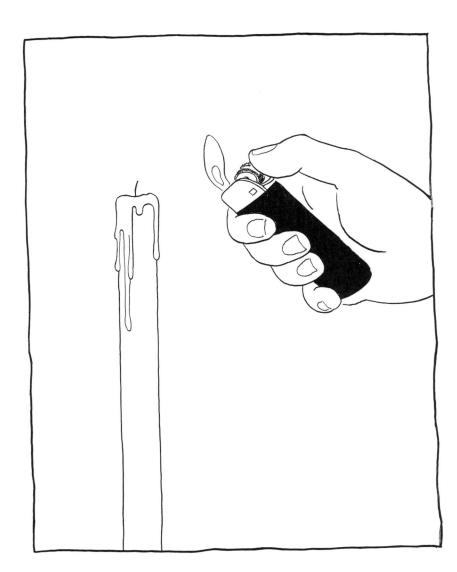

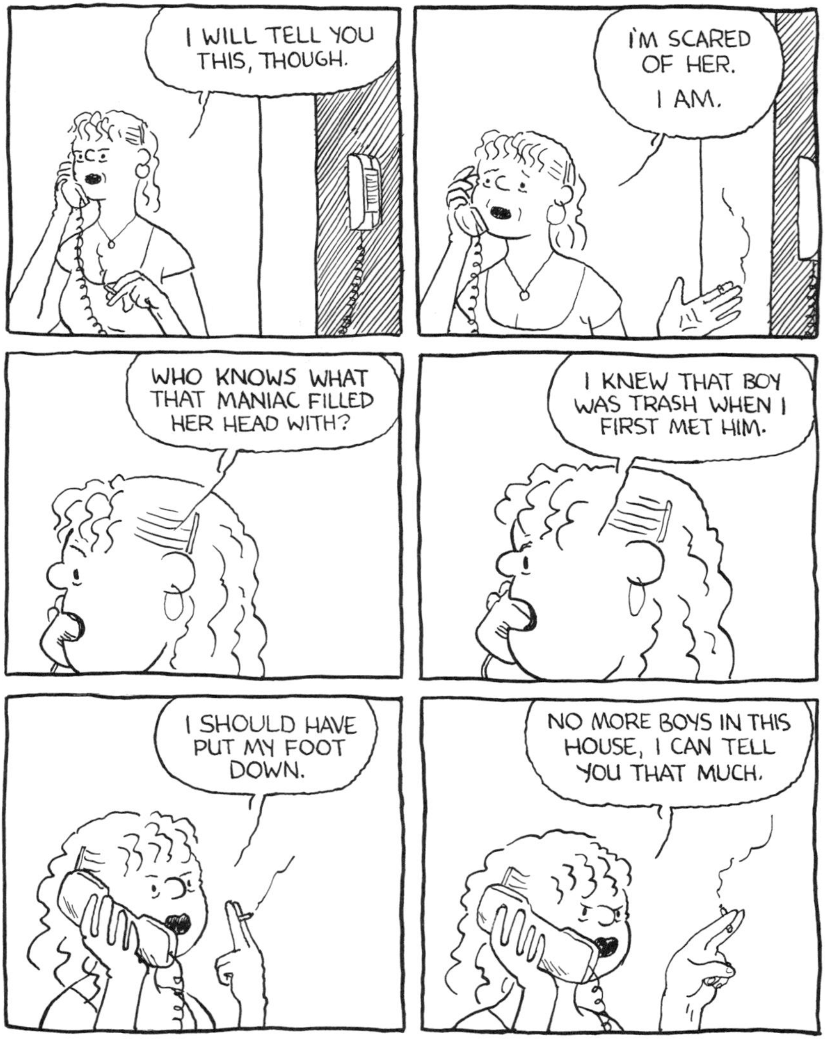
I WILL TELL YOU THIS, THOUGH.
I'M SCARED OF HER.
I AM.
WHO KNOWS WHAT THAT MANIAC FILLED HER HEAD WITH?
I KNEW THAT BOY WAS TRASH WHEN I FIRST MET HIM.
I SHOULD HAVE PUT MY FOOT DOWN.
NO MORE BOYS IN THIS HOUSE, I CAN TELL YOU THAT MUCH.

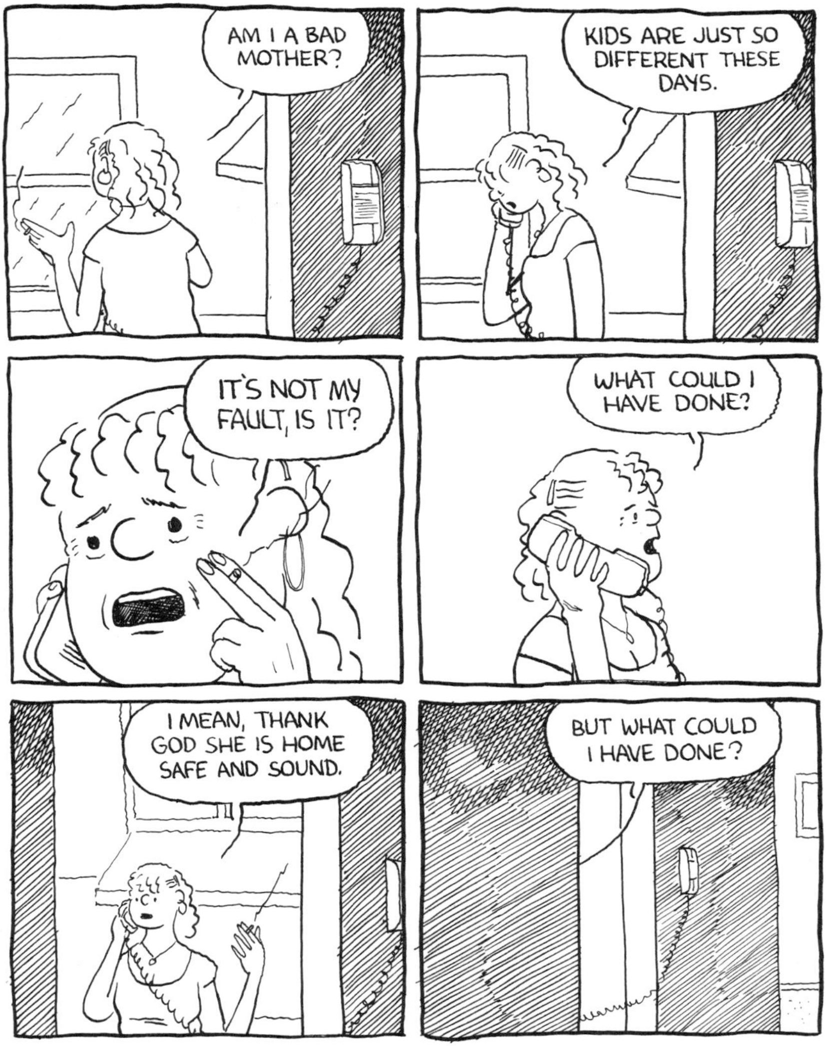
AM I A BAD MOTHER?
KIDS ARE JUST SO DIFFERENT THESE DAYS.
IT'S NOT MY FAULT, IS IT?
WHAT COULD I HAVE DONE?
I MEAN, THANK GOD SHE IS HOME SAFE AND SOUND.
BUT WHAT COULD I HAVE DONE?

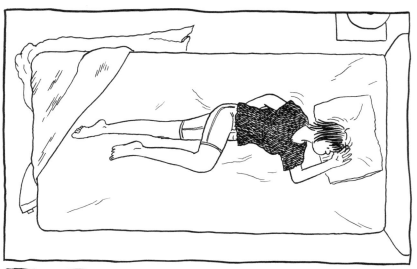

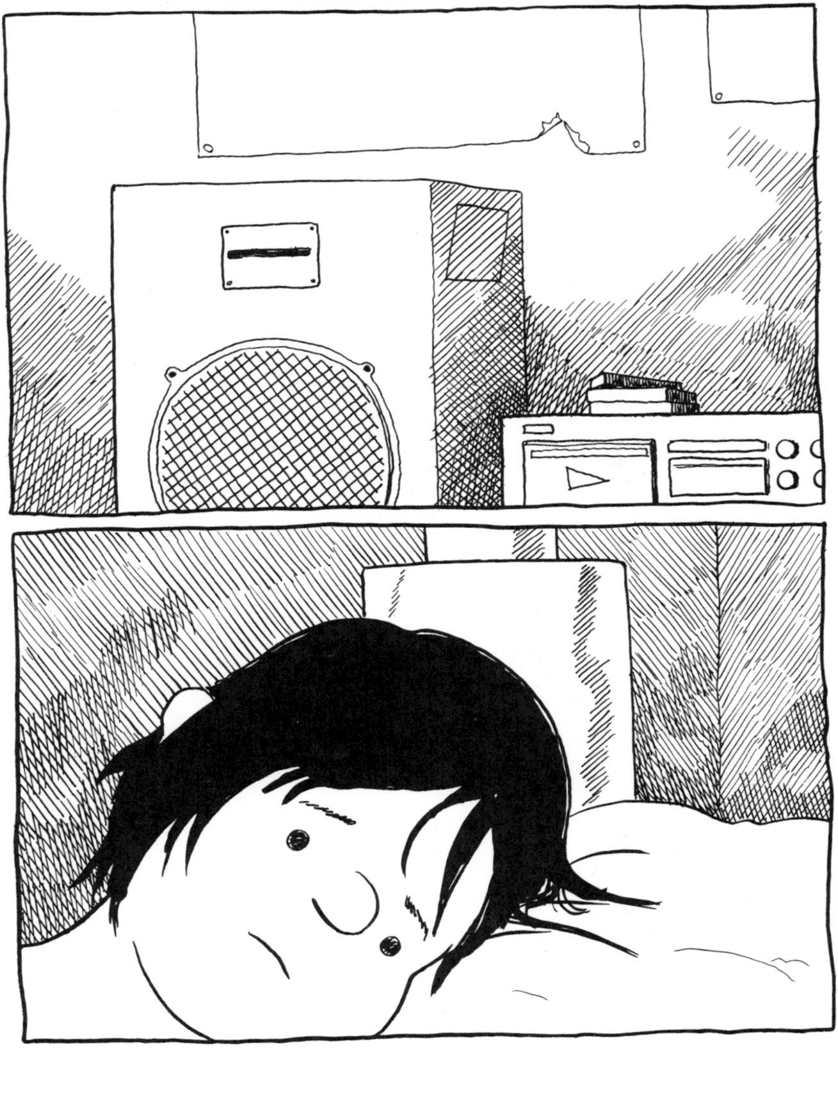

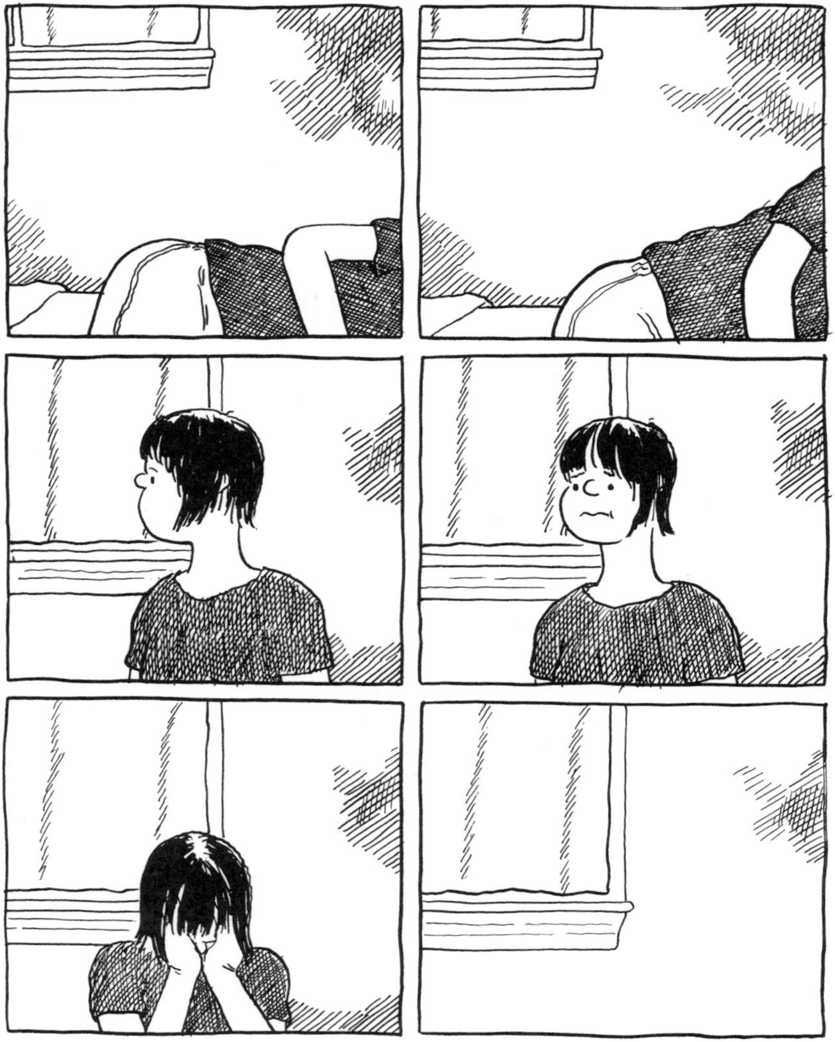

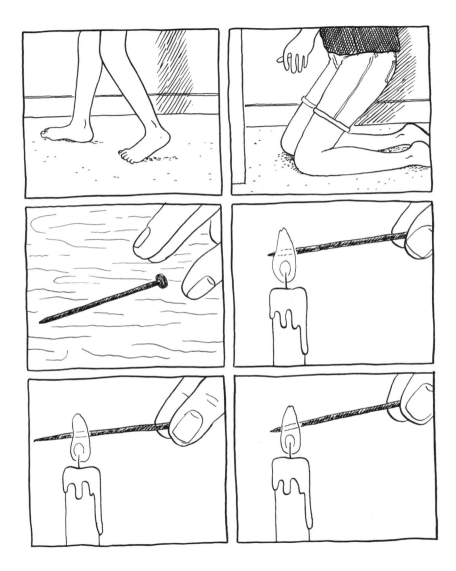

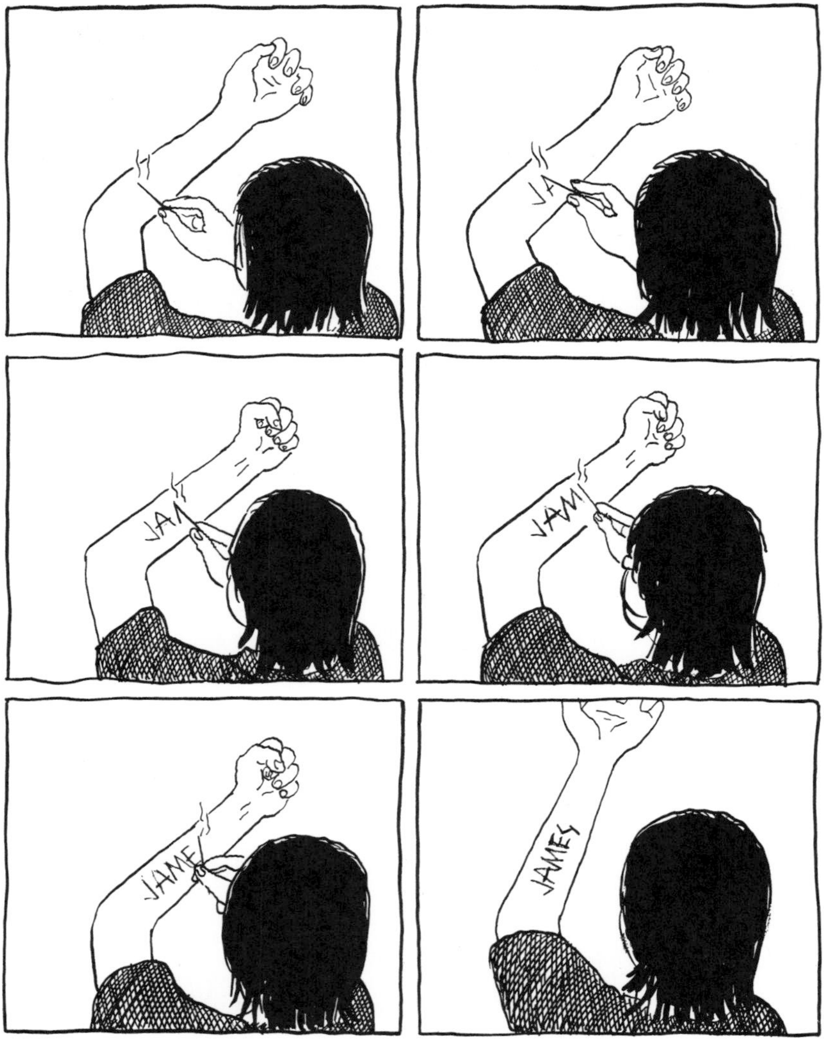
JA
JAM
JAME
JAMES

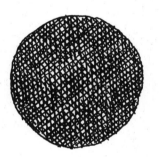

CHARLES FORSMAN (b.1982) IS A GRADUATE OF THE CENTER FOR CARTOON STUDIES. HIS OTHER COMIC BOOKS INCLUDE *REVENGER*, *SLASHER*, AND *CELEBRATED SUMMER*.